Malignancy

Science Traveler Series

Book 4

Malignancy

Science Traveler Series

Book 4

J. L. Greger

Bug Press

New Mexico

Malignancy

Bug Press
An imprint of IngramSpark
Bernalillo, New Mexico 87004
http://www.jlgreger.com

Copyright, second edition © 2019 by J. L. Greger
First edition © October 2014
Cover design by Barbara Hodges for Got You Covered Bookcover
Design © 2019

ISBN (paperback): 9780960028528
ISBN (EPUB): 9780960028535
Library of Congress Catalogue Number: 2019905234

DEDICATION

To Bug for his constant companionship and to a rigid tour guide who forced me to see Cuba from her viewpoint.

ACKNOWLEDGEMENTS

I want to thank:

Barbara Hodges for designing the cover,

The late Billie Johnson and Oak Tree Press, publisher of the first edition of *Malignancy*,

Zelda Gatuskin, Lorna Collins, and reviewers of all my books in the Science Traveler Series.

The Public Safety Writer's Association (PSWA) for awarding first place in their annual writing competition for published novels in 2015 to the first edition of *Malignancy*.

CHAPTER 1 Sara Almquist in the Albuquerque area in late October

The gray plastic garbage cans lined up along the street looked like teeth on a broken zipper. Sara Almquist realized if the garbage cans were out in her community of La Bendita, today must be Tuesday.

On Sunday — no it was Monday — anyway yesterday, she had returned from Bolivia in time to hear her sister Linda testify at Abel Raines's murder trial at the courthouse in Albuquerque. Today the events of the last week swirled in her head. When she agreed to serve as an epidemiologist on a public health mission to Bolivia, she thought the assignment might be a little rough because of the high altitude of thirteen thousand feet and the grinding poverty, but she had figured it wouldn't be any tougher than several other international consulting assignments she'd completed as a professor. She was wrong. This mission, at least the part in which she served as bait so U.S. agents could capture the notorious drug czar Jim Mazzone, had been a nightmare. She smiled wistfully as she remembered one bright spot — she survived because of Xave Zack.

She willed herself to stop thinking about Xave. She'd promised her sister Linda that she'd go listen to Ethan Wilson, dean of the medical school and Linda's boss, testify at the murder trial of Abel Raines today. Assistant DA Zelda Zane had forbidden Linda from attending the trial because she planned to call Linda back for further testimony if Dean Wilson's testimony was weak. The dean had been a friend of Raines since their days as medical interns. Linda, as the associate dean of the medical school, feared he would muddle the case by using his usual "dean speak" to hide all the ways he had covered for Raines during the last thirty years. Sergeant Elsa Grasso, the lead officer in Raines's arrest, agreed with Linda and offered to reserve a seat for Sara at the trial today so she could be her sister's eyes and ears

Sara felt a paw gently tap her bare feet and looked down. Bug, her black and white Japanese Chin, stared at her, and then ran toward the kitchen. He looked over his shoulder and wagged his tail held high over his back. When she didn't move, he returned to his original position at her feet, wagged his tail, and then raced toward the kitchen again. He was hungry.

As she fumbled through routine tasks, she tried to focus her thoughts but couldn't. She was exhausted and yet exhilarated by her adventures in Bolivia. She wondered whether she'd hear from Xave today, as he had promised.

***

Dean Ethan Wilson, a tall, thin man with silvery hair, gazed purposefully at the judge, jury, and other key players in the courtroom after he regally lowered himself onto the witness chair. Assistant DA Zelda Zane in an amethyst silk suit strutted forward, while he lowered his head slightly and brought his long graceful hands into a rather prayerful position. Linda had complained many times he assumed this affectation when he planned to be particularly evasive. Sara hated to admit it but the man exuded authority. No wonder Linda and everyone in the medical school simply called him "the Dean," and those outside the school always used his title when they referred to him.

Wilson claimed he couldn't remember details as he avoided answering Zelda's first question. Zelda's usual shrill tones turned into a screech as she asked her second question. Her face lost all color during his second evasive answer. She continued for two minutes to question her supposed prosecution witness before she stormed to her chair and whispered to Elsa who was sitting in the row behind the prosecution lawyers. Elsa raced from the room.

Wilson lowered his hands and stared at Raines before he began to answer the first question from the defense lawyer. He seemed to remember all sorts of details and sarcastically said, "My current Associate Dean Linda Almquist can't quite fill Dr. Raines's shoes. Her testimony yesterday reflects her jealousy."

Sara had thought Linda was being pessimistic when she frequently complained the Dean didn't respect her as his associate dean. Now she realized he considered Linda to be little more than cannon fodder.

Zelda asked one question in her counter to Wilson's responses to the defense lawyer. "Are you sure you don't want to clarify any of your statements?" When Wilson said no, she asked for a fifteen-minute break.

After a break Sally Wilson, the Dean's wife, was called to the stand. Sara sighed as Sally took the oath. They both were tall blondes, but Sara doubted anyone would call her a Grace Kelly look-alike. She was sure Sally was often described that way.

Raines for the first time today lowered his head and whispered into his lawyer's ear when Sally was seated. Sara thought this was good sign. She knew Sally and Linda had worked together to force the Dean to act on at least two issues during the last six months.

Sally Wilson stared only at Zelda during her detailed testimony. She corroborated Linda's comments from the previous day and provided information on Raines's behavior thirty years before when the Dean and Raines were interns and she was a nurse.

The defense lawyer asked her only one question. "Everything you know about Dr. Raines is hearsay. Right?" Sally stared at Raines for a moment and responded angrily and with more details, until the defense attorney stopped her.

Zelda didn't counter the defense's question, but instead announced the prosecution was resting its case.

Elsa had slid into an empty seat by Sara when Sally entered the courtroom. As soon as Zelda rested her case, Elsa snorted. "Zelda, takes chances when she's not the one at risk. If Raines isn't convicted, Sally Wilson and your sister are walking dead." She shook her head and pulled her long black hair into a clip. "Better not tell Linda what I said." She raced down the aisle and around the outer corridor of the courtroom so she was standing by the prosecutors when the judge adjourned the trial for the day.

The audience in the courtroom exploded. Sara didn't want to be jostled in the packed aisles. Instead she studied the key characters from her seat. Many in the audience took photos with their phone cameras of Raines and Sally. Raines waved to the crowd, as he was led from the room. Sally tried to speak to Zelda, but Zelda brushed her aside as she swept out of the courtroom. Elsa, at least, spoke to Sally for a moment before she bolted out the same door as Zelda. Sally sank onto the bench where the prosecution had sat.

Sara debated her options. Her head felt as if it would split in two from weariness and stress. The news from the trial was too bleak to deliver to Linda by phone. Maybe she should swing by the medical school, which was less than two miles away, and convince Linda to go lunch at Hurricanes Restaurant. They could eat in the car where no one would hear their conversation.

She noted Sally was alone. Maybe she might like to come too. She'd like to get to know Sally better, and Linda liked her.

Gunshots erupted from space behind the front door of the courtroom. Screams. The next shots echoed differently.

Only she and Sally were left in the courtroom. She called to Sally. "Let's get out of here."

Sally took a step toward the side front entrance.

"Better go out the rear entrance."

Sally nodded.

"By the way I'm Sara, Linda's sister."

Before Sally responded, a uniformed police officer, young and with his black hair shorn into a buzz cut, threw open the front side door. Sara couldn't believe her eyes. He was waving a gun.

The experiences of the last week in Bolivia had conditioned Sara's response. She dropped to the floor and crept toward the far aisle.

Two shots. A scream. Panting and footsteps coming toward her.

She saw nothing because she was busy crawling behind a wooden pillar at the end of the aisle. She shivered as she shrank behind it.

The front side door slammed open again. "Stop! Stop or I'll shoot!"

Running footsteps. The shooter was getting nearer. She peeked around the post and saw his hand with the gun pointing toward her. She pulled back. She heard a shot. Several shots, but from another gun. A moan as something or someone hit the ground. Another shot.

She leaned forward. The shooter was lying on the floor. Blood was trickling from his mouth.

She knew if she rose quickly, the other shooter might shoot her. "I'm an innocent bystander. Is it safe to come out? "

Silence for a couple of seconds. "Prove it."

"I'm Sara Almquist."

"Prove it."

A door slammed. Light footsteps as someone new entered the courtroom.

"I'm the sister of the witness yesterday."

"You can stand." Sara recognized Elsa's low tones.

Sara's legs were as stable as Jell-O. She grabbed the post to hoist herself.

She could see only Elsa's back as she leaned over someone on the floor at the front of the room. A uniformed officer with his gun drawn stood over the fallen shooter. Almost immediately, the back doors of the courtroom slammed open, and two officers from the Albuquerque Police Department, generally called APD, ran toward Elsa.

Paramedics with a gurney raced through the courtroom seconds later. They lifted Sally onto the stretcher. Her face was like snow, and blood was matted on the front of her light blue cashmere sweater.

Sara had experienced enough excitement in Bolivia during the last week and knew she couldn't be of use. She walked to the back of the courtroom, away from the action. When she emerged, a police officer grabbed her arm and detained her behind the line of policemen who were keeping the crowd in abeyance from the courtroom. She sat on the floor and watched as Sally was whizzed out on a gurney and as another crew of paramedics rushed into and then out of the courtroom with the gunman.

A familiar face appeared after ten minutes. She had worked with Chuy Bargas during the quarantine of La Bendita because of the flu epidemic two years before. The attractive, thirty-year old police officer had wanted a chance to advance his career and had recently transferred to the New Mexico Gangs Task Force and now worked with Elsa.

Chuy gave her a wink and guided her back into the courtroom. Crime scene technicians were busy bees gathering samples from the two puddles of blood on the floor. Sara and Chuy emerged from the front side exit of the courtroom into a hallway marked off with yellow tape. Police were interviewing people. At the edge of the crowd Elsa stood directing traffic. She gave a high sign to Chuy, and he led Sara to a waiting squad car.

As the car roared off, he explained. Four people had been shot — Abel Raines, Sally Wilson, and the two shooters. Chuy cursed the officers at the scene. As usual they responded over zealously, and both shooters were critically injured. Elsa had been unable to gain any information from them, but she had noted they wore the standard uniforms issued by the APD and were elaborately tattooed. Chuy and Elsa assumed all witnesses in the trial against Raines, especially Linda, were at risk.

His phone rang before he finished his comments. His reassuring grin disappeared and his unlined face turned gray as he listened.

CHAPTER 2: Sara at Linda Almquist's office in the medical school

Chuy leapt out of the squad car as soon as it screeched to a stop at the emergency entrance of the hospital. Sara ran after him as he raced down the main corridor of the emergency rooms, past the atrium with the fast food restaurants, and out a back door of the hospital. She lost sight of him as he entered the Basic Medical Sciences Building where the deans' offices for the medical school were located, but she heard him banging on the locked door to dean's suite once she entered the building. Audrey, the dean's secretary, was cautiously examining his badge through a window on the door to the deans' office suite when Sara caught up with him.

Sara slid through the door after Chuy grabbed Audrey's arm and dragged her toward Dean Wilson's private office. Sara threw open the door to Linda's office. A petite woman with auburn hair turned away from her computer screen. Her face was whiter than usual with puffiness around the eyes.

"How much do you know?"

Linda Almquist wiped her eyes and blew her nose. "The Dean swept by my office after his testimony with a self-satisfied look. I figured he'd avoided answering Zelda's questions," she sighed, "and accordingly made a fool of me. Also figured I'd be called to testify again, but Elsa called ten minutes ago."

Before Linda continued, Chuy yelled as he ran out the door of the outer office. "Keep this door locked until I bring your fool boss back. That means all three of you ladies. Open the door only for the police after they show you their badges."

Sara gulped and turned back to Linda. "Anything else from Elsa?"

Linda nodded. "Sally and Raines were shot. The Dean and I could be next, so we were to stay in the office until Chuy arrived. Then I handed the phone to the Dean."

"So?"

"He only listened to Elsa for a couple of seconds. He muttered, 'I told her not to testify,' and ran out of the office."

Sara leaned across the desk to stroke her sister's arm as she told her details about the courtroom drama this morning. Linda sobbed quietly.

Finally, Sara said, "The shootings don't make sense. I could imagine Raines hiring someone to shoot Sally for testifying against him, but then why was he shot? Or was Raines the target, and Sally was blocking the shooter's exit?"

Linda gained her composure enough to speak. "Zelda hasn't allowed anyone but the defense lawyer to see Raines during the last two weeks, ever since the police uncovered his communication scheme using crossword puzzles with Diego Rivera." She gulped. "Diego has been locked up since then too because he didn't raise bail. So, both Raines and Diego have been isolated for two weeks. Besides, Raines wouldn't order a hit on himself."

Someone banged on the outer door to the deans' office suite. Sara peeked out of Linda's office. Two uniformed policemen with their guns out were at the outer door. As Sara closed the door, she whispered, "Call Elsa. I think we're about to be ambushed." She pushed a chair under the door handle.

The banging on the door stopped. Tapping on the window came at a more rapid pace until a loud bang shattered the glass. The seconds seemed long as Linda and Sara crawled behind the metal desk in Linda's small gray office. Gunshots. Bullets splintered Linda's door. Sara hugged Linda closer as they both lay on the floor.

Then the clatter of feet running in leather-soled shoes. A tenor voice, Sara thought Chuy's, yelled, "Police. Get your hands up."

Gunshots. A groan and a thud outside Linda's door. More gunshots.

The tenor voice again. "Stop shooting. Cuff them." Silence. Sara was sure it was Chuy's voice when he said, "Are you ladies okay?"

"Yes," screamed Sara and Linda simultaneously. A hoarse moan came from Audrey in Dean Wilson's private office.

"Stay put until I get this mess cleaned up."

The wait seemed long. Chuy seemed to have backup because Sara heard him roaring orders and questions. Sara tired of laying on the floor raised herself to her knees and began to crawl away from the desk. Linda tried to assume a squat position but fell backward and grabbed for support. Her hand must have grazed the coffee cup on her desk, and the brown, creamy liquid dripped down on her hair. As Linda spluttered, Sara began to giggle. In a few seconds both women were giggling as they sopped up the liquid and looked about the room.

Sara found holes in the binding of one volume of *Brenner and Rector's The Kidney* and handed the book to Linda.

Linda opened the book, and loose pages fluttered to the floor. "Wonder whether my insurance will cover this loss?"

Sara convulsed in laughter. She recognized her giggles were a way to release tension, not a reflection of humor.

Linda, with her arms akimbo in mock annoyance, said, "Do you realize those two volumes cost five hundred dollars?" She too began to chuckle.

Sara continued to remove books with holes in their binding from the shelf until she found six bullets wedged in the gray concrete wall behind the open bookshelf. When Linda plunked herself in her black office chair, both women stopped laughing because they realized the bullets would have hit Linda's head if she had been sitting at her computer.

They pulled two cans of soda from the little refrigerator beside Linda's desk and were enjoying the fizz when the outer door of the office suite slammed open again. More glass splintered under heavy footsteps. Sara and Linda heard the creaking wheels of gurneys. The moaning outside Linda's door ceased.

Raps on the door. "Ladies, this is Chuy. You can come out now."

Sara slid the chair from under the doorknob and opened the door. She almost stepped into a pool of congealing blood. Streaks of red stretched across the gray carpet from the pool. Evidently a gurney had rolled into the blood and had left the red tracks. All the windows at the front of the deans' office suite were broken. Two APD officers stood by the now defunct outer door to the office suite.

Wilson sat on a chair in the middle of the room with a campus police officer on either side of him. His hair was rumpled, and blood was streaked across his white shirt and his black wool jacket. His secretary Audrey was scurrying to get him a glass of water. Crime scene investigators in marked jackets were snapping photos and measuring the room. Sara wandered, looking but not touching, about the chaotic scene.

Chuy stepped into Linda's office and gently poked Linda's shoulder. "How are you holding up?"

"I'm alive, barely." Linda pointed to the books and the bullets imbedded in the wall.

Chuy looked around the small office. "How did you avoid being shot?"

"Sara pulled me to the floor. We hid behind the desk."

Chuy nodded. "After seeing her in the courthouse today and here, I know why Xave Zack said his gal Sara has the right instincts."

Linda pulled at her damp, sticky hair. "Don't encourage her recklessness."

Before Chuy answered, Sara bustled into the office and shoved several wet paper towels at Linda. "Figured you needed to clean up a bit." She flashed a grin. "Don't worry, you look a lot better than your bastard boss."

"Shhh. He'll hear you." Linda wiped the sticky coffee mixture from her forehead.

"Bet Sally calls him worse after this morning in court." Sara suddenly looked serious and turned to Chuy. "Is she going to survive?"

"Too early to tell. She, Raines, and the shooter in the courtroom are in surgery. Touch-and-go. The man who shot Raines is dead."

"What about the two here?"

Chuy puffed a bit. "Hit the one at your door in the shoulder twice. He'll live." He deflated and shook his head. "His partner wasn't as lucky. When he aimed at me, the backup officers peppered him. Don't understand these APD officers. They're gun-happy. Doubt he'll make it."

"So, what about Linda?" Sara pointed to the outer office. "And Dean Wilson? How are you going to protect them?"

Chuy pulled a computer tablet from his coat pocket and sighed. "The FBI will be joining us soon. They claim the mess this morning is related to the drug running you stumbled into in Bolivia." He straightened. "Until they get here, we wait."

He stepped into the outer office and pointed toward Linda's office. "Guys, you'd better take some measurements in here too."

Sara followed him. "I heard you mention Xave. I'm worried. How is he recovering from his wounds?"

Chuy blanched. "I thought you knew. He was transferred to a hospital in Albuquerque to recover. I... I thought to be near you."

Sara's lips trembled. "Which one?"

Chuy gulped. "That info is above my pay grade. I know he's using an alias." He frowned as a tall blonde woman and men with FBI emblazoned on their jackets strode in. He placed a hand on Sara's shoulder. "You know, he's been a loner so long. He's not apt to change."

CHAPTER 3: FBI agent Rachel Jones

FBI agent Rachel Jones stepped across yellow tape to enter the deans' office suite in the medical school. She was glad she wore thick-soled boots. Shattered glass, splinters of wood, and loose sheets of paper covered the floor and desks. She carefully avoided brushing her butter yellow leather jacket or brown tweed slacks against the remnants of two chairs, splattered with blood.

The rest of the scene was better than she expected — only a moderate amount of blood and gore. Elsa and Chuy had insisted the office remained locked and all staff, except Dean Wilson, his secretary, and Linda, be assigned to work elsewhere during the last two days. The order, designed to protect Linda and Dean Wilson before they testified at Raines's murder trial, had saved lives.

Although few medical school personnel were present, the suite was a beehive of activity. Rachel quickly identified the characters amid the rubble. The ones standing by the door with queasy expressions on their faces were campus police, who probably hadn't seen this much blood before. Those monitoring the witnesses were members of APD. Those actively gathering samples and taking measurements were crime lab personnel. The obvious person in charge was Chuy Bargas.

Chuy had matured a lot as an officer in the last two years. When she had first met him during the Philippine flu epidemic, he was an enthusiastic but nervous beginner who had a crush on her. Now he greeted her without allowing his dark eyes to gaze at her legs or torso. Maybe he was currently discretely courting Elsa Grasso, as rumored. She thought it was more. He looked determined and wasn't gulping constantly.

His stance close to Sara suggested he trusted her. Not surprising. She had been his ace in the hole twice. Sara had worked with Chuy during the flu epidemic two years ago to maintain the quarantine in the small community of La Bendita, which was under the jurisdiction of the Mercado Police Department and was where Sara lived. As Sara traced the spread of flu through the community, she had inadvertently identified Jim Mazzone, then using a different alias, as the leader of the drug trade in Albuquerque. The bureaucratic nightmare created by a quarantine had slowed Mazzone's arrest. In retrospect the local Mercado police, including Chuy, had handled the situation admirably, but her boss at the FBI had not. Mazzone outsmarted him and eluded capture. Five FBI agents were killed, her old boss took early retirement, and she became the associate director of the Albuquerque office of the FBI. Chuy was given the opportunity to transfer from the podunk Mercado Police Department to the prestigious New Mexico Gangs Task Force.

Sara had also helped Chuy burnish his image recently. About ten days ago, Sara spotted Mazzone on a flight to Bolivia out of Miami. She was beginning a public health assignment in La Paz and Potosí in Bolivia. Mazzone was strengthening his business connections with coca producers and processors in Bolivia. The FBI and other government agencies quickly realized Sara might be the key to capturing Mazzone and decreasing the amount of cocaine streaming into the U.S. from Bolivia. Unfortunately, Sara, Chuy, and a seedy undercover agent called Xave Zack received most of the credit for bringing Mazzone back to Albuquerque for trial.

Rachel arched her back with pride. However, as the FBI person coordinating Mazzone's capture, she would be up for another promotion when he was convicted. One reason why she was standing in this mess instead of sending other agents was she wanted to hear Sara's opinion on whether Mazzone was involved somehow in the shootings at the courthouse and in the medical school.

Rachel studied Sara for a moment. It was hard for her to identify what the male officers saw in her. She was just a semi-retired professor of epidemiology. However, she did have guts, but she had no style. Her pixie haircut accentuated the small sags in her jaw line. Her slightly droopy eyelids and her ten pounds of extra weight made her look like a woman past her prime.

Rachel noted Sara kept looking nervously into a small side room with a bullet-riddled door. Sara would be motivated to be helpful because she was concerned about her sister.

Dean Wilson sat slumped over a desk in the middle of the room. He certainly didn't look like a powerful medical school dean now. This upper-class snob had no guts. Someone got to him before he testified at the Raines's trial this morning. Rachel thought assistant DA Zelda Zane had been smart to have Sally Wilson lined up to testify if her husband chickened-out. If she were Zelda, she'd charge him with obstruction of justice or perjury for his performance in court.

The perfectly dressed woman wiping his forehead must be his secretary Audrey. She didn't resemble her nickname, the Dean's dragon. She looked worried. Rachel figured Audrey knew she'd be demoted if Dean Wilson lost his deanship. Maybe she didn't care because she planned to be his next wife.

Rachel nodded to Chuy but directed her first question to Sara, "What made you suspect the men at the door?"

"Their guns were already drawn."

Rachel grimaced and turned to Chuy. "Anything about the shooters here?"

"Hispanics in APD uniforms. Same as at the courthouse. The one I shot spoke like a boy from the L.A. gangs. The other one never said a word." He scrolled through notes on his tablet. "I want to be there when they come out of surgery because patients often let things slip when anesthesia is wearing off, but I stayed with my flock," he winked at Sara, "until you arrived."

Rachel snapped her fingers and pointed at Dean Wilson and his secretary. The FBI agents who accompanied her stopped talking to the APD officers. One led Wilson back to his office; the other steered the secretary to an intact pair of chairs at the back of the room. Rachel gave a tight-lipped smile to Chuy. "You might as well be on your way."

She stepped to the doorway with the defunct wood door. Linda had looked better the last time Rachel saw her a few days ago. Then, Linda had been arguing that her sister Sara shouldn't be pulled into any more schemes to trap Mazzone but should be sent back to Albuquerque immediately. The short, lithe woman with long auburn hair was now folded over her desk. Occasionally, she emitted a sniffle.

Rachel thought Linda didn't deserve the trouble heaped on her, whereas she felt no sympathy for Sara who actively looked for trouble. Linda didn't. She had stepped into a quagmire when she replaced Abel Raines as associate dean of the medical school after Dean Wilson had been forced to fire Raines for repeatedly harassing, actually raping, women employees and students. Linda, while investigating two cases of scientific misconduct in the medical school, had turned up the evidence needed by police to solve several murders. Unfortunately for Linda, Raines had planned these murders and now sought revenge. She knew now why local police groaned when they got calls from the university. Brilliant but psychologically warped people, such as Raines and his helper Diego Rivera, were difficult to trap and convict. The police needed insights from a peer like Linda.

Rachel cleared her throat. "Sara, you might as well join us." As she studied the two straight-backed chairs in Linda's cramped office, she understood why Elsa often commented Dean Wilson didn't appreciate Linda. "Let's talk."

Linda sat up, rubbed her eyes, and readjusted the clip in her hair. "I'm ready. I've cried myself out." Sara rubbed Linda's shoulders before she sank into the remaining chair.

"I assume Chuy recorded all the facts already. I want to get you two thinking — no brainstorming. Let's assume the same person enlisted the shooters at the courthouse and here. Who do you suspect was the mastermind?"

Linda gave a small smile. "Not Raines. He might have wanted all the witnesses against him eliminated, but he wouldn't have risked being shot himself."

Sara frowned. "Maybe, but Raines was desperate. He knew he couldn't survive in the general prison environment. He probably realized he'd be better off in solitary, in the hospital, or even dead." Sara frowned. "Funny, the two men shot at Linda's door but not Dean Wilson's. Was he being rewarded for his cooperation this morning in court?"

Rachel relaxed as much as possible in the chair and pulled out a computer tablet. "Good summary of my conflicting thoughts. Do you think Sally Wilson might have been a target for reasons other than the trial?"

Linda rubbed her eyes again. "What are you suggesting?"

Before Rachel replied, Sara smirked. "I noticed Audrey was more attentive than usual to Dean Wilson, and it's obvious Sally and he disagree about Raines."

Linda shook her head. "You're wrong. He was devastated when he heard his wife was shot." She pointed at Sara. "And you have an innate hatred for bossy secretaries. Granted Audrey only values men as bosses," she sighed, "as I've learned repeatedly in this job."

Rachel finished typing. "Enough. Who in the medical school had reason to want Raines dead?"

Sara laughed. "Take a number. He screwed almost everyone literally or figuratively."

Linda grabbed a pen and was jotting names and then crossing most of them out. "She's right. So, let's limit the discussion to those who might benefit from his death and who are, I'll say, psychologically unstable." She studied her list. "Three young professors here were driven by ambition and Raines's, I guess, Svengali power over them."

Rachel nodded. "Not apt to be the diet doctor who pled guilty and is in prison. From what I heard, he wasn't smart enough to coordinate four shooters."

Linda shrugged.

"Bet it's Diego Rivera. He's a planner. Hasn't gone to trial yet and probably won't be found guilty if Raines isn't around to testify." Rachel leaned back and sighed.

Linda handed her list to Rachel. "Don't be hasty. Another assistant prof George Kummer lost his job and is employable only at private clinics because of Raines's schemes."

Rachel whistled as she began to tap the keys on her tablet. "Yes, I talked to him during the investigation of Raines. Creepy and vindictive neurologist, but I can't imagine he'd work with others."

"True," said Linda, "but then there's all the women Raines humiliated. Individually or as a group, they might have sought revenge."

Rachel talked as she continued to type. "Who would be angry with you?"

Linda shivered a bit and pulled on her jacket. "The same three men."

"Mmm." She turned to Sara. "I'm surprised you were so patient. Now let's talk about the most obvious suspect Mazzone."

Sara stood and began to pace. She held up one finger. "Mazzone has to be pissed at Raines because Raines's schemes, unintentionally of course, got Mazzone arrested." She held up two fingers. "Mazzone has good reason to hate me. I identified him during the quarantine and again in Bolivia." She lifted a third finger. "He was my neighbor in La Bendita at one time. He knows the best way to hurt me is to kill Linda," she stopped, "or Bug." She lifted an additional finger. "He's got the contacts to order shootings. The jails in Albuquerque are merely an inconvenience to him." She closed her hand and shook her head. "Although he's a killer, he doesn't order innocent bystanders, such as Sally, to be shot for no reason."

"Good help is hard to find," said Rachel, "especially when you're in jail awaiting trial. Sara, I think we need to think more about the characters you annoyed while in Bolivia."

Sara reddened. "I pleased a lot of people too."

Rachel's phone rang. She listened for a few seconds. "I'll tell her."

CHAPTER 4: Sergeant Chuy Bargas of the New Mexico Gangs Task Force

Chuy finally tracked down the right nurse. "Did either shooter from the courthouse say anything before he died?"

The emergency room nurse pulled off his blood-splattered gloves. "Wrong question. They were unconscious when they arrived." The nurse guided Chuy out of the doorway to a vacant corner in the emergency room. "The shooters in the medical school were a different story. When your APD officers stepped away so we could prep the guy with the shoulder wound for surgery, the patient said 'Jorge.' The one with the gut wound must have heard him from the other side of the curtain and stopped shrieking with pain and gasped, "Shut up." He paused. "Only intelligible utterance the guy's made except for curses in Spanish."

"Did you tell the APD officers?"

"No, better." The nurse leaned back with one foot against the wall. "Asked the shooter who said Jorge if he wanted to get anything off his chest. Hinted he might not make it, even though the wound wasn't close to a major vessel and hadn't collapsed the lung."

Chuy withheld a groan. Nurses in the ER sometimes played detective. The problem was they usually didn't ask the right questions when there was only time for one or two questions. He looked at the nurse's sunken eyes and gray, creased skin underneath his eyes. Chuy heard screams behind him and turned. A patient was thrashing on her gurney as two staff dressed all in dull green held her while a nurse threaded a needle into her arm. Groans of different timbres were coming from two side rooms. He turned back to the nurse who looked expectantly at him. This man needed encouragement not criticism. "Good. What'd he say?"

"He said, 'Tell Jorge, I tried.' I leaned closer and said 'Jorge who?' Pretty smart of me?" The nurse smiled and his crow's feet deepened.

"And?"

"He kept saying 'my bro Jorge' as the anesthesia took effect and I wheeled him up to surgery." He shook his head. "If I'd known that was all I'd get, I'd let aides roll him up to surgery without me."

"It's a lead. Any tattoos."

"Plenty. police officers took photos of them already" Moaning and yelling surged in the background. "I got to get back to my patients."

***

Chuy found Elsa sitting in the waiting room outside the surgery suites on the second floor of the hospital. She scooched over on the bench to make room for him. He sighed as he slid into the narrow space. "These attacks were well planned."

Elsa nodded. "My crew and I interviewed the twenty-three witnesses to the first shooting at the courthouse. Total bust. No one saw anything but the obvious. Cameras around the courthouse showed when and where the shooters passed through courthouse security. So far, no evidence either of them talked to anyone but in a perfunctory manner prior to the shootings. We caught them on tape only once together. Shortly before the first one made his move."

"Strange. They certainly were coordinated."

"Agreed. Officers are tracking down all those shown on tapes talking to the two shooters or even near them. I also saw your emails to the FBI and L.A. police. What made you think all four shooters were from the same Sureños gang in LA?"

"The similarity in the style of the M's and thirteens tattooed on them. Thought it might be the same tattoo artist." He paused, "Let's hope I'm right. There are about five hundred of those gangs. Anyway, I'm guessing someone, maybe the Jorge character, coached all of them. The two left alive won't even give us their names. Of course, we'll know them soon because of fingerprints and DNA swabs."

Elsa sniffed as she started to fiddle with her tablet. "So unnecessary. Five shots in each of the dead shooters at the courthouse. Sometimes, I think my fellow police officers are my worst enemies."

Chuy casually swung his arm around her shoulder. "Know the feeling." He gave her a squeeze, looked around the room, and put his arm back at his side. "I want you to talk to both shooters from the med school, especially the one with the shoulder wound. See if you can get more on the man whom one called Jorge." He blushed slightly. "Take the clip out of your hair. They might respond better to woman with long black hair than me."

She glared at him. He was thankful when his phone rang. After saying hello, he wasn't sure he'd done anything right. He breathed heavily and shifted uncomfortably on the bench as he tried to get a word in occasionally.

When he ended the call, Elsa said, "What's up?"

"That was Eric Sanders, the director of USAID activities in Bolivia." He paused and scratched his chin. "Though that wasn't the title he gave. Anyway, he's upset, no mad, because he wasn't notified until two hours after the shooting in the courthouse." Chuy shrugged. "I thought I was being nice to send him an email while I waited for Rachel to show up at the emergency room. He also about bit my head off when I called him Eric. He made it clear that he wants to be called Sanders."

"Part of his power trip."

"I guess. Just now Sanders was so sure of himself that he convinced me."

"About what?"

"He thinks Sally was shot by mistake. The shooter was supposed to kill Sara. Both Sally and Sara are tall blondes." Chuy pulled his hands through his hair. "Come to think of it, Sara said the shooter waved the gun in a confused manner before he shot Sally. Sara and I both figured he was nervous."

"What does he expect you to do?"

Chuy again swung his arm around Elsa's shoulder and pulled her closer. "He wants Sara out of Albuquerque before more gang members arrive for more shootings. He was strangely protective of Sara. Kept mumbling, she was much too valuable an asset to lose."

Elsa pulled away a bit. "What about Linda?"

Chuy whispered in her ear. "He wants her out too. He's convinced ABQ police killed the shooter in the courtroom for one of two reasons. They're stupid or at least one of them is in league with the gangs. He's betting on the latter."

Elsa shivered. "Something we all fear. I'll talk to my lieutenant as soon as I finish with the two shooters in post-surgery."

"Good. One thing was funny about the call. There was an odd echo sometimes. I figured Sanders's phone was on speakerphone mode, but then I heard an announcement of a blue code alert faintly in the background."

Elsa breathed in deeply. "Know what you're thinking. Xave was listening in from a hospital in Albuquerque."

"Sneaky bastards."

"Worse. Sanders and Xave are paranoid." She grabbed Chuy's arms and looked into his eyes. "Be careful, very careful when you work with them. They... Well at least that Xave character is as crazy as the gang members."

Chuy felt his Adam's apple bobbing in his throat as he gazed at Elsa. He blinked, and she squeezed his arms before she released them and stood.

Elsa took the clip out of her hair. "Let's see what I can pull from the remaining gunmen." She sped off to the surgical recovery room.

As Chuy sent messages, an orderly ran up. "Follow me."

The surgeon who headed the team working on Raines was waiting behind the swinging doors. He neither frowned nor smiled as he pulled off his gloves, slung them into a basket, and pulled his hand over his gray buzz cut. "Dr. Raines is dead. I admired the man professionally. He was a brilliant oncologist and the brains behind most of the expansions in the medical school during the last fifteen years. But I couldn't save him. Gut wounds are always difficult, so many bleeders. And he had four."

"Did he say anything?"

The surgeon looked at Chuy for a moment. "Yeah, right before they anesthetized him when I told him I would be his surgeon. Odd. I think he said, 'Sorry Ethan.' I know he and the Dean go way back. The Dean overlooked lots of Raines's foibles because Raines delivered as his associate dean. Still, not what I expected. Course his nearest relative is a sister somewhere in the Midwest. They weren't close."

Chuy couldn't force him himself to console the surgeon. Raines had caused the deaths of three women, granted one murder had occurred more than thirty years ago, and he had harassed and raped dozens of other women. Elsa had noted during his arrest that he was proud and unrepentant. Chuy thought Raines's murder prevented the state from wasting more money on finishing his trial and imprisoning him.

Chuy instantly regretted his hard heartedness and touched the surgeon's shoulder. "You tried. Any news on Sally Wilson?"

"Nice lady. Don't know how she put up with the Dean all these years. I checked on the other team before I came out. One simple shoulder wound. The other bullet punctured a lung. They were working on the last bleeder when I came out and should have her in recovery soon."

"Will she survive?"

J. L. Greger

"Should, but won't be able to talk for a couple of hours, maybe longer. They almost lost her in surgery."

"Thanks Doc."

The surgeon cleared his throat and hung his head. "I should clarify my earlier comments. I respected Raines's professional abilities, but he was ruthless. He always said, 'You have to destroy malignancies wherever you find them in the body or anywhere in life before they spread.' And he called anything or anyone who thwarted his plans a malignancy. Not good to be on his bad side. He made a lot of people, especially women like my daughter when she was a medical student here, miserable." He shook his head. "Odd he should be shot with Sally Wilson. He had a particular aversion to her. Only person he hated more was Linda Almquist."

CHAPTER 5: Sara at the medical school

Rachel had settled into a chair facing Sara before her phone rang. "Rachel Jones here." She slid forward in her chair. "Yes, Mr. Sanders." She was silent during the one-sided conversation, but occasionally she meekly said, "I see."

Sara enjoyed watching the diva be reduced to quietness. Sara had observed Rachel was a bully around local police officers. Maybe her behavior was an integral part of being an FBI agent and a supervisor to boot. Interesting to see how she caved to someone with more authority.

Sara was glad for a chance to think about the day. Linda was in danger. She probably was too. The Hispanic gangs were an almost inexhaustible source of young men who would willingly risk death to gain status in the Mexican Mafia. Whoever had hired the first gunmen would probably hire more if his goals hadn't been met.

Rachel's phone buzzed. She looked relieved to put Sanders on hold at first. Then her lips quivered. "I'll tell Sanders. I have him on hold."

Sara was surprised by the softness of Rachel's voice.

Rachel swallowed hard. "We lost Raines." She listened. "Probably too late, but I will try to keep the news from the press for an hour." As she spoke, she stood, scribbled a note, and lunged for the door. She screamed at the two FBI agents as she passed through the doorway. "Get more back up here. And call this number."

As soon as the door slammed shut, Sara walked to Linda's office. Linda appeared to be studying a complicated document on her computer screen, but only a short memo was visible. "I'm hungry. You obviously aren't able concentrate anymore. Let's get out of this office complex."

Without glancing at Sara, Linda opened the refrigerator beside her desk and held up a plastic bag with a couple stalks of celery blackened at the ends.

"Not that hungry. I also need to get my car from the courthouse."

J. L. Greger

Linda sighed and continued to stare at the screen.

"Raines died."

"I know. Elsa emailed me." She turned to Sara with tears in her eyes. "I was trying to sort out how I felt."

Sara snorted as she plunked down onto a chair. "Relieved. There's one less bad guy trying to kill you. Maybe even happy. Those emotions made you feel guilty and brought tears."

Linda rubbed her eyes. "I know I'm being silly. Elsa emailed me because she wanted to contact his relatives. So, I checked his personnel file. He listed the Dean as his contact in case of an emergency. Guess that makes sense. They worked together for almost thirty years."

"No relatives?"

"One of the surgeons told Chuy that Raines had an estranged sister." She swallowed. "I heard him snicker about two ex-wives when he was with the Dean and wanted to describe something bad. So, I searched his personnel file until I found their names." Linda typed the names of Raines's sister and ex-wives and tapped the reply button.

Sara stood. "I don't want to talk about the events of today. If I started crying, I might not stop for hours. The worst may be ahead. We haven't heard news on Sally Wilson yet. And let's face it — more gunmen are apt to come after us. We won't be safe until the reasons for shootings today are known and arrests are made." She looked upward and muttered a prayer. "Let's eat."

Sara stomped to the outer office and announced to the two FBI agents she was going to the cafeteria. They claimed that was impossible. She laughed and threw open the door, which had a sheet of plywood where a pane of glass was supposed to be, and stalked down the hall. In less than a couple of seconds, she heard an agent fuming and fussing on his phone as he ran after her and Linda calling for her to slow down. Three campus police joined them before they reached the cafeteria.

The choices were limited. Lunch was over. Servers were cleaning the steam table before they placed the dinner entrees on display. Even so, Linda and Sara both selected a bowl of green chili chicken soup. Linda also bought crackers. Sara chose a hot chocolate chip cookie.

Few were in the lunchroom, but Sara noticed those present were staring at Linda. Not surprising. The courtroom dramas of the last two days had to be the chief item of gossip in the med school. Then too, anyone who knew them would be amused to see four men protectively flanking the sisters.

The FBI agent's phone buzzed. He listened briefly and handed the phone to Sara. She was greeted by Sanders's clipped words. "You owe me a report on your trip to Bolivia tomorrow. Today would be better."

Sara wasn't in the mood to take any guff. "You'll get it. Why did you call?"

Sanders chuckled. "I think you and your sister should leave Albuquerque until the FBI and local police have control of the situation. I want you to work on two projects. One is the continuation of your work in Bolivia. The other is in Cuba."

Sara noted the officers had stopped talking and were staring at her. She turned her back to them. "Don't know anything about the latter."

"Mmm. I understand. People are listening. You'll get the standard government consulting fee." He coughed. "Not what you deserve."

"Money's not the problem per se. What about Linda and Bug?"

Sanders cleared his throat. "I'll hire her as a consultant too. Is Bug your pet name for Xave?"

Linda snorted. "Bug is my Japanese Chin. Don't insult him by comparing him to Xave who hasn't bothered to contact me, as he promised." She almost added she knew Xave was in Albuquerque but decided withholding some information was smart when she was negotiating with Sanders.

"Is this Bug the usual nip and yip?"

"No. He's flown many times at my feet and never barks. Do you want to give me details on what I'd be doing? I'm easy."

Sanders groaned. "I doubt it."

Sara ignored his comment. "Linda is hard to blast out of her house. So, you'd better spike her interest."

"Hand the phone to Linda, please."

Linda moved down two chairs and sat by the window after listening to Sanders for only a few seconds. The FBI agent stared at Sara. "Well?"

Sara had learned in Bolivia that Sanders expected his conversations to be private. "Nothing to tell." As usual, she thought Sanders was right. If she could keep the four men from staring at Linda, he would be more apt to succeed in coaxing her sister away from Albuquerque. "I'll buy cookies and beverages for all of you, but I'll need help to carry the beverages back to the table."

The three campus police officers cast quick glances at the FBI agent and followed Sara to the cafeteria line. When they returned, Linda had her head braced between her hands with her elbows on the table. Sara thought she saw a trace of a smile on Linda's lips. A good sign.

Sara was ready to give up on keeping the officers distracted when Linda handed the phone to the FBI agent and started to walk to the cafeteria entrance. When Sara caught up with her, Linda whispered, "We're going tomorrow. He's talked to everyone who needs to know. We can only discuss our travel plans with Chuy, Elsa, and Rachel."

"Bug, too?"

"Of course." She lowered her voice even more. "He hypothesized the shootings could be related to something you saw or did in Bolivia. Something you thought was insignificant."

CHAPTER 6: Sara traveling to Washington on Day 2

"I don't think this is a good idea."

Sara pulled a rolling bag behind her and ignored Linda as she looked for a seat within hearing range of their gate and where no one could easily get behind them. After she found two seats in front of a window, she opened the bottle of water she purchased after the security check and poured a bit into a red cup. She unzipped the bag and shoved the cup in before Bug could pop out. Sanders had warned her it was important to keep Bug out of sight because he was so easily identifiable.

"Is he all right?" Linda, wearing a short black wig, settled next to Sara and peered anxiously at the bag.

"He's fine. Don't stare at the bag. We don't want to be noticed. I'm thankful Sanders allowed me to bring Bug to Washington and got a reservation for him under my seat. You know there can only be one pet per compartment. I usually spend more than an hour trying to arrange Bug's reservation when he flies with me."

Linda uncapped her bottle of water. "The TSA pre-check that he arranged for us made security a snap today." She gulped her drink and scratched at the hairline behind her ear. "I feel pretty obvious with this itchy wig, and you look ridiculous with long brown hair."

Sara tucked the hair behind one ear. "Thought it looked pretty good."

"Hmmf. You do look different. Maybe odd is a better word. It would have been easier if I'd stayed here with Bug. You know I'm a homebody."

Sara whispered, "Sanders is right. We'll be safer out of Albuquerque, and the police are more apt to get your boss to talk if they can isolate him from his usual support system. Now he's waiting on Sally instead of vice versa. You're not handling situations in the medical school." Sara chuckled. "And Audrey isn't cooing over him because she has given up hope of being the next Mrs. Wilson."

Linda pulled a novel from her case. "Not funny. Audrey can be a bitch, but no one can convince me she was in on any plan to shoot Sally and Raines. It was mean of Elsa to threaten to charge her as an accessory to murder if she didn't relate all of the Dean's confidences to her."

"You're the only one who feels sorry for Audrey. I think Dean Wilson is hiding a lot. And she knows it."

"Cynic."

"No, he verbally abuses you, and he wouldn't have tolerated Raines, unless he shared some of Raines's attitudes. Yesterday, he showed more of a change in mood when Raines's death was announced than when told his wife survived surgery."

Sanders had promised a federal air marshal would be on both the flight to Denver and the next one to Washington. He warned her flight delays might signal the air marshal was incapacitated. Accordingly, Sara scanned the crowd at the gate. The crowd was large. She quickly discounted anyone traveling with children and focused on business travelers. Sara assumed most single individuals wearing suits or hunched over their computer were business travelers. She studied faces to see if she recognized anyone. No one caught her eye, but she suspected most air marshals were expert at traveling incognito.

Several couples caught her interest. A young man and a young woman with her blonde hair sprayed into a stiff updo were pacing at the edge of the crowd. The woman was carrying a zippered, white clothes bag labeled David's Bridal. Oddly, they never smiled as they spoke to each other. She couldn't imagine this would be a happy marriage.

Three Hispanic teens wearing green camouflage do-rags boisterously pushed at each other, but said nothing intelligible, at least to Sara. The hit men yesterday were young Hispanic gang members, but these seemed too obvious to be a danger.

A big-shouldered, thirtyish man with a crew cut pushed an old man in a wheelchair to the desk and spoke to the gate agent and then edged back in the crowd. The old man was slumped in the chair and wore a black stocking cap with a black knit scarf pulled up around his face, even though the waiting area wasn't chilly. Occasionally he lifted his cane to thump on his attendant's shoulder.

Sara stood ostensibly to stretch and walked haphazardly through the crowd so she could get a closer view of the three interesting groups and hear their conversations.

The "bridal pair" was nervous about pleasing John, but they never spoke of a wedding or reception and never kissed or hugged each other. The "teens" were catching a bus from Denver to Boulder to visit the University of Colorado campus. The "guy in the wheelchair" wore heavy boots and looked sturdy despite his slumped position in the chair. The first and third pairs weren't what they pretended to be.

"Person with specials needs can now board the flight to Denver." The whole crowd around the gate became more animated.

Sara hurried back to claim her rolling bag from Linda who was tugging at her wig. She decided any comment would only increase Linda's nervousness. Instead, she slipped her hand inside the bag and tickled Bug's silky ears. He nuzzled her and uttered a soft snort. "Let's go."

The early boarders were families with small children. Sara and Linda approached the podium at the same time as the man in a wheelchair and his attendant. For the first time, the man looked up, so Sara could see his eyes. Sara stifled a gasp. The man looked down immediately. The attendant waved Linda and Sara to go first.

Sara debated her options and pushed Linda ahead of her. The man in the chair was Xave. At least, he looked like Xave. The attendant looked like Xave's military cohorts in Bolivia — strong with the same ugly crew cut. Halfway down the jetway, as the last family member was disappearing into the plane, she stopped and faced the wheel chair attendant. "Watch the bridal couple." She wanted to pull the scarf away from the face of the man in the chair but resisted the urge.

The attendant's eyes narrowed. "Lady, don't know what you're talking about?"

The man in the chair raised his cane without lifting his head. Sara considered questions she wanted answered, but the "bridal" couple was barreling down the jetway toward them. She wiped a tear from her eye and hurried to catch up with Linda.

***

The man in the wheelchair and his attendant were seated a few rows behind Sara and Linda in the economy class. Sara thought that was odd. Usually those with wheel chairs were in the first row of coach. The "bridal" couple was seated in first-class. That meant Sara couldn't observe either during the flight because the pilot kept the seat belt light on throughout the flight even though the flight felt smooth.

The flight to Denver lasted less than hour but seemed endless. Sara kept replaying in her mind Xave's instructions before the flight from Bolivia only three days before. "Get off every flight as fast as you can. Duck into a washroom. Change your appearance with the props I gave you, and get on the next flight as fast as you can. No matter what you hear or see, keep moving and never approach me in airports because I'm probably trying to be incognito." Obviously, he didn't want to talk to her now.

She looked over to her sister in the next seat. Linda was alternately chewing on her fingernails and pulling at her wig. She wondered how had she and Linda gotten into such a muddle. They hadn't set out to annoy anyone. She prayed no one was pissed off enough to try again.

***

As Sara and Linda raced into the boarding area for the flight to Washington, Sara spotted the "bridal" couple near the gate. She hoped they wouldn't recognize her because now she and Linda wore trench coats and were gray-haired. She chose a seat in the waiting area as far from the suspicious couple as possible and studied the crowd. She saw only four others, not counting the suspicious couple, who had been on the flight from Albuquerque. No wheelchairs or canes.

Sara poked Linda hoping to engage her in conversation, but Linda only grunted and continued to stare at a book. Linda wasn't reading because she hadn't turned a page in over five minutes, but the swollen knuckles on her hand were white from clenching the book. "Does your arthritis make your hands hurt more during flights?"

Linda gave a disgusted shake of her head. "Yes, and they will ache in Washington because of the low pressure system centered there." She returned to staring at her book.

Linda was always grouchy when they flew because she hated the process. In contrast, Sara loved airports. So many people to watch, endless possibilities to imagine, and lots of memories.

Although Sara enjoyed the frantic pace of airports, she loved Washington more. She was looking forward to wandering with Bug around neighborhoods near DuPont Circle and in Georgetown and studying the various styles of architecture and reading obscure historic plaques. But there was a glitch in her plans. Bug was a desert dog, and he lowered his head and pulled her toward their home whenever rain began to soak through his long coat of fur on their walks. It was seldom a problem in the Albuquerque area because it seldom rained for more than ten minutes at a time. Weather reporters forecast rain daily for the next week in Washington. She felt sorry for Bug and shoved a handful of pellets into the rolling carrier.

Linda peered over the top of her book. "Glad you finally settled down. For a while, I thought I was traveling with a two-year-old."

Sara slouched down in her seat.

The agent at the desk announced that the flight would be delayed.

Sara gulped as she remembered Sanders's comments about the air marshals. What could have delayed the air marshal? She'd never identified him on the last flight. Sara stood and scanned the crowd again.

Linda grabbed her sleeve and pulled her down. "Stop the spy routine."

The plane took off ten minutes late. The seat belt signs remained on for most of the flight, although only the last half of the flight was rough. The "bridal" couple was again located in first-class. Sara dozed because she knew Linda sitting by the aisle would remain alert. She awoke and gazed out the window as the plane thudded on the tarmac at Ronald Reagan Airport. She'd traded a landscape of brown and tan for one in shades of gray. Even the sky was gray as rain pelted down. She nudged Linda. "Let's not take the Metro to Federal Triangle and then walk to Sanders's office in the Ronald Reagan Building. Let's splurge and take a cab."

"Best idea you've had today."

CHAPTER 7: Sara in Washington

Sara was surprised when Sanders, not an aide, came to the front desk of the Ronald Reagan Building to claim them. When he stiffly bent down to pat Bug after being introduced to Linda, Bug shook his bedraggled, wet fur and splattered dirty water and sand across Sanders's black pinstriped suit. Sanders snorted and pulled out a white handkerchief and brushed the grit from his sleeve. Bug sat down and began to lick his paws.

"Sorry. He got wet during his bathroom break." Sara tickled Bug's ear.

Sanders waved his hand to direct them to the elevator. "My ex-wife would have said that's why I avoid children and pets." He then proceeded to explain his plans for the next few days. Linda and Sara would work separately. One reason he'd been in such a hurry to get them to Washington was that the director of USAID had convened representatives from several Latin American and Caribbean countries to discuss their countries' public health needs. Sanders thought an associate dean from a medical school in the Southwest might be an addition to the mix because several of the representatives had already requested more training opportunities for their staff. The conference had begun two hours ago.

They stopped at a large desk on the third floor. Sanders snapped his fingers, and a young man whisked Linda away. Sara dragged both her and Linda's bags and followed Sanders into a noisy room. One woman was packing books into boxes. Another was giving orders to two uniformed workmen with a hand trolley. She hardly glanced at Sara before she pointed to the suitcases and told the workmen to take them with the boxes. Sara grabbed Bug's rolling carrier and the tote with her papers as Sanders waved her to a small table. Bug stalked around the room and before settling at Sara's feet.

"I'm in a transition phase from being the director of USAID in Bolivia to working for the Under Secretary for Political Affairs in the State Department on issues related to Latin America and the Caribbean.

This room, my old office, is where we'll start today." He pulled a file from his desk and sat down at the table. "I read the report you sent late yesterday afternoon on the public health mission to Bolivia." He smirked. "Gave you a chance to forget being shot at again."

Sara ignored the jibe. She had struggled to complete the report among the chaos of Linda's office yesterday. "I hope the report met your needs."

He shuffled pages. "I noted you sent the report electronically to all the committee members. All replied to me already. The water expert said he expected to be appointed the chair of any new committee formulated to improve water purification systems in Bolivia." He sighed. "Bit of an ego problem. The survey expert from the committee volunteered to serve on a new committee if you chaired it, but not if the water expert was the chair." He cleared his throat. "She said he made her nervous."

"How did the chairman of our original committee reply? He's too sick to respond to emails."

"He didn't answer per se. His wife did." Sanders fumbled with a page and read, "I'm pleased something positive came out of my husband's last project." He continued to look at the page. "I have to respect him for persisting to the end. Real guts. Actually, I'm amazed by the professionalism of all of the members of the committee. You performed well in difficult situations, and the Bolivian government for the first time in years is pleased about a U.S. project in Bolivia." He handed the collection of responses to Sara and returned to his desk to check messages on his computer.

"So?"

He kept tapping keys on his computer and reading his messages. "I filed your report already and put through the initial request to re-formulate the committee. Takes less paperwork than creating a new committee." He snorted as he read a message on his computer and deleted it. "The director of USAID will send thank you letters to all of the committee members today with copies to their Congressional reps." He lingered on a message on his computer. "Interesting."

"So, why am I here?"

"Mmm." He finally looked at Sara. "In your down time this week, you'll work with a USAID staffer to re-formulate the committee and plan the next goals for the committee. I agree with the original committee's assessment. The scope of the committee should be narrowed from 'improving child health in Bolivia' to "upgrading water quality to improve child health in Bolivia.' Questions?"

"Can I enlist public health officials we met in Bolivia to join the committee?"

"Good idea. Talk to them and have them clear their participation with their bosses. Then a USAID staffer will do the tricky paperwork for including non-US citizens on government-appointed committees. I can see already that you don't need my help."

Sara shook her head. "A control freak like you doesn't sign off easily. What's the real story?"

The smirk again. "I won't, as you say, sign off easily, but I have confidence in your judgment." He sniffed. "Don't be kind. Pick people who will work with you as the chair of the restructured committee. If the water expert from the old committee can't, he's out." He started to walk toward the door. "Now for your major project." He looked back over his shoulder. "Better bring your coat and whatever the dog needs. My staff will see your other bags are transferred to the appropriate place."

Sara guessed Sanders would race along at top speed because his patience and politeness didn't appear to be improved by being in the U.S. instead of Bolivia. She put Bug in the rolling carrier, grabbed her coat and tote, and raced after him. At the doorway, she looked both ways. Sanders was almost to the elevator.

"I usually take the State Department shuttle to C Street, but a cab is faster, especially," he stared at the rolling cart, "with your dog and the rain."

Once in the cab Sanders immersed himself in the messages on his laptop. He growled before he typed a sentence or two in response to most messages and pushed the send button. Finally, he slowed his pace and chuckled. "Seems you gave the air marshal and more importantly the man I assigned to watch you this morning conniptions."

"Was one of them the attendant for the guy in the wheel chair?"

Sanders's eyes remained focused on his computer. "What gave him away?"

"He was muscular with a crew cut like the guys you used in Bolivia. The supposed invalid in the chair wore heavy boots and kept his face covered."

Sanders finally looked at her. "I told you only one air marshal would be on the flights. Why did you even notice the pair?"

Sara checked Bug in the rolling cart by her feet as she debated whether to be honest. She decided she had nothing to lose. "I think the man disguised as an invalid was Xave. I've gotten the brush off before, but I never had a man hide from me."

Sanders smirked. "Seems my man became concerned when the couple with the David's Bridal bag skipped the baggage claim and followed you to the cab stand."

"I didn't see the wheelchair attendant on the second flight. What happened?"

"I'll make a long story short. Bridal gear is a good way to move stolen jewelry. Amazing what can be sewn into those gowns." He closed the lid of his computer. "You weren't the only one changing your appearance between flights this morning. At least you didn't spot the air marshal." He pulled cash from his pocket to pay the cab driver. "Believe me, Xave didn't want to hide from you. Follow me."

Sanders bounded from the cab. The cab was under a canopy, and Sara saw no reason to rush blindly after him. After she met Bug's needs and passed through the security check, she found Sanders leaning against the wall by the elevators and checking his messages. He didn't complain. When they reached a room on the fourth floor, he said, "Two others will be going through this orientation on Cuba with you."

Sara gasped as she entered the small conference room. At the table sat Shantelle Eaton, the USAID officer who had made serious mistakes in Bolivia, and the wheelchair attendant now dressed as a naval officer. "Shantelle, why are you working for Sanders? I thought he fired you from USAID."

Shantelle grimaced. "I'm now an independent contractor employed by the State Department."

Sara turned to Sanders who was pouring himself a cup of coffee at the beverage tray. "I don't understand."

Sanders put his cup down, pulled a can of Diet Coke off the beverage tray, and handed it to Sara. "Your favorite source of caffeine as I remember." He picked up his cup of coffee and nonchalantly nodded at Shantelle. "Tell her."

Shantelle hiccuped as she stared back at Sanders. "I've learned a lot in the last three days. I'm in the purgatory where all potentially useful State Department employees go after they've made highly visible mistakes in the field. Once our careers are ruined, we're given an opportunity to accept," she paused, "assignments as contractors so our bosses can disclaim us, if necessary."

               J. L. Greger

Sara eyed Sanders. He really was a manipulative bastard. "Am I in that category?"

Sanders seemed to savor his mouthful of coffee. "Quite the opposite. You and the naval officer here are the squeaky clean parts of this plan. Shantelle and another character, I'll say with a couple of past mistakes under his belt, add another dimension to our retinue."

Sara thought for a few seconds as she put her can of cola and her tote on the table. Then she stood with arms akimbo and spoke slowly and distinctly. "I'm an epidemiologist, not a spy or whatever you call those doing your dirty work. I plan to stay that way."

Sanders flashed a broad smile. "Exactly the right response. Use the same tone if anyone asks you about your association with me."

Sara suppressed a gasp. She debated whether she'd received a compliment or had been disciplined. She guessed it didn't matter and unzipped Bug's carrier. Bug snorted as he emerged and circled the room before sitting at Sara's feet.

Sanders put down his coffee cup, waved for the rest to sit while he remained standing, and went into lecture mode. "Despite our embargo of Cuba, our government has allowed Cuba's best artists to tour the U.S." He paced as he explained how the artist exchange program worked despite a trade embargo and travel restrictions. "These artists have provided us useful insights into modern Cuba and have taken many ideas back to Cuba. What we expected and wanted."

He stopped pacing. "Now we want to encourage another exchange — an exchange of scientists in key areas, such as medical research. Nixon and Kissinger encouraged scientific exchanges as they opened up trade with China. We believe the Cuban government will be receptive to this suggestion because its leaders are proud of Cuba's public health and medical efforts. Several of their scientists received extensive training at universities here, particularly Harvard and Tulane."

Sara waved her hand. "Wasn't this training prior to 1960 and the Bay of Pigs?"

Sanders smiled. "No, I'm talking about training in the last ten years. Now, scientists at our National Institutes of Health are eager to visit Cuban facilities." He frowned. "These scientific exchanges must be managed carefully. The differences between new medical treatments and a biological toxins are often not large. We don't want to duplicate our past mistakes. We shouldn't have been surprised when Pakistan and Iran built nuclear devices, considering how many Irani and Pakistani students received doctoral degrees in physics and nuclear engineering in the U.S."

Sara waved her hand. "I can guess where this might be going. I've read a Cuban research group received a patent for a new cancer drug. I'm the wrong person for this assignment. I'm not a molecular biologist who can understand the details of the drug's development."

Sanders glared at her. "You aren't an expert on water purification systems either, but you performed well on the USAID committee for Bolivia."

Sara suppressed her annoyance and her voice was only a little louder than usual as she replied. "That committee was designed to look at factors affecting child health in Bolivia. I signed on as an epidemiologist to sort through a large amount of data and help the committee focus on the most important factors."

"Exactly what you'll be doing here — helping us identify experts and writing a charge for scientific, maybe medical is a better word, exchanges." He pointed to the naval officer and Shantelle. "They're preparing for related missions in Cuba. Yours, actually ours, is the first step."

Sara knew that the question buzzing in her mind was inappropriate. She blurted it out anyway, "Why did you rehire Shantelle after you fired her?" Sara cast a quick glance of Shantelle. "Sorry."

Shantelle nodded. "I said that too."

Sanders gave a benevolent smile. Sara thought his smile might be called a shit-eating grin. "Ladies, fire is such a harsh word. The records in USAID headquarters show Shantelle resigned to seek other opportunities."

Sara waved her hand. "What about the other mystery member?" She glanced around the room. "When will he or she show up?"

"He'll be here when he needs to be." He cleared his throat. "Don't worry. He has a master's degree in public health and experience in South America. He'll appear to be a logical choice. Furthermore, I promise you Shantelle won't make the same mistakes as before."

Shantelle shivered and seemed to shrink in her chair. The naval officer chewed his gum at a slow, steady pace and stared at Shantelle. Sara wondered about his expertise.

During the next hour, Sanders displayed an encyclopedic knowledge of Cuban history and politics. Sara guessed he secretly dreamed of being a professor because he addressed the three in his audience as if they were fifty. She smiled to herself. He obviously wouldn't be a popular professor because his authoritarian tone without humor was boring.

J. L. Greger

Thus, Sara was relieved, and she suspected so were Shantelle and the naval officer when two experts on health care and medical research in developing countries joined the group. One was a scholar from the Library of Congress; one was a State Department employee. They reeled off health statistics for one-half hour and showed lots of colorful charts.

Sara figured they were trying to convince their audience that health problems in Cuba were similar to those in the U.S. They made two main points. The average life expectancy in Cuba and the U.S. was the same, about seventy-nine years in 2016. Cardiovascular disease and malignancies were the leading causes of the death in both countries. Their most interesting comments were on the cost of health care. Cubans spent about $800 per person on health care in 2016; American spent about $9,400. That translated into eleven percent of the gross domestic product (GDP) in Cuba and seventeen percent of the GDP in the U.S.

Shantelle had alternated between taking notes and nodding off to sleep during the lecture. The naval officer had sat motionless with his eyes glazed. He reminded Sara of pre-med students in her classes. Usually they were bright, bored, arrogant, and a pain-in-the-ass to work with unless you sparked their interest. She doubted either of their assignments were related to medical issues in Cuba.

In contrast, Sanders took notes throughout the session. He also occasionally asked questions and listened to answers without his usual impatient interruptions. Some of his questions confounded the experts who complained they'd only been apprised of this meeting yesterday. Sanders shrugged when they repeated their complaint a second time. "Things evolved quickly in Bolivia and here."

Sara was puzzled. She wondered what in Bolivia had prompted Sanders's interest in Cuba and his shift in position from USAID to the State Department. She knew the leaders of Bolivia, Cuba, and Venezuela shared leftist political views, and the three countries were in some sort of trading alliance. The State Department probably eyed this pact skeptically, but these well-established connections hadn't sparked Sanders's current interest. More importantly, she assumed he had an ulterior motive for his interest in health care and medical research in Cuba.

She decided it was time to get answers. That meant provoking or at least surprising Sanders and his experts. Besides she wanted to learn more about the announcement she'd seen in a scientific newsletter.

"What do you know about the new cancer drug patented by the Cubans? How hard would it be for a large drug company to break the patent?"

The expert from the Library of Congress sucked in his breath and exploded with information. During his answer, he revealed he was a professor of pharmacology at the University of California-San Francisco on sabbatical leave for a year to examine potential drug development ideas in third world countries using the resources at the Library of Congress.

Sanders winked at her when she asked the question, almost like he expected her to ask the question. During the answer, he took notes on his laptop.

Sara sighed. She'd underestimated Sanders, and she'd not provoked him to reveal his ulterior motives. As the lecturers returned to their dry recitation, Sara kept wondering what in Bolivia aroused Sanders's interest in Cuba?

Suddenly, a potential answer hit her. The majority of coca-derived products entering the U.S. from South America went through Columbia. What if a new major trade route was emerging through Cuba? She'd heard the black market in Cuba was thriving. Instead of listening to the lecturers, she thought about how to test her hypothesis that Sanders's interest in Cuba was related to the movement of drugs from Bolivia to the U.S.

Sanders must have noticed her inattention because he pointed at Bug who was gazing intently at him. "I see the dog is the only one with an intelligent look on his face at this point. Let's break." He thanked the experts and requested a summary of their comments. Then he rushed from the room with Shantelle and the naval officer in tow, and the experts trailing after them.

Almost immediately, a man rolled in a new refreshment cart stocked with beverages, chips, crackers, cheese, and even little sandwiches. Sara was playing with Bug when Shantelle strolled back in and began to wolf down the ham salad sandwiches. She looked sheepishly at Sara as she grabbed her third. "Don't know when I'll next get a chance to eat."

"Shantelle, there's a lot I don't understand. Let's start with — why were you picked for a mission to Cuba?"

Shantelle glanced at the door and finished her sandwich. "I speak Spanish fluently and have a degree in public health." She poured herself a cup of coffee.

J. L. Greger

"Mmm." Sara recognized Shantelle was being evasive. "What about the naval officer?"

"He's from an upper-class Cuban family of Spanish descent. His family owns a cigar factory in the Ybor district of Tampa and has frequent contact with associates in Cuba."

"Now back to you."

Shantelle sipped her coffee. "I'm black, and a large proportion of Cubans are mulattos with a black heritage."

"Shantelle, forget the practiced answers. What is the real reason Sanders wants you to work in Cuba?"

Shantelle gulped. "I met several men in Bolivia with Cuban contacts. They might make me seem more accessible to those... to those...."

Sara stepped closer. "Involved in the black market in Cuba."

"Why do you ask?"

Sara shrugged. "I've seen the black markets in China and Russia. Cubans must have found ways around the embargo. I was hoping Sanders would bring in an expert on the Cuban economy, particularly on the ways the people circumvent state controls. Bet it's fascinating and ingenious."

Shantelle flinched and looked at the floor.

Sara guessed she might be getting close to the truth, so she barged ahead. "Your friend from high school Diego Rivera forced you to contact drug runners in Bolivia. Are these the contacts Sanders wants you to develop?"

Shantelle knelt and began to tease Bug with a bit of a chip.

"My sister Linda believed Diego had broken his ties with the L.A. gangs before he was hired as an assistant professor in the medical school in Albuquerque. However, when Raines was charged with a couple of murders, he blackmailed Diego into using his adolescent ties to the gangs in order to court favor with the drug lord Mazzone."

Shantelle petted Bug. "I'm well aware how strong Diego's contacts are. Sanders moved my grandmother out of L.A. away from the reach Diego's friends."

Sara knelt by Shantelle. "Do you know about the shootings in Albuquerque yesterday? L.A. gang members killed Raines. Diego is apt to be involved. Don't let Sanders drag you back into Diego's web."

"Hmmf." The noise came from the doorway.

Sara jumped to her feet and stepped toward Sanders. "How much did you hear?"

"Enough. I was told twice in the last fifteen minutes that you and your sister are much too nice to be drawn into any clandestine activities. I agree your sister is, but you have a proclivity for understanding and possibly even seeking the dark side of issues."

Sara looked down. She quickly realized she had no reason to feel ashamed and jerked her head up. "I'm more practical than most academics."

"Exactly why you're so useful," he laughed, "and fascinating. You will be pleased our next expert will address the Cuban economy, both legal and illegal."

Sara looked directly into his eyes. "You told me once I was a nosy do-gooder. Maybe you were right, but I don't want to end up dead or in a Cuban prison."

"That's a given." He started to turn away and then he laughed. "The biggest inconsistency in your life is," he pointed at Bug, "your dog. He's a gentleman through and through. You, well you, seem to enjoy going head to head with men who are not being gentlemanly."

CHAPTER 8: Sergeant Elsa Grasso of Albuquerque Police Department (APD)

"Raines lowered my conviction rate." Assistant DA Zelda Zane scanned the group assembled around the oval table in her office. Chuy and Elsa both reddened as they suppressed laughter. Two FBI agents were less polite and guffawed openly.

Rachel yawned. "I doubt he arranged his own murder just to annoy you." She too looked around the table as if all were her minions. "The shootout in the courtroom occurred twenty-five hours ago, where do we stand?"

Elsa feared this would be a bumpy meeting because both divas were ready to fight. Secretly she found Zelda to be the more disagreeable of the two, which wasn't to say she liked Rachel.

Zelda must have stood on her tiptoes because she suddenly seemed taller. "Don't laugh. The victims and their families deserve closure. More importantly, Raines's conviction would have sent a message to high-handed university administrators, such as his friend Dean Wilson. You saw the man in court yesterday. He withheld evidence and lied. Now potential jurors will consider him a victim because his wife was shot." She bounced into her chair.

Elsa was hesitant to speak because she realized the one activity the two divas relished more than sparring with each other was skewering her. "Police cars regularly drove past not only Linda's house but also the Wilsons' house during the last week. They noted no unusual visitors, but..."

Zelda pounded her fist on the table. "About what I expected from the APD. Too little, too late."

Elsa flushed and bit her lip. "As I was saying, no visitors came to the Wilsons' home, but Chuy went over Dean Wilson's schedule in detail with his secretary Audrey late yesterday."

Chuy gulped. "A man called Dean Wilson's office at four the day before the Dean testified. Audrey refused to put through the call when the man wouldn't give his name." Chuy shook his head. "In her usual uppity style, Audrey said he wasn't a senior faculty member because she would have recognized the voice. She also thought the voice sounded young."

Elsa consulted her tablet. "We decided the individual might have called Dean Wilson's directly. I checked the calls to and from his cell phone, which is paid for by the university. Two incoming and one outgoing calls looked interesting. One incoming call was from a burner phone. APD officers should be talking to the second caller now. I spoke to the third person, the university counsel. Seems Dean Wilson called him at home after he received the other calls two night ago."

"Damn." Rachel finished pouring herself a cup of coffee and glided back to her chair. "Bet he claimed attorney-client privilege."

Elsa didn't bother to look up from her tablet. "Yes, but his heart wasn't in it."

Zelda leaned forward aggressively, but she was no longer scowling. "What do you mean?"

"He said he was 'uncomfortable' about the tenor of Dean Wilson's questions and referred him to a private defense lawyer." Elsa stared at Zelda. "I pushed a bit. He admitted he had closely followed the Raines's trial. He said something odd." Elsa cleared her throat and read from her notes. "I quote, 'In the last ten years, the only straight-forward answers I've gotten from the administration of the med school have been from Linda Almquist.' I think he's hinting Dean Wilson lied, but of course he'd never say so in court."

Rachel yawned. "Tell us something we don't know."

Elsa's tablet emitted a chirp. She silently read the message. "Not what I hoped." She looked around the table. "The second caller was a woman detective working for the lawyer defending Diego Rivera. The APD officers, who questioned her, reported she was legit and the call was routine. That's all I've got." Elsa turned to Chuy. "He was luckier."

He winked at Rachel. "I too noted Audrey seemed to regard the shooting of Sally Wilson as an opportunity. She couldn't fawn over the Dean Wilson enough yesterday."

As Chuy chuckled, Rachel turned to Zelda to explain. "Talk about optimism. Audrey is an over-dressed, over-made up stub of a woman. As you know, Sally Wilson is a gracefully aging beauty." Rachel pointed to Chuy. "So?"

"The more I thought about Audrey's answers to my questions yesterday, the more I doubted her. Last night I checked the calls to her desk for the last two days." Chuy examined his notes. "I love how employees of public universities know that they have no right to expect privacy in their communications on university-owned phones but still act as if their calls are private." He traced his finger along a line on his tablet. "She received a call around four the day before Dean Wilson's testimony as she said, but the call lasted almost five minutes. I know she can stop anyone in less than a minute." He cocked her head. "I decided an indirect approach was best this morning. I brought her a scoop of butter-pecan ice cream from the cafeteria." He lowered his voice. "Linda told me that was how she bribed Audrey when she was desperate for her cooperation."

Elsa interrupted, "I made a big show of having two APD officers escort Dean Wilson to see his wife in the surgical recovery area. Then Chuy turned on the charm. What a ham." Elsa chuckled.

"Not funny. It worked. She eventually remembered she had heard the voice of the unidentified caller before, and he had left a message. I guess she didn't lie to me before because I didn't specifically ask if he left a message when I questioned her earlier. The message was: 'Forgetfulness is a kind of freedom.' That's all. "

Zelda gasped.

"It gets better." Chuy puffed his chest a bit. "I prodded Audrey a bit. I exaggerated how eager Dean Wilson was to visit Sally today. I kept saying Sally was a wonderful lady until Audrey began to cry. For a moment, I almost felt sorry for her. After a few tears, okay a lot of tears, she said the caller sounded similar to the assistant professor in neurology who had yelled a lot at Linda."

"George Kummer." Elsa stood, threw her Styrofoam coffee cup in the trash, and stuffed her tablet in her bag. "I've already sent officers talk to him."

CHAPTER 9: Sergeant Chuy Bargas

The facts had accumulated but not added up in the almost thirty hours since the shootings. The fingerprints of all four shooters were on file with the Los Angeles Police Department, but their offenses were minor. They were members of four different Sureños gangs from south L.A., the area bounded by 10 Freeway on the north and Harbor 110 Freeway on the west. The two surviving shooters weren't talking. Of course, one was barely breathing.

Originally Chuy expected all four shooters to be from one gang because their tattoos were similar in style. Now he figured the key to the case was to identify the organizer of the attacks, the so-called Jorge. Although Chuy increasingly found Rachel's style abrasive, perhaps because Elsa complained of Rachel's uppity behavior frequently, he appreciated her help in mobilizing FBI agents and police in L.A.

L.A. police and FBI agents questioned ten Jorges in the four gangs represented by the shooters and concluded the Jorge that they wanted was in another south L.A. gang. Now they were focusing on two Jorges in the gang Diego Rivera was associated with as a teen.

FBI agents had scanned videotapes at the airport, bus station, and train depot in Albuquerque to ascertain how the shooters had arrived. One of the shooters killed at the courthouse came by plane. One of the shooters in the medical school by train. The FBI assumed one or both of the other shooters drove all the guns to Albuquerque, and one those men was dead. Accordingly, Agustin Falto, the only conscious shooter, was the best source of information.

Chuy thought he'd set the stage well for his interview of Falto. He'd kept the two living shooters isolated in guarded hospital rooms. Falto didn't know the fates of his compatriots. He chose Rachel to join him for the interview because Elsa was busy tracking down leads related to Dean Wilson and the tapes of all activities at the courthouse on the days of the trial. Then too, Rachel had a harder edge and that made her a better bad cop to offset his good cop routine.

J. L. Greger

He opened Falto's door, and Rachel breezed into the barren room with her blonde hair streaming. The chairs, bed table, and usual accoutrements in a hospital room had been removed. Only the bed remained. Her heeled boots echoed on the tiled floor as she paced about the room checking to see the closet and bathroom were empty.

Falto, as he lay in the metal hospital bed with his left arm chained to the rail, seemed to be the runt of the litter. He was only five-foot-two and bit his lip repeatedly. A kid pretending to be tough. His right shoulder and arm were in a cast, and the arm was raised in some sort of sling attached to a pole above the bed.

Chuy grimaced as he looked at the uncomfortable-looking contraption. He had purposely shot Falto in his right shoulder during the melee in the deans' offices to ruin Falto's shot but not kill him. Unintentionally he had destroyed Falto's shoulder joint. The kid would probably be crippled for life, which meant he would be defenseless in prison.

"You again." Falto closed his eyes.

Chuy gulped. He had a job to do. "Hey Falto, your friends are talking. They're saying you planned the shootings with Jorge. We know your partner at the med school took the train two days ago, so we think you drove in with the guns."

The dark-haired kid of twenty stared blankly at the ceiling as Chuy made the required legal comments. Falto didn't request a lawyer.

Rachel abruptly cranked down the head of the bed, stretching Falto's arm in the sling, and leaned over the helpless man. "You're mine. While New Mexico courts don't hand out the death sentence, federal ones will give you the injection."

Falto blinked in surprise. "I got lucky and popped one of the women behind the door?"

Chuy laughed. "Not even close little buster, but someone was killed at the courthouse. Because you drove ammo used in murders across state lines, the feds can charge you with murder."

Blood trickled down the kid's chin from his raw lips as he chewed them.

Chuy felt sorry for this boy trying to be a man. "You failed at your assignment. I bet you won't get any of the rewards promised by the guy who hired you." Chuy adjusted the bed to a more comfortable position for Falto. "Now if you help me, I might be able to help you

Falto closed his eyes. "You're bluffing."

Chuy knew he wasn't good at bluffing and tried not to gulp. "We got some revealing videos. Whoever talks first get a deal."

The teen grimaced.

Rachel slapped Falto's cast. "You're wasting your time on this peewee. He knows squat about where we can find Jorge or who paid for this operation. Too bad. The old cons in the federal pen are going to love this pretty little baby."

Chuy's phone rang. He'd instructed the guard outside the door to call him after five minutes. He smiled as he said, "Really. The other shooter in the med school talked and we don't need...."

"Wait."

The resulting conversation almost proved Rachel right. Falto didn't know Jorge's last name or gang affiliation, but he'd seen him around "the hood" in L.A. but not often. Falto reported Jorge seemed to know he needed money to pay for his mother's cancer treatments when he called three days before. He was told to tell no one and to bring a suitcase with a change of clothes to a bodega a mile from his home.

When he arrived at the bodega, Jorge led Falto to a white 2000 Subaru Impreza coupe, opened the trunk, and instructed him to throw his bag next to the four already in the trunk. Before Jorge closed the trunk, he pointed to keys attached by twine to each bag and instructed Falto to deliver the bags to the lockers indicated on the keys at the bus station on First Street in Albuquerque and to lock the keys in Locker 4G.

"Then Jorge surprised me. He pushed me in the car and told me to put on a blindfold. Drove around for a while before he pulled into a garage and closed the door."

"Can you give us any details about types of roads or how long?"

Falto scrunched his face. "Slow, lot of turns, never on a highway. Mmm. Less than ten minutes, about five. I guess. I wasn't paying attention. I was trying to remember what he told me to do. If I killed my target and kept my mouth shut, he'd take care of my mother's bills."

Chuy glanced at Rachel. She was texting, probably telling FBI agents in L.A. to center their search of Jorge to within ten blocks of the bodega. He continued to try to jog Jorge's memory.

Falto claimed Jorge had dissed him. Jorge made Falto prove he could shoot a gun and made him repack his suitcase three times until Jorge was satisfied a gun and ammo were hidden underneath the police uniform, which Jorge gave him. Falto noted the uniform included a shirt, pants, a belt, socks, and shoes. "I told him I don't wear belts, but he wouldn't listen."

Chuy attempted to focus Falto's ramblings on the plans for the shootings. Falto kept complaining about the car that he was forced to drive. With patience and frequent prompting, Chuy learned Jorge gave Falto a map with his route marked, told him where to stay in Albuquerque, and told him when to show up at the medical school the next day. He also instructed Falto where to park his car so he could claim it afterwards.

Chuy thought he finally had concrete clues. The car and map should have Jorge's fingerprints. Chuy watched Rachel out of the corner of his eye. Her facial expressions alternated between disgust and boredom until Falto told where he'd left the car. She began to text immediately. He bet the car would be found within the hour.

"Any details you remember about Jorge?"

The response was slow and useless until the end. "He was weird and wore gloves. You know hospital type gloves. All the time I was with him."

"Shit." Obviously, Rachel was hoping for fingerprints too.

Falto continued to speak in a halting manner. "At the end, he blindfolded me... Drove me to the bodega and gave me a thousand dollars. Said my mother would get nine thousand dollars... when I completed the task." Falto smiled.

"Anything else?"

"Warned me that he or his friends would be watching me all the time." Falto closed his eyes. "He'd know if I goofed up. Would kill me if I made a mistake."

"Do you think you were watched?'

"Yeah, I saw the same black Camry behind me on and off on my way to Albuquerque."

"Are you sure? They're pretty common."

"This one was dented along the right side." Falto's eyes blinked. Saw it in the parking lot when I arrived yesterday morning to do my job." He frowned. "But if I didn't pop one of the women, I won't get the money."

As Falto lamented his lost money, Chuy looked at a list of questions on his tablet. He'd missed a couple. "How well did you know the other shooter in the med school?"

Falto looked surprised at the question and pressed his lips together and twisted in the bed.

Chuy figured either this was a stupid question or Falto didn't know him. "I... I want to see if your answer matches what he said."

Falto twisted more in his bed to look at Rachel.

Chuy was thankful when Rachel broke the silence. She leaned closer to Falto with her finger twisting blonde strands of hair. "Mmm, let's try a not-so-stupid question. You said you were supposed to kill one of the women? Which one?"

Falto continued to chew his lips.

She brushed a few strands of her hair across his face. "Come on. Did you get more if you hit the right woman?

"Jorge wanted both dead."

"I would have thought he wanted...." Rachel licked her lips slowly and gave a slow smile.

Chuy hoped she guessed right. Falto's meager information suggested a tie in to the L.A. Hispanic gangs and indicated detailed planning. Chuy had concluded Diego Rivera was the instigator of the killings, and Linda was the main target. She would be a major witness against Diego when he came to trial for abetting Raines's murderous plans and for plotting the murders of three other women, including Sara.

"So, you were aiming at the tall, blonde?"

Chuy stifled a cough. He wondered whether Rachel had intentionally given Falto a chance to prove her wrong? Linda was short with long, dark red hair.

Falto stopped biting his lips long enough to say. "You cops are dumb." He closed his eyes and remained motionless, except for biting his lip, for the next fifteen minutes despite Chuy's and Rachel's' attempts to arouse him. He even ignored the blood that seeped from his lips and trickled down his chin.

CHAPTER 10: FBI agent Rachel Jones on Day 3

Rachel sped past a large room with ringing phones, crying victims, and yelling arrestees protesting police decisions. No wonder APD officers were eager to rise to a rank where they shared an office with only one or two others, even if those offices resembled jail cells.

She stopped in front of an open door to an office shared by Chuy and Elsa. She'd heard Elsa say their office became a sauna if they kept the door closed and the temperature rose above fifty outside. Elsa sat staring at a computer screen. Chuy's arm was slung on her left shoulder as he also looked at the computer screen.

They looked comfortable. The rumors were true. They were an item. "I'm here to receive Sanders's message." She sniffed. "I wonder whether the guy is as bossy in person as over the phone."

Chuy straightened immediately, gulped, and pulled a cheap blue plastic chair from a corner for Rachel. He checked his watch and hesitated before he plunked into his desk chair. "He should call in five minutes."

Elsa continued to futz with her computer. "While we wait, I might as well update you on Dean Wilson. He's a hard nut to crack so I focused on his wife Sally. I've talked to her three times now. For a couple of minutes after she came out of surgery. My second interview yesterday was interrupted when her husband swooped through the ICU but stayed less than five minutes. A third time this morning, after she was moved to a private room."

Rachel tapped her nails polished in a silvery pink on the side of her tablet. "I don't suppose you thought to assign a police guard at her door."

Elsa gave her a quick look of annoyance. "Of course, I know my job."

"What did you learn?"

Elsa took her time as she perused her computer screen. "Sally confirmed what we knew about the calls to the house but added a bit more. Dean Wilson departed the house around seven in the evening twice in the last week. Both times he returned about two hours later with a gift for her. One night three red roses. One night a pint of Ben and Jerry's Cherry Garcia ice cream. She called them 'guilt' gifts."

"So, he's cheap on top of being a jerk. What does she suspect?"

Elsa tapped her unpolished nails on her desk. "She figures he's hiding something about Raines and feels guilty about it." Elsa stopped and frowned. "Guilty might be the wrong word." She checked her computer screen. "Her exact words were he'd only 'commit sins of omission' to protect Raines."

"I would have thought she'd be annoyed because his omissions forced her to testify and ultimately got her shot."

"No, she seemed sad. I think she suspects more but isn't ready to talk yet about feelings not facts. Besides, we can't force her to testify against him."

"Isn't love grand?" Rachel looked back and forth between Elsa and Chuy. Chuy gulped. Elsa turned back to her computer. "That's it? Nothing useful."

Chuy pointed his finger at Rachel. "You talked to Dean Wilson right after the shootings. You know he admits nothing unless you have three-quarters of the evidence already. Elsa was smart to focus on Sally."

Elsa scanned her computer screen. "Dean Wilson claims both evening meetings were with Raines's estate, not defense, attorney. Seems Raines updated his will two weeks before his trial and wanted Dean Wilson, as the executor of his will, to know. "

"Strange," said Rachel. "A man on trial for murder usually doesn't worry about his will until after the trial. And estate lawyers don't generally meet with the executor of a will of a healthy client."

Elsa nodded. "I thought Raines was trying to get a message to Dean Wilson through his will. When I asked to see the will, Dean Wilson did his praying act with his hands and claimed only the attorney could release it. I called the estate lawyer, the type of lawyer who gives them a bad name, but he wouldn't release the will until he received a copy of Raines's autopsy. I pushed the medical examiner."

Rachel flounced her hair. "Another couple days wasted."

Elsa gloated. "No, as favor to me, he'll have the autopsy report available tomorrow morning. The autopsies on the two gang members won't be done until next week."

Chuy glanced at his watch. "You can set your clock by Sanders's calls. The guy is..."

"Anal retentive." Rachel smirked as the office phone rang.

Chuy kicked the door shut before he put the phone on speaker mode. "All three of us are here."

Sanders voice was clipped and clear but not loud. "As you know, Shantelle Eaton was physically threatened by Hispanic gang members in the U.S. and by thugs processing coca in Bolivia upon the request of Diego Rivera. Yesterday as I told you, she remembered Diego mentioned one of his buddies from the L.A. gangs was now on the Albuquerque police force." He cleared his throat. "What have you learned?"

Elsa responded immediately. "We have eight officers with a history of at one time living in the south L.A. area. Unfortunately, our records wouldn't mention summers spent with relatives in L.A. None of the eight are named Jorge or its derivatives."

"Too bad but thank you. Chuy promised me yesterday you'd get answers."

"I've been thinking too," said Chuy. "Bit embarrassing. Before I turned the corner to the deans' offices in the med school on Tuesday, I heard pounding and the sound of glass breaking and called for help. Two campus police and one APD officer arrived unusually fast, but I didn't think about it at the time. I couldn't have saved Sara and Linda without their assistance, but I had to stop the APD officer from being gun happy and shooting the second shooter a third time after he was down. I meant to get his name but didn't in the excitement."

Rachel stifled a laugh as Elsa immediately tried to protect Chuy. "Almost simultaneously, I sent a second cadre of officers to the site. One officer could have easily disappeared in the crowd."

Sanders coughed. "Elsa, you don't have to cover for your partner. I'm well aware of the confusion in tense situations. Your follow-up?"

"I started last night." Chuy wiped his brow. "Talked to the campus policemen who appeared at almost the same time as the lone APD officer. They were clueless about his name or assignment. In fact, they never saw him before. Like me, they weren't sure when he disappeared, but they thought almost as soon as the other APD officers arrived. Disappointing but not surprising."

Rachel straightened in her chair. "You should have told me."

"Nothing to tell, " said Chuy. "Today Elsa checked with the officers she summoned to the scene, while I talked to the crime lab people at the scene. We've enumerated everyone present, except the one officer. Only two of the APD officers remember seeing a lone officer standing over the second shooter when they first walked in. When he excused himself to go to the bathroom, they figured he was a rookie and had never discharged his gun before in the line of duty. They said they took charge of the second gang shooter because I was busy monitoring the one I'd shot."

Rachel tucked her blonde hair back. "Not a well-managed crime scene."

Sanders audibly sucked in his breath. "I don't believe criticism will help. Chuy rather remarkably saved our prime witnesses and both shooters. He was more successful than the FBI and the police at the courthouse."

Now Rachel sucked in her breath audibly.

Sanders continued, "Tell me about the officer."

Chuy sighed. "Six-foot, medium build, probably in his early thirties with cropped black hair and a large aquiline nose. The ABQ and campus police officers couldn't add much, except one officer called an hour ago. He said he'd suddenly remembered the guy's name badge had a G initial with a last name starting with L. We were checking the APD roster when Rachel arrived. So far, we identified five."

Elsa stopped scanning her computer screen and interrupted, "I've notified my lieutenant, and he gave me the go ahead to question each of these officers."

"Good. Let me know what you learn." The speakerphone emitted a loud click as Sanders hung up.

Chuy looked at the ceiling. "I didn't get a chance to tell him that an hour ago the third shooter, the one from the medical school who never talked, died. Means assistant DA Zelda Zane could charge our mystery officer with murder if he wasn't an APD officer."

CHAPTER 11: Sara in Washington

Sara with Bug trotting by her side turned right off Constitution Avenue onto Seventh Street. It wasn't raining, but Sara soon realized Bug wasn't used to wet pavements. The poor dog tried valiantly to sidestep puddles but regularly shook muddy water from his fur.

She and Bug had arrived at Sanders's old USAID office on Pennsylvania Avenue before seven-thirty this morning. After a brief phone conversation with Sanders, she, the assigned USAID staffer, and Sanders's secretary worked all day at restructuring the USAID project in Bolivia. At three, she mumbled she was going for a walk. The secretary said, "You can't."

Sara responded, "I'm going to visit an old friend. I'll be back by six when Linda should arrive after a day at her meeting."

As the secretary kept repeating "You can't," Sara stormed out of the building with Bug. She felt a bit ashamed now. This secretary's comments had reminded her that she had lost control of her life and that made her defiant.

It all began two years ago during the Philippine flu epidemic. Using her skills as an epidemiologist, she not only helped to develop an effective vaccine against the deadly Philippine flu but also unintentionally identified her neighbor Jim Mazzone as the chief drug lord in the Albuquerque area. He'd escaped, and her life returned to normal. Then she'd agreed to serve as epidemiology consultant in Bolivia and stumbled into Mazzone again.

Although Sanders and Xave had "saved" her from Mazzone in Bolivia, she wondered whether their "help" had actually made her more of a target. Perhaps working with them was a mistake. It was time to assess her concerns one by one.

Her questions about Xave were typical of ones about an unstable relationship. Why hadn't he contacted her? Would she ever see him again? Would she be better off if she never saw him again? She suspected the old adage, "Be careful what you wish for, you might get it," summed up her thoughts on him. The rogue was intriguing but scary.

Her thoughts about Sanders and his projects were less clear. Although she'd spent a lot of time thinking about Sanders's expectations in Cuba, she knew they weren't *her* problems. But she knew she would intellectually enjoy the challenge of arranging a scientific exchange between the U.S. and Cuba. Besides, a trip to Cuba didn't seem particularly dangerous and might be fun.

She was progressing well in revamping the Bolivian project. Sanders was pleased, as he should be. She had guaranteed the support of Bolivian officials for the project and USAID in general by involving them as she restructured the committee and its goals. More importantly, she felt the USAID project was a "good thing" to do. It would help people in need help themselves.

Then there was Mazzone. Sanders had speculated if Mazzone ordered the shootings in Albuquerque as a warning to those meddling in his business, he might initiate retaliations in Bolivia too. She agreed that Mazzone was capable of malevolent retaliations. But only one Bolivian mentioned Mazzone in all her conversations with Bolivian officials today. He noted the coca trade in Bolivia seemed unaffected by Mazzone's extradition to the U.S.

Maybe Mazzone wasn't a threat to her safety, at least if she stayed out of his way. But Linda said that Raines often said, "It's important to eliminate all malignancies." She feared that Mazzone and even Diego Rivera might consider her and Linda malignancies to be eliminated. Moreover, Raines had proven he could operate through intermediaries while awaiting his trial in a jail cell in Albuquerque. She assumed Mazzone and Diego Rivera could, too. That meant they were a constant threat to Linda and her until they were convicted and put in isolation in a federal prison. Their trials were probably a year away. Until then, she and Linda were almost powerless to protect themselves.

She wouldn't mind living under some sort of disguise in Washington, but Linda was building her career. She needed to get back to Albuquerque. Consequently, she was traceable through Linda, and Linda was a target in her own right. Besides, Sara wasn't sure Washington was safer. Diego had arranged for gang members in Washington to attack Shantelle prior to the trip to Bolivia.

She paused to stare through the fence into the National Gallery of Art Sculpture Garden. The "Thinker on the Rock" with a hare substituting for a man seemed dumb not funny to her today. She guessed that proved she was in a bad mood.

This walk was probably a stupid idea too, but she knew her old friend would help her analyze her problems. She had first met him in Washington more than thirty years ago. She had slipped away from a scientific conference at the National Institutes of Health and taken the Metro to the National Gallery. There she'd fallen in love with her old friend — Rembrandt's self-portrait as an old man. She had come back almost every time she had been in Washington since then, probably close to a hundred times. Each time she saw Rembrandt's face differently. Sometimes his eyes seemed sad and he seemed to sympathize as she mentally told him her problems. Sometimes he looked peeved and seemed to chide her for her actions. Mostly, he allowed her to think through her choices better than live listeners.

As she trudged up the stone stairs to the front entrance of the National Gallery West Wing, she suddenly realized the guard wouldn't allow Bug in the museum. More proof of her general confusion. She found a clean spot, not covered by bird droppings, on the stone shelf to the side of the stairs and plunked down. Bug lay down beside her and let her run her fingers through his tangled hair. Amazing how comforting his presence was when she was tired — maybe weary was a better word.

Her mind drifted through the last few days. What a whirlwind of travel, shootings, and intrigue. She idly watched the crowd on this gray, late October day. Most of the individuals in the sparse crowd weren't tourists. They didn't wear circus shades of red, yellow, or blue, and almost no children were present. Most were probably government employees sneaking a break into their day.

The relative quietness of the passersby and the grayness of the sky fit her mood. She thought a sniper might be aiming a rifle at her even now. Then realism set in. A gang member was more apt to stab her as she stood in a crowd. She wondered whether both she and Linda would survive the next month. The next year.

She spotted a man dressed too formally to fit into the crowd. He was dressed in a gray pinstripe suit with a gray fedora. He was walking straight toward her. Although he wore dark glasses, she thought he was focusing on her.

She picked up Bug and ran to the door of the museum. As she grabbed the door, she took one look over her shoulder at the man who was now only six feet away. The man was Sanders.

"Your initial reflexes were good, but you shouldn't have taken the last look over your shoulder." He smirked. "Your old friend is late."

Sara reddened because now she had to admit the truth. "Rembrandt is where he usually is, but I couldn't go in with Bug. Stupid mistake on my part."

Sanders bent down, scooped up Bug, grabbed her upper arm, and led her down the stairs to a bench by the East Wing of the National Gallery. "I expected your sister to be the first to crack under the stress."

She sniffed. "Linda's tougher than she looks. Besides, she doesn't feel she has any choice but to proceed as normal after this Washington interlude. I have options, and when I have hard choices I find Rembrandt is helpful. He's quiet. Allows me to talk."

"Does he answer back?" His lips quivered as he placed Bug on her lap.

"No, I'm not crazy." Sara glared at him. "I feel trapped probably because I am. I'd be willing to disappear in a witness protection program, but Linda isn't. She's building her career."

Sanders flicked a leaf off his sleeve. "Too early to talk about such a dire decision."

Sara nodded. "I like to plan ahead. With my luck, they'd say I couldn't take Bug, and I can't manage all alone again. I was successful but alone for most of my years at Michigan State."

Sanders removed his dark glasses. "I know about your marriage."

"Yeah, to a guy who wouldn't admit he was gay to himself let alone me. The worst part was he is a genuinely nice guy. I have no one to blame."

"I was told a different story. I heard that years of harassment from your colleagues in the Department of Statistics at Michigan State toughened you into a resourceful epidemiologist, especially in field situations and on interdisciplinary teams, but made you way too independent to be in a staid academic department.

Sara tickled behind Bug's ears. "Who's been talking?"

Sanders pulled a phone from a pocket and started to text. "Seems to be common knowledge." He cast a quick glance at her. "Don't worry. I'm the butt of similar stories."

Sara smiled. "Time to 'fess up."

Sanders frowned. Sara wasn't sure if he was responding to her comment or something he was reading on the tablet. "Short marriage. My ex-wife, a lovely woman, said I was gone too much. The last straw was an assignment at the embassy in Asunción in Paraguay. Big difference is I have a daughter. We're not close. I only see her three times a year, but changes are afoot. She began law school at Georgetown last month." He responded to a message on his tablet with a few strokes. "Now what did you and Rembrandt decide?"

"Not to hide out doing make-work activities."

Sanders continued to text. "You aren't. The tasks I assigned need to be done quickly. Linda is a good addition to the ongoing conference."

"I made my living on making predictions with limited data, but I'm not patient enough to be a good mind reader. What's your real agenda?"

Sanders pursed his lips as if confused and finally looked at her.

"What's Shantelle's role? Her answers didn't add up. What about the young naval officer at your training sessions?" She thought for a moment. "And what are the chances of getting both Diego Rivera and Mazzone isolated in federal prisons. Realistically, what should Linda and I do until that happens? We're in constant danger."

Sanders shook his head, tucked his tablet in a pocket, and stood. "The first question shouldn't be answered here. The young naval officer is about to be assigned to a security detail at what serves as the U.S. embassy in Cuba, commonly called the U.S. Interests Section. I don't have the other answers. We'll know more after the Albuquerque police sort out the mole in their own organization."

Sara placed Bug gently on the ground. "Since this may be my last chance to ask such direct questions, might as well go for one more. Will I ever see Xave again?" She looked down, embarrassed. "Not sure how I feel about him, but I hate dangling in the breeze for someone."

Sanders looked across the National Mall toward the National Air and Space Museum. "I think the mall is best in late October and early November because there are fewer tourists and the weather is pleasant. I can see why you wanted to walk today, but it's time to get back."

He directed her toward the mirrored pyramids between the east and west wings of the National Gallery. As they looked down into the pit that became the cascade of water in front of the cafeteria in the art museum below, he said, "If you insist on taking long walks, we should work on disguises, though the mutt will be hard to camouflage."

"I bet the mutt has a better pedigree than you. They can document Japanese chins in Japan over six hundred years ago. And Bug's parents' and grandparents' were all show dogs."

"Oh, I don't know." He placed Bug in the crook of his arm and set a brisk pace west on Constitution Avenue. As they walked, Sara and Sanders played a game of one-upmanship to see who could tell the best story about each building they passed.

While they waited for a light change at Twelfth Street, he said, "Unfortunately you will see Xave again. The ghosts from his past make ours look like child's play. There's a reason why his undercover moniker is Lady Killer."

CHAPTER 12: Sergeant Chuy Bargas on Day 4

Chuy drove slowly past Barelas Coffee House on Fourth Street. Ten people were milling under a green awning in front of the inauspicious, tan stucco building, even though it was only seven-thirty in the morning. He turned right onto Simpier Lane and nosed his car into the last place in the lot.

After Sanders's call late yesterday afternoon, Elsa and Chuy combed through APD files for data on the police officers with initials of G. L. Gerald Laughlin was a redhead, and Geoff Ling was Oriental. According to their records neither had ever lived in L.A. Elsa eliminated them from the list of suspects after brief phone calls.

The next two on their list had potential, so Elsa and Chuy had invented a story and talked to them at their homes last night. Greg Lago, a beat cop, worked in the Southeast Area Command and was forty-five. Thirty-year-old Gino Lara was assigned to the ABQ Family Advocacy Center. Both officers admitted several of their relatives had connections to Sureños gangs in the south L.A. barrio, but they appeared to have no obvious connections to Diego Rivera. Neither was the ABQ police officer Chuy remembered from the medical school.

Chuy and Elsa debated whether to call or visit the home of the last police officer with the initials G. L. George Lehar was an administrator in Internal Affairs. He was fifty-two with no traceable relatives in L.A., but his departmental photo showed he had a large, hooked nose, like the unidentified cop from the medical school shootings. Elsa won. They stopped by Lehar's home last night around nine. Lehar's non-Hispanic wife said he was out of town, and she didn't know when he would return. She noted "no matter what," he would breakfast tomorrow morning around eight at Barelas Coffee House. "They reserve him a spot at the counter. He says he can't face the day without their *huevos rancheros* smothered in red sauce. Personally, red chili sauce gives me heartburn."

Afterward Chuy volunteered to find George Lehar the next morning while Elsa worked the Wilson side of the Raines murder case.

Now, as he looked at the full counter and several rooms overflowing with diners, he thought he had made a bad decision.

He spoke to the manager, who agreed to point out Lehar when he arrived, and grabbed a seat at the counter when a customer left. People came here for a lively start to the day. Sounds reverberated from room to room in the cavernous restaurant. Chuy looked around. Most of those at the counter almost had their noses in plates covered with either green or red chili. No one was eating only a bagel. The pungent odor of the chili sauces and the aroma of sizzling bacon permeating the restaurant tempted him, but he didn't want to end up like most cops with a paunch by forty.

The manager nudged him when a thin, stooped man with scraggly, dyed-black hair took a seat at the counter and ordered *huevos rancheros* with red sauce. Chuy discretely studied the man as he sipped his coffee. The man was an older version of the file photo of George Lehar. His only resemblance to the unaccounted APD officer at the medical school was the nose. Not a typical Hispanic nose, longer and narrower with a hook.

Chuy was convinced this interview would be a bust too, but he attempted to project a positive attitude. He waited until the man began to eat before he stepped behind his stool. "Jorge, is that you? You're Jorge from the old neighborhood in L.A."

The man glanced at Chuy and then turned his brown eyes back toward his overflowing plate.

"Or don't you go by Jorge anymore?" Chuy squeezed into the space between the man's stool and the next.

"Do I know you? Only two old friends call me Jorge."

Chuy continued the bluff. He willed himself not to blink or gulp and flashed a smile. "Would one of those be Diego Rivera?"

The man almost buried his face in his plate as he shoveled food into his mouth. He continued to eat as Chuy pushed his badge at him and mentioned the discussion could be continued at police headquarters. Suddenly Lehar stopped shoveling food into his mouth. "Are you sure you want to continue this discussion with someone from Internal Affairs?"

"Sir, that's irrelevant."

"Am I being charged?"

"Not yet."

"I'll finish my breakfast while you call my union rep."

***

Chuy jumped into a waiting car around two. "Boy, talk about unpleasant." He shook his head. "Lehar will lose his job and pension, in essence, because he was a student teacher who helped a bright Hispanic teen over twenty years ago."

Elsa stepped on the gas and headed the car toward Hurricanes Restaurant on Lomas. "I figured you'd want to blow off steam. Where do we stand?"

"I talked to Lehar and then his wife again. Do you want the long story or short story?"

"Short."

"Lehar got a girl pregnant in the L.A. barrio thirty-three years ago when he spent a summer with his grandparents. His parents shipped him off to the army. He lost all contact with the girl but after his army stint and college returned to the barrio to student teach. There he pushed a bright, street-wise kid named Diego Rivera to consider college."

"I thought this was the short version." She nosed the car into one of the slots under the canopy at Hurricanes Restaurant. "What do you want?"

"My usual, the tuna sandwich."

She pressed the button and ordered a tuna sandwich, a BLT, and two iced teas."

"Hmm. You usually order a salad."

Elsa shrugged. "I can tell I'll have plenty of time to eat."

Chuy grimaced. "The story won't make sense without the details. About seventeen years ago, out of the blue, Diego called Lehar and told him his ex-girlfriend had died in a fire, and his son needed a home. Lehar was married, went by George not Jorge, and worked for APD, but he did the right thing. He brought the kid called Jorge to Albuquerque."

"Think short."

Chuy cleared his throat. "Mrs. Lehar summed up the next seventeen years this way. Young Jorge was continually 'out of control.' He ran away at seventeen but continued to regularly ask for money until he got a job at Community Outreach Medical Services in L.A. 'doing something with computers' five years ago. Lehar admitted he hadn't seen young Jorge for years, even though Jorge knew George was battling lung cancer. He showed up again ten days ago."

The carhop delivered their lunches, and Chuy suspended his recitation while food was sorted. Elsa pulled a slice of bacon from her sandwich and nibbled the crisp strip. "What did the son want?"

"Told his dad he was paying off his debt to drug dealers by providing a few services to Diego Rivera. Indicated his dad wouldn't have to worry about lung cancer killing him if he didn't comply with his request."

"George was foolish not to have turned the kid in. What happened next."

"Jorge demanded APD uniforms for six men. He gave his dad the sizes but no names. The older Lehar also gave his son badges with names of men who had left the force in the last two years." Chuy bit into a spear of dill pickle "Now comes the sad part. Granted George Lehar knew the uniforms would be used for felonious purposes, but he didn't want to steal. He paid for them. If he hadn't, APD couldn't have proven he was the source of them. Sad." Chuy finished his pickle and ate several bites of his sandwich. "Doesn't taste as good as usual."

Elsa coughed. "Might be spoiled. Don't eat it. Do you want me to re-order?

He shook his head as he wadded up the remaining sandwich in its wrapper."

"You left out the most important part. Where's the son?"

"Lehar and his wife don't know. Here's a weird part. Jorge ordered the uniforms ten days ago — before Diego and Mazzone were arrested."

"As usual, Diego planned ahead." Elsa swallowed the last bit of her sandwich

"I guess." Chuy shoved her garbage with his into the paper bag." Another quirk to his story. Lehar didn't give Jorge his own badge but noticed it was missing five days ago after Jorge breezed through Albuquerque."

"Why would Jorge take it? He had to realize the badge would help police trace him."

He sipped his iced tea. "I'll ask him if we ever locate him. His smile widened as he studied Elsa's face. He felt lucky to be her man. "So, how was your day?"

"Weird. I'll show you Raines's will when we get back to the office. I assume there are encrypted messages in it considering Raines's use of them before, but I can't find them."

CHAPTER 13: Linda Almquist in Washington

Linda stood at the threshold of Sanders's old office in USAID. Sounds echoed because movers had removed all his books and upholstered furniture from the room. Sara and a staff person sat at a six-foot, oak table pounding at computers keypads in front of them. Occasionally they spoke to each other or to the speakerphone, which emitted crackling sounds with irregular short clipped phrases from Sanders.

Sara announced the final document was to be delivered to the USAID director in the next hour. She handed Linda the current draft of the document and the original proposal, which was the basis of Sara's trip to Bolivia. Bug jumped from an extra desk chair and ambled over to Linda when she sat down on the only other chair to peruse the documents. He returned to his chair once he realized she had no treats.

Linda was surprised by the document. The new document, labeled *Revised Proposal for Improving Child Health in Bolivia through Upgrades in Water Processing*, bore little resemblance to the original proposal *Improving Child Health in Bolivia*. Evidently, researchers from the University of Oklahoma had convinced committee members and Bolivian officials they could purify mine run-off with their prototype passive water purification system near Potosí. The document also contained lots of facts and figures on how clean water would reduce parasitic infestations as well mercury toxicity in miners and their children in Bolivia.

The revised proposal contained concrete suggestions based on the pilot project. First, USAID agreed to fund construction of passive water purification systems at five key sites of pollution with the proviso Bolivian officials would maintain the systems after the first two years of their operation if the systems produced water meeting the stated standards for water purity. Second, USAID would issue a call for proposals on low-tech ways to monitor a variety of water pollutants, including mercury and parasites. Third, USAID would help the Bolivian government train local people to build more sustainable water purification systems throughout Bolivia.

One aspect of the new document wasn't surprising. USAID restructured the committee. The original water and survey experts remained on the committee, which Sara would chair. Two public health officials from Bolivia and a hydrology engineer from Universidad Mayor de San Andrés in Bolivia would join the committee.

Linda watched Sara as she cursed typos and read sentences from the document out loud. Sara hadn't said much about the actual project. Before going to Bolivia, Sara had complained the plan lacked focus because the previous chairman of the committee had lost his edge, the USAID staff person on the committee Shantelle Eaton was distracted, and the expert on water quality had difficulty "playing in the sandbox" with others, particularly women. After her return from Bolivia, Sara had talked about being chased by Mazzone across Bolivia and saved by Xave and Sanders, with wistful remarks about Xave. Linda thought a second. Actually, Sara hadn't talked much about Bolivia since her trip because the shootings at the Raines's trial and the medical school had occurred the day after her return from Bolivia. That was too bad. The new proposal was interesting, well at least for a scientific document.

Linda also decided as she perused the document that this trip to Washington was exactly what Sara needed — a chance to forget Mazzone and all the problems in Albuquerque. Even under the pressure of completing the document, Sara was smiling more than usual.

Linda was less sure this trip had provided what she needed. The two-and-a-half-day conference on public health needs in Latin America and Caribbean countries had been professionally worthwhile. Linda now understood the types of educational opportunities desired and needed by public health workers in Latin America. She knew faculty in the medical school, particularly in the Department of Family and Community Medicine, could provide this type of training. Now, she could coach them on how to secure funds for their efforts. Not a bad result for her time in Washington.

However, Linda didn't want to be a consultant. She didn't enjoy traveling overseas. She belonged back in Albuquerque. But doing what? She wanted to become the interim dean of the medical school if Dean Wilson stepped down to care for Sally or if he was charged for some entanglement in the Raines's mess. More likely, the Dean would dismiss her as his associate dean first. His testimony on her at Raines's trial was damning. She wondered what she had done wrong.

"This might be the break they need on the shootings in Albuquerque." Sanders voice rang from the speaker more clearly now.

"Linda, I'm faxing documents to you. Chuy will call in an hour to get your comments."

Linda grabbed the pages as they buzzed out of the printer and moved to Sanders's old desk to study them. The scene at the table quickly returned to normal with Sara and the USAID staff person scanning their computers screens and conversing with each other and Sanders.

The first five pages in Linda's pile were the pathologist's report on his autopsy of Raines. Linda would have skipped those pages, if she hadn't noticed the underlined area. She almost choked. Raines was dying with pancreatic cancer at the time he was killed. The pathologist predicted he would have survived at most another six months.

Next were notes, dated about two months previously, from an oncologist in Utah. They looked more detailed than usual. Linda surmised the physician was uneasy about the situation. He had visited Raines two months ago in the Albuquerque jail, had reconfirmed Raines's self-diagnosis of pancreatic cancer, and had prescribed medications. He'd concluded his report with:

> Per patient's insistence, the medications are generalized chemotherapy drugs, not the best ones for pancreatic cancer. An abbreviated report was given the nurse at the jail.

"Abbreviated" was an understatement. The report from the oncologist to the nurse was:

> The patient has elevated PSA (prostate-specific antigen) levels, perhaps from an earlier bout with prostate cancer. Against my advice, he wants only standard prophylactic therapy.

The last set of pages was Raines's will and codicils. Linda was astonished by Raines's wealth. She figured he must have invested well, had an outside income, and/or earned a lot higher salary than hers. He left the bulk of his fortune, four million dollars, to the medical school to create two professorships named after himself and the Dean. He left fifty thousand dollars to his lone sister, and stated that his ex-wives and any other relatives "deserved nothing." He named the Dean his executor after he waxed effusively about his "loyalty and unquestioning support" for more than thirty years.

The codicils were succinct. Raines per the first one, dated four months before his death, gave George Kummer an old neurology text as a "guide." In the second codicil, dated two weeks before his death, he gave the Dean two old medical texts as "keepsakes." He requested both codicils be enacted immediately after they were written. Linda suspected the codicils contained secret messages, like the rest of Raines's communications, but was too tired to guess their meanings.

Suddenly there was a flurry of activity at the table as the printer churned out pages. "We'll be back in thirty minutes." Sara and the USAID staffer slammed the door shut as they raced out of the room.

Linda looked over at Bug who was gazing at the door. "Guess they finished their report."

The phone rang.

Linda cut Chuy's pleasantries short. "Why didn't the medical staff at the jail inform you of Raines's illness? I thought you had talked to all of Raines visitors while in jail awaiting trial. You must have missed the oncologist. How did you get the oncologist's notes?"

"Wait. One question at a time. The nurse at the jail told Elsa that Raines was receiving chemotherapy to prevent the recurrence of prostate cancer about two months or so ago. Elsa was busy. She didn't think it necessary to talk to the physician who visited Raines and forgot to check his medical records. When she received the pathologist report today, she turned into a super sleuth. She rechecked the list of those who visited Raines in jail during the last five months and called every physician who had treated Raines during the last twenty years. The oncologist from Utah was eager to cooperate. He realized the report that he'd filed with prison nurse, per Raines's request, was misleading."

"Now about the will."

"I guess I should start with Elsa's distrust of the estate lawyer. She describes him as slimy. First, he refused to release the will until he received the autopsy report. He even denied his visits to the jail until she showed him his signature on the jail's visitor logs four months and two weeks before Raines's death. Evidently, he came in with the defense lawyer and passed himself off to the attendants in the jail as an assistant to the defense. He claimed client-attorney privilege and refused to answer her questions on the codicils. Elsa asked assistant DA Zelda Zane to consider charging him with abetting murder, but Zelda laughed at her."

Linda groaned. "Why would the estate lawyer have the neurology text in his possession and give it to Kummer four months ago? Raines was still communicating through crossword puzzles with Diego Rivera then. Similarly, why would he give keepsakes to the Dean before he was dead?"

"Something smells, but we can't seem to get straight answers. Let's start with Elsa's questions. Do you know whether Dean Wilson ever met George Kummer or Diego Rivera?"

"Mmm. He saw Kummer one time outside my office say six months ago, and guessed he was an assistant prof but didn't seem to know his name. I don't know whether he'd met either of them at other times. But I...."

"Don't apologize. Earlier we dropped all charges against George Kummer for abetting Raines's and Diego's scheme to eliminate all witnesses against Raines because his involvement seemed minor."

Linda interrupted, "And because we all thought he was too naïve to know what was going on."

"We're reassessing our previous decision. Any thoughts?"

"Glad he's off the med school pay roll already. That way the med school will look good in the press. Sounds like Raines was either trying to frame Kummer or Kummer was more involved than we thought. Both are equally probable."

"We have one more small problem. The APD officers sent to his apartment didn't find him."

"Probably because he's working at a private clinic." Linda gave Chuy the name and address of the clinic.

"On to the next problem." Chuy snorted. "Dean Wilson is cooperating, sorta. He agreed not to file the will for probate for several days, but we caught him in a lie. His wife said he went out twice in the evenings of the week before the trial. He claimed he went to see the estate lawyer both times. The lawyer said he saw him once. Any ideas?"

Linda gulped. "How would I know? You heard what he said about me at the trial." She was silent for a moment. "Probably he's afraid. Possibly he's trying to get an offer of protection against prosecution."

"Zelda said hell could freeze over first. Rachel and Elsa agreed for once." He lowered his voice. "They hope Sally will divorce him and will testify against him."

"Isn't going to happen."

"Mmm. Elsa pulled one useful comment from your boss. He griped that you and Sally shared the same bad trait — trying to control him with your righteous indignation."

Linda heard women's voices in the background. Probably Elsa and Rachel.

Chuy cleared his throat. "Now for the big question. Will you be back in Albuquerque by Monday? We think Dean Wilson would cave in and tell the truth if both you and Sally confronted him. Sorta a double whammy guilt trip.

CHAPTER 14: Sara in Georgetown and Washington on Day 5

Bug found a small strip of particularly fragrant grass in front of townhouse with its brick façade painted white. Sara used his dawdling as an excuse to study the nearby three-story townhouse where she and Linda were staying. The building's brown brick exterior and gray tile, dormered roof and the brown brick front yard fit perfectly into this backstreet neighborhood of Georgetown.

She observed the exterior, while not welcoming, was well kept. The front door and casings around the windows and doors were painted brown to match the garage door. Neatly trimmed hedges of boxwood lined both sides of the lot. The smell of boxwood made her think of historic cemeteries and of cat urine, but Bug savored the aroma. At least, he seemed to visit every boxwood bush on their walks around the neighborhood.

The townhouse was an ideal safe house. It faded into the scenery and the exterior gave no clue to the interior. On their first night in Washington, Sanders's assistant had opened the front door with a key and immediately left. Sarah and Linda stood alone in a strange entryway.

The space must have been elegant once with its lacquered light gray walls, gray slate floor, and wide white moldings in the traditional egg and dart style around the ceiling, but it was now partitioned. A large, smoked mirror covered much of a more recently added wall six feet in front of the door. A door, small sliding window, an intercom buzzer, and a code pad were on another wall within two feet on the right of the front door.

Seconds after they pushed the intercom button, a middle-aged man with a limp had silently admitted them into the rest of the original entry through the side door. The walls, floor, and ceiling were the same in this space as in the original entryway, but it was apparent the large mirror in the front entryway was a window. A modern, square stainless steel table and four chairs sat underneath the window.

The man had motioned them to sit as he told them the "house rules." He'd reminded Sara of the military guards in Bolivia — stern, taciturn men with crew cuts and big shoulders — but he was an older version.

He'd pointed to a second white door on the right. "You may use the laundry facilities and soda vending machine anytime." He'd jabbed toward a center door. "Someone will be available at all times." Finally, he handed them a key and a card with two numbers. "The key opens the front door." He'd pointed to a door on the far left. "The first number gives you access to the stairs and elevator. The second number opens Apartment B on the second floor." Before he had sent them up on the elevator, he said, "Don't share the numbers with anyone. Don't try to explore this building."

Bug's tug on his leash brought Sara back to the present. It was Saturday and neither she nor Linda had work to do today. By now Linda would have charted the sites she wanted to visit and neatened the apartment to her satisfaction. Sara shrugged. She wasn't a neaknik, like her sister. She took one last look around the neighborhood, pulled the key from her pocket, and headed for the brown door.

She couldn't explain her emotions but the safe house made her nervous. She didn't even want to imagine who the other residents were. Yesterday she decided to return to Albuquerque with Linda on Sunday rather than remain here alone with Bug. Sanders raised his eyebrow in surprise when she told him late yesterday afternoon. He reminded her she would accomplish her work on what he called the "Cuba mission" faster here than at her home.

***

A rap on the door. Next the phone rang. Sara grabbed the phone and sucked in her breath. Linda came running from the bedroom. Sanders had told her to expect a visitor today before nine-thirty but to be cautious when answering the door. She felt heat rising up her neck, as she listened, but she said in as steady a tone as she could muster, "What's the code?"

She ignored Linda's questions and Bug with his tail wagging so hard he almost fell over as she pulled her hands through her hair in an ineffective attempt to improve the style before she unlocked the triple locks on the front door of the two-bedroom apartment. A man squeezed through the partially open doorway and slammed the door behind him.

Sara gasped. Xave tanned faced looked gray and more lined than usual. Not surprising, he'd been shot six days before. He moved cautiously and his shoulders, especially the left one, uncharacteristically slumped forward. However, he was groomed to impress. His black hair was slicked back to show a bit of silver at the temples. He wore gray flannel slacks, burnished leather slip-ons, and a Navy sports jacket with a blue suit shirt left open at the collar. He carried a small leather briefcase and a cane.

She grabbed his free left hand. "Xave, are you sure you're up to this visit? How did you get a jacket on over the bandages?" She reached to touch his shoulder.

He jerked back. The wrinkles at the outer corners of his eyes deepened. "That's my gal. Always practical. May I sit?" He pointed his cane toward the worn brown sofa. He uttered a small groan when he lowered himself onto the sofa and placed the case at his feet.

Sara felt the heat rising up her neck and assumed her face was red as she awkwardly introduced Linda and joined him on the sofa, albeit at the other end. "I hoped I'd see you before we left tomorrow but gave up hope." She scanned the lines of his face. "Where do I begin with my questions? The easy ones first. Were you the man in the wheelchair on our flight from Albuquerque to Denver earlier this week?'

Xave smiled. "You impressed my attendant. He was sure you wouldn't recognize me. Sanders and I weren't sure, but I needed to see a specialist in Denver and couldn't manage alone. Sanders thought the attendant would learn valuable lessons from observing you before he met you for the discussions on Cuba."

"What did you think of Linda's and my disguises?" Sara looked at Linda who sat at a tiny dining table near the sofa.

Xave bent forward and offered his hand to Bug who wagged his tail but stayed tucked at Sara's feet. "You would start with the one thing you've done during the last five days that wasn't spot on. Let's say, someone needs to work with you on using wigs and creating disguises."

Sara shrunk in her seat. Linda chortled. "I told you we looked like fools."

"Fools no, but bag ladies maybe." He looked around the dull beige room with fake walnut cabinets and cleared his throat. "I saw the proposal you finished yesterday for restructuring the USAID committee to Bolivia. The bigwigs were impressed. Sanders said the director stayed late, read it, and sent a copy over to the Bolivian embassy." He cocked his head. "Sanders would gladly find a permanent job for you here if you wanted it."

Sara nodded. "I prefer the flexibility of retirement and only taking interesting, short-term consulting assignments." She focused on Xave.

He looked down and seemed to inspect the slightly worn brown and black tweed carpet. "Figured you'd say that. Will you take on the Cuba mission?"

"Did you come to recruit me?"

"No." He raised his head. "Not sure you should get involved, but this consultation should be much calmer than the one in Bolivia. Sanders wants someone like himself, but with a science background, to help him evaluate the situation."

Sara wondered what Xave meant by saying she was "like" Sanders but ignored the comment. She wanted to relax him and engage him in the easy banter they had enjoyed in Bolivia. "You act as if you're wearing a wire and Sanders is listening."

He smirked showing his teeth. "I'd be glad to undress to prove I'm not." He started to rub his left upper chest.

Linda coughed. Sara laughed but was worried by the half smile. She learned in Bolivia that he generally wasn't sincere when his teeth showed as he smiled. "For the first time, you sound like the Xave I met in Bolivia."

He continued to rub his left chest and shoulder.

"Wounds often itch as they heal."

He stopped rubbing his chest immediately and looked down. Sara thought she saw a bit of color rising up his neck.

"Would you be more comfortable with the jacket off? They said you took two bullets in the shoulder during Mazzone's attempted escape while you were bringing him back from Bolivia. I'm surprised you're up and walking without an aide." She leaned forward to stroke his hand. "Do you want to talk about it?"

"No." He pulled his hand away and opened the case. "But I would be more comfortable in a sweater than a jacket." As he stood fumbling with his jacket, he muttered, "Didn't want to look like an old man."

Sara felt wonderful — relaxed, desirable. "You put the jacket on to impress me. Wow, you wanted to see me for a reason besides business." She jumped up, stepped behind him, and began to pull the jacket off his shoulder.

"Whoa girl. Gentle."

The next fifteen minutes were a lively interchange of stories from the last ten days. Although no one had updated her on Xave's whereabouts or on details of the ongoing investigation in Albuquerque, he seemed to have been briefed on all her activities since they worked together in Bolivia.

Sara and Linda were both shocked and pleased by his last piece of news. Mazzone and his compatriot Diego Rivera had been transferred to a federal prison in Florence, Colorado yesterday. Sara immediately thought of her conversation with Sanders two days before. "So, Sanders' acted on my question?"

Xave smirked. "Yes, and we're getting the expected results. Our boy Diego isn't doing well there. Much too pretty."

Linda gasped and hurried to the small refrigerator. As she pulled out a bottle of Diet Pepsi, Xave walked from the sofa to her. "Don't feel bad about being duped by his conscientious assistant professor act. FBI psychiatrists think Diego's one of the most brilliant cons they've seen. He probably was an excellent lecturer."

Sara knew he was being honest and not merely trying to soothe Linda. "Linda, listen to him. He smiled without showing his teeth this time."

Xave chuckled as he glanced at Sara. "You got my number in Bolivia." He looked back at Linda. "Diego's weaknesses are his perfect face, slight stature, arrogance, and fear of Mazzone, The feds, particularly Rachel Jones, will use his weaknesses to break him. It has to be done." He grabbed a bottle of water from the refrigerator.

"I know." Linda sipped from her bottle of Diet Pepsi. "He was so enthusiastic about his research, such a good lecturer, and in general so talented. Best assistant professor I've worked with. It's a shame."

Xave leaned against the counter separating the kitchenette from the rest of the room. "Where do you gals plan to spend the day? I thought I might tag along."

Linda shoved a page across the counter at Xave. "We made a list of our favorite sites. There's a mum show at the Botanical Garden on Capitol Hill. The National Gallery of Art, the Lincoln and Vietnam Memorials, and Eastern Market are our favorite places."

Sara noticed Xave winced when Linda said Vietnam. "We're flexible, and don't have to hit all the spots." She jumped up and began to fuss with Bug's food and water dishes. "We're leaving Bug here so we can take the Metro. Thought we might start at Eastern Market. For my money, the stand there has the best crab cakes in town."

"All the elegant places and you pick Eastern Market." Xave shook his head. "Why am I not surprised?"

Sara stopped. "What would you prefer?"

"No, no, I agree about the crab cakes. Hope we don't run into Sanders. He lives not far from there." Xave shook his head and muttered, "No wonder Sanders sent me."

Sara decided to ignore the comment.

***

The three wound their way through the crowds surrounding the vendors under blue and white umbrellas. They were on their way to the red brick Eastern Market until Linda stopped at a display of paper mache masks. "Look at these." She pointed to a mask with curls cut from Diet Pepsi cans. The irises of the mask's eyes were Diet Pepsi logos. A band around the neck said, "Do you think I drink too much Diet Pepsi?"

"Why don't you get it for your office?' Sara pulled the mask from its hanger and handed it to Linda. "It would add humor and color to your office."

Xave snorted and stepped backward out of the hubbub around the display.

Linda fingered the mask and put it back on the rack. "I'll think about it." She added more softly, "I think he's bored."

Sara leaned toward her sister. "Hope not. We have to see if we have anything in common besides the dangers of Bolivia." She stepped back to Xave's side and shaded her eyes with her hand to admire the building. "I know about the fire in 2007, but Eastern Market, at least on the outside, looks the same to me. Brings back memories."

Xave rested a hand on her left shoulder "Good memories?"

Sara put her hand on top of his, and they moved in step toward the long wood tables in front of the Market's lunch area. "Wow. The inside is modernized. When I first saw the Eastern Market in the early 1980s, it reminded me of an old European market with fish and meat piled on barrels of crushed ice because refrigeration facilities were limited."

"Yeah, and a hundred years of cooking grease stains on the walls. Looks and smells cleaner now."

Sara squeezed his hand. "Funny, I enjoyed its old charm. Eastern Market was a nice contrast to the grandeur of U.S. Capitol and the Library of Congress only a few blocks away. Seemed to ground them."

As they stood in front of the chalkboard with the menu, Xave whispered in her ear. "First time, I've seen your sentimental side. You worried about food safety in Bolivia whenever we stopped at vendors' carts."

"Big difference. Although the old Eastern Market looked primitive, I figured USDA inspectors checked the food here regularly to see low temperatures were maintained. They wouldn't want a Congressman to get food poisoning and vote against their next appropriation. Street food vendors in Bolivia deserve 'buyer beware' signs, and the hospitals aren't good."

Xave blew into her ear as he sighed. "Good thing you only do short consulting blitzes in developing nations."

Sara pulled away. She wanted to cry because nothing she said came off right this morning.

Xave touched her cheek. "But I agree." He turned to Linda. "I'll order three crab cake sandwiches with sides?"

Linda continued to study the blackboard for a few seconds more. "No, only the sandwich and iced tea for me. Then…"

Sara completed her sentence. "We can stop for dessert elsewhere or pick up bakery items here." Suddenly she lurched toward the far end of the table when a couple started to rise from their stools. Xave ambled up to the counter with Linda who immediately began to assemble napkins and plastic forks.

***

Sara watched Xave from a distance as he sat on a wood bench almost hidden by plants. On his left, the large white-flecked leaves of Dieffenbachia plants spread over a low stone wall. Behind him palm trees, bamboo, and fig trees reached upward in the glass dome of the Botanic Garden Conservatory on Capitol Hill. On his right, a profusion of ferns completely obliterated any sight of a wall. She thought the high humidity and the intense light on the hundreds of different types of green foliage was intoxicating. He sat with his head drooping. She couldn't decide whether he was bored, his wounds ached, or both.

After a brief conversation with Linda, Sara ambled on a wet stone path toward Xave, and Linda hurried toward the entrance of the conservatory. When she reached the bench, Xave was hunched forward.

"Linda wanted to walk down to the Vietnam Memorial and the Lincoln Memorial."

The look in his uplifted eyes was of pain.

"I figured we'd rather sit here and relax in the warmth." She gently pushed him to one side of the bench and scrunched into the open space.

"Not sure she should be alone." He pulled out his phone and texted as he said, "Will she come back here or do we need to walk down there?"

"We'll meet at the National Gallery of Art Sculpture Garden in an hour and a half. Figured we can catch a cab on Constitution Avenue on the backside of the sculpture garden."

He put his phone in his pocket but didn't look at her. Instead, he wheezed a bit and placed his large hand over hers, which were uncharacteristically folded on her lap.

She leaned toward him. "If you don't want to walk, we can catch a cab on Independence at the side of this building. Whatever you're in the mood for."

"Hate to have you see me like this. I'm not bouncing back from these wounds as I usually do. Old age."

"Nonsense, the wounds were serious. I pushed you too hard today. I'm sorry."

Xave raised his hand and traced his pointer finger under her chin. "I enjoyed seeing you in your native environment. Your face glows when you look around scenes in Washington. I can tell you've enjoyed past visits here. I also liked watching you and your sister together. So different in looks and temperament but so in sync."

"Yeah, I'm a talkative version of Oscar to her quiet rendition of Felix in the *Odd Couple*." She stroked his stubbly cheeks. "Now, you have to lower your guard. You admitted earlier you joined the navy after a fun-loving semester of college." She paused. "How did you say it? Mmm. 'I liked the look of the Marine dress uniform, but thought a biology major would make a good medic.' So, you joined the Navy because they served as medics for the Marines."

"I forgot how even though you often didn't appear to be listening, you could usually quote my words back to me in Bolivia." He gently squeezed her right ear lobe between his calloused fingers. "Not sure if that's a good or bad trait in a woman."

"By my calculations, you must had landed in Vietnam in seventy-four at the age of nineteen."

"Eighteen, I graduated a year early from high school." He paused. "I was one of the lucky ones," he winked, "who was airlifted out in 1975 when Saigon fell."

She lowered her voice. "Is that when you moved from the military to the CIA or whatever you're in now?"

"What makes you ask?" He pulled his hand away from her face.

"Shantelle called you a spook once. You aren't in the military now. On the surface, you were an embassy official with USAID in Bolivia, but your activities seemed clandestine." She put her hand under his chin and raised his head. "How am I doing?"

He stood and pulled Sara to her feet. "I think it's time we walk over to the sculpture garden."

"I'm not through with my questions. Did you earn the nickname Lady Killer in Vietnam?"

He dropped her hands, the wrinkles on his face deepened, and his black eyes bore into her. "Who told you?"

"Doesn't matter, but I need to know the story behind your troubled look now."

"I'll tell you as we walk. As you guessed, my adventures started in Vietnam. I was assigned to work as a military advisor with tribesman, mainly Hmong, on the Cambodian border. Usually my contacts were men, but one of my contacts was wounded so badly that he sent his sixteen-year old daughter to guide us."

After they cleared the humid warmth of the conservatory, she drew in a chestful of crisp fall air and put her arm around his waist. "Tell me about her."

"Smart, fearless, more ruthless than her father."

"And you fell in love with her?"

He stopped and seemed to gaze at the yellow trees around the Capitol. "I depended on her, and she on me. I made a mistake, and the Viet Cong captured her. We heard her screams through the jungle that night, but she must not have talked because we were able to escape."

Sara squeezed his waist. Now wasn't the time to ask more about Vietnam or his alias. "What about your story in Bolivia about having a master's degree in public health?"

"True. I started college again in fall of seventy-five. Didn't want to be a physician and didn't seem to fit into the U.S. scene. Decided public health work overseas was right for me. My friends," he coughed, "in government thought that would be a good cover. Gave me versatility. After college, I worked all over Latin America and the

Caribbean ostensibly in public health programs and clinics. Sometimes in posts in DC, like Shantelle's at USAID."

"Were you happy?"

He stopped and pushed her onto the edge of large concrete flowerpot in front of the Capitol. "What an odd question?

She jumped up. "How so?"

"It deceptive like this flowerpot. The pot seems decorative on the surface. In reality, it's heavy enough to stop any vehicle but a tank from approaching the Capitol. Your question is also deceptive."

She tugged on his unbuttoned sweater and pulled him toward her. "My question was an honest one."

She placed her hand on his shoulder and lightly kissed his cheek. He turned his head, teased her lips open with his tongue, and slipped his tongue in her mouth. She felt the muscles of her abdomen tighten and warmth move up her torso. He lowered his arms to her hips and pressed her against his thighs, which swayed slightly. Next his tongue flicked her left ear. Then he gently tickled her earlobe as his hot breath warmed her cheek. "I'm bad luck."

She stifled a moan. "Don't brag." She began to worm her tongue into his mouth.

Suddenly he braced both arms on her shoulders and pushed away. He gasped, "You won't want me after you hear the rest of the story."

The warm glow faded from her gut as he continued to hold her at arm's-length and stare at her with unflinching black eyes. Tears began to trickle down her face. He loosened his grip on one shoulder and handed her a large, white handkerchief from his trouser pocket. As she dabbed her eyes, he grabbed her free arm and set off at a rapid pace across the National Mall.

He slowed the pace to scan a group of men playing touch football on the brown grass in the center of the mall, as Sara watched a young couple rolling on a blanket. When she nudged him to look at parents doling out ice cream treats to children standing impatiently by a snack truck, he looked away. His eyes constantly swept the Mall as they moved toward the sculpture garden, and he only said "aha" occasionally to Sara's attempts to start a conversation.

They stopped in the garden in front of a large orange metal sculpture by Alexander Calder. Sara read the sign. "Red Horse. Should be two orange horses."

He snorted. Suddenly he tensed. Sara turned to follow his gaze and gasped. Linda was running toward them. As soon as she was near enough, Linda shoved a yellow, lined page into Sara's hand. In capital letters, the note said:

You can't hide from us.

Xave gripped Sara's bicep with his right hand and handed her his cane and case in a few swift strokes. Then he grabbed Linda's arm as he pulled her forward.

CHAPTER 15: Sergeant Elsa Grasso on Day 7

"Damn. Damn."

Elsa had never heard Chuy curse so much as today. They had leads, but most weren't yielding answers. In fact, they were sliding backward in several ways.

Chuy was pleased when Sanders arranged for Sara and Linda to be in Washington because then he had two less worries. Now on Monday, they were back. He tensed whenever she mentioned their names. She and Chuy needed a break in the case and fast.

The chances of recovering information from Dean Wilson plummeted Saturday. Sally Wilson threw a blood clot from her wounds and had a stroke. She was paralyzed on her left side, and physicians in the intensive care unit weren't optimistic about her recovering the ability to speak. Elsa doubted she would pull much from Dean Wilson without Sally, even with Linda's help.

She and Chuy had wanted to move Diego and Mazzone from a jail in Albuquerque to the federal prison (a high security unit but not a super max security unit) to reduce their channels of communication with the outside world, but Rachel had opposed them. Sanders went over Rachel's head and called Ulysses Howe, the director of the Albuquerque office of the FBI, on Thursday night. Diego and Mazzone were transferred on Friday morning.

This advance was partially reversed when Rachel convinced the warden at the high security unit of the federal prison in Florence, Colorado to put both men into the general prison population late on Friday afternoon. Elsa suspected after Ulysses Howe had gone home for the weekend.

A prisoner slashed Diego's arm with a makeshift shiv during a morning outdoor exercise period on Saturday morning. Rachel claimed this experience would scare Diego into talking and drove to Florence to interview him on Sunday. Despite extensive bruises and cuts from what he called "falls," he remained silent. Rachel informed Chuy Sunday night that she was interviewing Mazzone and Diego together today after she

J. L. Greger

"set the stage." Elsa shuddered to think what Rachel would do to set the stage. She knew Chuy was worried too because last night he moaned in his sleep "Rachel don't" repeatedly.

She took a sip of her coffee. Enough of the negatives. They had made limited progress on several fronts.

APD technicians had spent hours examining all the tapes from the courthouse on the days of the trial but found the two dead gunmen appeared on the tapes only on the day of the shootings. She guessed they had not cased out the scene themselves.

APD officers had studied the tapes and interviewed everyone who spoke to the gunmen or stood by them for more than a minute on the day of the shooting. She had brought in for questioning the four most likely suspects: the officer who had shot the second gunmen, two bailiffs, and one of assistant DA Zelda Zane's aides.

She doubted the APD officer had been bribed but recommended he receive psychological counseling. The aide was innocent of anything but incompetence.

The male bailiff was uncooperative until Elsa mentioned his history of gambling. Then she quickly learned that a man, who refused to identify himself, had called the bailiff on the day before Raines's trial commenced. "All I had to do was admit an APD officer with a certain name badge to the roped off area behind the courtroom. An officer with the badge came at least twice during the trail. Once on the day of the shootings." The bailiff gave a name matching the badge on the gunman who shot Raines, but he thought different men wore the badges on the two days. "I found an envelope with one thousand dollars in my locker on the first day of the trial with a note saying, 'You're dead if you talk.' I found two thousand dollars in my locker and a similar note after the shootings." Elsa garnered little more. The man had been too frightened or dumb to study the faces of the officers wearing the badges. He'd already gambled away the cash and discarded the notes.

The second bailiff was also resistant to Elsa's first set of questions but cooperative after Elsa threatened to charge her with abetting murder. She told a similar tale as the first bailiff, except she admitted only one man to the restricted area by the courtroom once, on the day of the shooting. She accurately described the man who shot Sally and turned over two envelopes with cash and notes. Elsa sent the envelopes and their contents to the lab to be checked for fingerprints.

Elsa was jolted from her thoughts when Chuy stopped shuffling papers and said, "We've missed the obvious. Dean Wilson and Raines have seen a lot of patients over the years."

Elsa put her cup of coffee down. "At least a few must have been dissatisfied."

Chuy stretched back in his chair. She couldn't decide whether he was showing off his well-toned torso or relaxing. He sat up quickly. She assumed he was merely stretching. "Might go back thirty years. But why the action now?"

"True. If you wanted revenge on Raines, letting him be sentenced to prison would almost be better than killing him outright. Nothing adds up logically in this case."

Elsa turned to her computer screen and began to type. "However, it's a lead we should consider. I'm on it. Think I'll stop by and see Sally again, too."

"Why?"

Elsa organized materials on her desk. "Linda found Sally could answer yes-and-no questions by blinking her eyes. Might be my last chance."

Chuy winked at Elsa. "You're not as tough as you pretend. You feel about Sally much as I feel about George Lehar. They don't deserve being dragged into this criminal investigation. Lehar looks ten years older this morning than when I first saw him at Barelas Coffee House on Friday, and he looked bad then." He checked his computer screen. "Why wouldn't he? He's lost everything." Chuy blinked repeatedly at the screen. "Message from Lehar. He may have a lead on his son's location."

***

She pushed the large square metal button. Both doors swung open. Elsa hated intensive care units. Walking into an intensive care unit was worse than walking into a jail lock up. The intensive care unit was scarier because the patients were generally tethered to noisy monitors with flashing lights. Prisoners, at worst, were shackled or handcuffed. Their monitors were usually silent, not constantly emitting unsettling noises. Sometimes the prisoners she interviewed were bruised and battered, but she seldom felt sympathy because she told herself they deserved their scars. The victims she interviewed in hospital beds were more pathetic and frightening.

Actually, pathetic wasn't the right word for Sally Wilson. She was a fighter, but Elsa was unsure what to expect after the stroke. Sally flashed a smile as Elsa neared the bed. Only the right side of Sally's

J. L. Greger

mouth turned upward while the left hung slack. Sally's lopsided grin sent a shiver down Elsa's back.

Elsa swallowed hard to control her nausea and stroked Sally's right hand. "Sally. I have a few questions. Linda says you can do this. If the answer is yes, blink your eyes twice. If the answer is no, blink once." They practiced the routine with a couple of routine questions. Then Elsa asked, "Does your husband ever talk about his patients to you?"

Sally blinked her right eye twice. The left lid remained drooped over most of the left eye.

Elsa thought a second. "Does he mention names?"

Sally blinked once.

"Damn."

Sally puckered her lips on the right side. A tear slid down her right cheek.

"Sorry. I know you're trying, but we're up against the wall. No leads, and we think the man who organized the shooters is still free."

A nurse pulled the curtain. "Time for you to go. Sally needs her rest."

Elsa started for the door, stopped, searched through the files in her tote, and shoved a photo, not used in any press release, in front of Sally. "Ever see this guy in person?"

Sally's right eye fluttered. Suddenly the heart monitor started to emit a piercing sound. Despite the nurse's scream, Elsa leaned down and asked the question again.

Sally blinked twice.

Elsa smiled. "Was the hair gray?"

One blink.

"Was the hair black?"

Two blinks.

Another nurse entered the alcove and dragged Elsa away from the bed as the first nurse began to slide the glass door to the alcove shut.

"God bless you, Sally," said Elsa as she departed the cubicle into the shared space of the intensive care unit. She turned to the nurse. "She may have given us the first big break of this case." Somewhat sheepishly, she added, "She deserves better than her husband."

The nurse shrugged. "We all agree, but you have to leave."

***

Elsa knew she needed to swallow her pride and get help from a woman whom she disliked. Chuy might be able to charm her into cooperation, but she and Chuy were swamped with work. They'd gone on separate paths most of the day. She was prepared to beg.

First, she found the report on the standard physical given Mazzone when he entered the federal prison last Friday. Then she beseeched assistant DA Zelda Zane to find a sympathetic judge who would allow her access to medical records of all the patients Raines and Dean Wilson had seen during the last thirty years. Normally such a request was impossible. Zelda called back in thirty minutes. The judge who had been trying Raines wanted answers and thought Elsa's hypothesis was logical.

Elsa marched into the office of the top administrator in the University Hospital with the search warrant in hand. Linda always claimed the man hated the Dean. Elsa knew Linda was right when he smirked and instantly granted her access to the records of all patients who had been treated by the two men.

Her next stop was the medical school deans' office complex. Life was back to normal. No broken furniture or shards of glass. The carpet must have been patched because no bloodstains were visible. The door to Dean Wilson's private office was closed, and Audrey guarded the entrance like a loyal Pekingese dog. She even snorted like a flat-faced dog when Elsa entered the office complex. Linda's door was open. Otherwise the office complex was empty.

Linda was not enthused about Elsa's plan until Elsa showed her the search warrant and the hospital administrator's signature. Suddenly Linda called Winston Chu, a computer technician who had worked with Linda and Elsa during the initial investigation of Raines, and set a fast clip out of the office complex, down stairs, and through long, dimly lit hallways in the basement. Elsa suspected Linda's enthusiasm stemmed from the realization she wouldn't have to confront her boss until the computer search was completed. Then too, Linda and the lively computer analyst seemed to be a mutual admiration society.

They entered a room lined with gray metal cabinets. Computer parts, screens, keyboards, and associated junk spilled out of boxes and covered most of the floor. They were looking about the room when Winston Chu popped in. "Welcome to the medical school's computer graveyard." He scooted a rolling chair toward Linda and gave a mock bow toward Elsa. "Long time since we work together. What fun today?"

Elsa thought Winston with his dry humor was unusual for a first-generation Chinese man. She noted his fake singsong English disappeared when he spoke to Linda who quickly outlined the first task.

Elsa had watched them do complicated computer searches before and stepped out of their way.

The first computer search was negative. No patient with Mazzone's name or any of his aliases was ever registered in the University Hospital. Elsa gave Winston the name and aliases of Mazzone's deceased wife. Nothing.

They zeroed in on patients seen by both Dean Wilson and Raines during the last thirty years. Winston's stream of wisecracks lessened after a couple minutes and then stopped as he began to type frantically. His harangue began again as his printer buzzed and spit out pages. He thumbed through the pages and ignored Elsa's questions. "I found one hundred, fifty-seven patients who were treated or at least seen by both Dean Wilson and Dr. Raines during the last thirty years at this hospital. Eliminated seventy-four," he smiled, "because they're dead. Printed only names, diagnosis, and the date of the last time they were seen by one of the two physicians."

Elsa looked over Linda's shoulder as she scanned the page. "Is Mazzone there?"

Linda mumbled. "Too early to tell. "

"Would this help?" She shoved her laptop toward Linda. "Seems the physician at the federal prison gave Mazzone a routine exam when he was admitted there."

Linda squinted as she read, coughed, wrote several words on a page, and handed it to Winston. "Let's try another approach. Please determine how many files among the Dean's and Raines's patients meet these criteria."

CHAPTER 16: Sergeant Chuy Bargas

Chuy opened the blue wood door in the adobe wall and stepped onto a narrow red brick patio. A tin roof, supported by faded blue square posts, shaded the front façade of the small house. Underlying adobe bricks showed though several chipped areas in the front wall of the house. Dead and dying plants drooped from four large, blue jardinières, the type locals bought at the New Mexican version of Pier One stores called Jackalope, near the front door.

He hadn't noticed before how the house cried for attention. George Lehar and his wife must have been too sick or tired to do necessary upkeep lately.

As soon as Chuy knocked, George Lehar swung open the front door and ushered him to a living room with an old style stamped, tin ceiling. George had walked slowly when Chuy first met him at Barelas Coffee House, but he hadn't used a cane as he did today. George plopped into a brown leather recliner and pointed to the matching sofa. Mrs. Lehar sat in one corner. Chuy moved the beige and rose striped, crocheted afghan before he sat on the other corner.

"We've been thinking." Mrs. Lehar's voice trembled as she repeatedly plumped a rose-colored decorator pillow in her lap. "If we cooperate, the city might let George retire. Then we wouldn't lose his insurance as we will if he is fired."

Chuy wanted to crawl through a hole in the floor. As far as he was concerned, George had made an unwise decision, but the loss of his insurance coverage and potential retirement benefits seemed extreme. However, assistant DA Zelda Zane had threatened to charge him with abetting murder, and APD in an effort to protect their reputation had started the proceeding to fire him.

Lehar cleared his throat. "We don't know where Jorge is, but we own a cottage, a tiny one near Nambe Falls. We stayed there most weekends in the summer when Jorge was a teen."

"It's a little cooler in the foothills of the Sangre de Cristo Mountains than here." Mrs. Lehar stood, brushed tears from her eyes, and rushed to the kitchen.

George handed Chuy a photo he pulled from a side pocket in his recliner. "Only time when Jorge seemed happy. See how handsome he looks in the photo." For the first time since Chuy arrived, George smiled. "Anyway, yesterday we thought we'd take a drive up there and get it ready to sell." He nodded toward the kitchen. "She'll need the money when I'm gone, and I may not be able to do simple repairs if we wait any longer. We tried to help Jorge, but he was lost by the time we got him at fourteen. Nothing worked." George seemed to go into a daze and kept repeating, "We tried."

Chuy hated to push George, but he couldn't withstand another verse of "we tried" and was sure he was out of comforting phrases. He cleared his throat loudly to interrupt George's litany. "You said you urgently needed to see me."

George pulled a map with a big red X on it out of the other pocket of his recliner. "The keys to the cabin are gone. Don't know when they disappeared." He pulled his hand through his sparse hair. "More we thought, the more we thought Jorge took them. The X marks the cabin's location."

Chuy studied the map as George continued to lament his "lost" son. The location was as close to the Nambe Falls and Reservoir as possible without being on the Nambe Pueblo. It would take him more than two hours to get to the location on a dirt road fifteen miles north of Santa Fe.

Mrs. Lehar returned with a pitcher of lemonade. "Do you want some? I just made it."

Chuy gulped as he stood. "Look folks, I'd let you retire with full benefits if it was up to me. I told my bosses what I thought, but my opinion doesn't matter." He looked at the pitcher of lemonade. Sugary beverages left a sour taste in his mouth, much like this pitiful situation. "I think the best I can do is get someone to Nambe fast."

George closed his eyelids as Mrs. Lehar sobbed.

"I will plaster my report with how much you cooperated. I... I'm so sorry about this whole mess."

***

Chuy texted Elsa. Her immediate response was:

Hot lead. Can't go to Nambe with you.

He called a state police officer, who was on the New Mexico Gangs Task Force with him, and explained the potentially explosive situation that might greet the first police officers to approach the Lehar's cabin in Nambe. After consultation, four members of the Nambe Police Department agreed to block the road to the cabin with their cars until officers from the New Mexico State Police and Santa Fe County Sheriff reached the cabin in probably about one-half hour.

No one thought Chuy could reach the location before the action was over, and he might as well stay in Albuquerque. He was relieved to miss another shootout.

Chuy figured Jorge must be desperate by now. Falto, the only shooter left alive from the medical school and courthouse shootings, had repeated many times that the shooters would only receive their payments if they succeeded in killing their targets. He assumed Jorge was under the same mandate. If Jorge had gotten enough uniforms for all his accomplices from George, he only had one accomplice left to help him kill at least one of the three women — Sally, Linda or Sara.

In the midst of the negotiations with the state police and sheriff, Sanders emailed him and reminded him of an earlier promise. Chuy wanted to ignore the message but knew Sanders would call within an hour to check. Originally Chuy planned on seeing Sara late in the afternoon after he had completed his other tasks, but Sanders was insistent in his email. Besides, her home in the gated community of La Bendita was only a few miles off I-25 and north of Albuquerque, basically on the way to Nambe. He swung by his office, picked up several items, and drove thirty minutes to Sara's house.

As usual the light in the front office was on. Bug sat on his perch in front of the window and surveyed the yard as Sara worked at her computer. An easy target for a drive-by shooting.

The office was transformed fifteen minutes later. The shade was down. A stuffed animal sat on the teak table in front of the window, and a life-size mannequin sat on a chair by the side of the window where Sara usually sat. He ran outside to confirm the shadow of the mannequin showed through the shade when the lights were on. The three file cabinets, previously lined up against the wall, now created an alcove for the table and computer at the back of the room. He figured the full, metal cabinets would stop bullets from handguns aimed at the mannequin by the window and might even stop rifle bullets.

He sensed the furniture realignment had heightened Sara's fear of being alone in the house when she asked him to stay for lunch. She

J. L. Greger

didn't need to beg because the aroma wafting from the slightly browned casserole with potatoes, green chili, carrots, chicken, and cheese in the oven was enticing.

He had eaten only part of his lunch when photos of the cabin in Nambe arrived on his phone. The so-called cabin was actually a rusty trailer almost hidden among large piñon pines. The path to the trailer was covered with crushed dry pine needles and pine cones but no debris. Inside was another story — pizza boxes, empty bags from McDonald's and Sonic, and unidentifiable debris covered the floor and counters. The scariest part of the photos of the messy trailer was a red X painted across a picture of the Lehars.

His colleagues reported they found no one inside. After sifting through the garbage, they concluded two people had inhabited the cabin for several days, maybe a week. They advised Chuy to mobilize protection for the Lehars while they combed through the rest of the debris at the Nambe site.

CHAPTER 17: Sara at home near Albuquerque

Sara had started Monday morning by reading an email from Sanders. Now, after hours of searching the Web, she was editing her response to his questions.

The first point in his email was he wanted a simple, the word was underlined, explanation of how research at the Cuban Center of Molecular Immunology had garnered a patent for an anti-cancer drug. She wrote:

> Most oncology drugs are poisons that kill all cells. However, they kill cancer cells faster than normal cells because cancer cells grow faster than normal cells.
> The drug developed by the Cuban Center of Molecular Immunology is an example of cancer immunotherapy. These new drugs attempt to harness the immune system of patients to battle their own tumors. They do this by causing the body to develop antibodies, which will attach to a unique compounds found on the membranes of cancer cells but not normal cells. Thus the antibodies cause the destruction of only the cells they're attached to.

She appended two pages from the December 2013 issue of *Science*, which announced the journal's decision to name cancer immunotherapy as the "Breakthrough of the Year" in 2013.

> Here's the weak point of cancer immunotherapy. Different cancers have different unique compounds on their membranes. Thus, the vaccine developed in Cuba will help a limited number of patients with a specific type of lung cancer. Similarly, the cancer vaccines developed in the U.S. are specific to certain cancers.

Scientists are looking for a universal compound on the surface of all cancer cells but nowhere else.

His second question was: how did scientists at this Cuban Center of Molecular Immunology become so sophisticated scientifically? This question annoyed her because she suspected he'd already gotten answers from people with far more expertise than hers. However, she traced the backgrounds of scientists listed on the Cuban patent and wrote:

> Despite the U.S. embargo, Harvard and Tulane Universities have brought many scholars in medicine, biology, and public heath to the U.S. to study and do research. One of these scholars is the lead researcher on work supporting the patent for the cancer immunotherapy drug.
>
> I think you could get more detailed information from your health experts in the Library of Congress or the State Department and from the National Institutes of Health (NIH). The Fogarty International Center of NIH announced the first government-supported, cooperative agreement between NIH and Cuban scientists interested in pediatric oncology in 2012.

Sara thought she'd conveyed her annoyance nicely. She'd warned him in Washington that she didn't want to do busy work. Then, she realized he probably hadn't understood the long treatises provided by experts in Washington and was too proud to admit it.

He also wanted to know how to learn more about the *Cuban Center of Molecular Immunology* and other medical research groups in Cuba. Again, she suspected others must have already supplied him with these data. Her advice was simple.

> Probably the State Department or USAID should provide funds to the Fogarty Center of NIH or a large international drug company and have them invite Cuban scientists to a conference in the U.S.

She felt peckish, so she added:

Many scientists don't want to work with USAID because CIA agents are rumored to use USAID as a cover. Hence, you might not want to list USAID as a source of funds for the conference.

She imagined his face reddening as he read her comments.

Sanders ended his email with a question that he'd asked all the experts on Cuba when she was in Washington: "Where can I get honest answers on drug usage in Cuba?" The experts had agreed on four points: 1) Cuba was a major trading partner with Bolivia, and coca was one of Bolivia's main exports. 2) Many Cubans in the U.S. were involved in drug trafficking, especially along the east coast of the U.S. 3) Castro executed several high-ranking individuals for drug running in Cuba in 1991. 4) Although Cuban scientists and physicians seldom mentioned drug addiction in their publications, drug addiction must be a problem.

Sara had thought about this question more and searched the Web a lot before she wrote:

HIV is fairly common among users of illicit injectable drugs in many countries. Cuban medical scientists, especially those at the Pedro Kourí Institute of Tropical Medicine in Havana, mention HIV a lot in their publications. Researchers studying the demographics of HIV transmission might be able to provide data on illicit drug use in Cuba. Unfortunately, the Cuban government may not be willing to send these physicians/scientists to an international medical conference.

I know this isn't a great idea, but I hope it's helpful. Call if you want me to brainstorm more.

She sent the email and was ready to walk Bug when Chuy appeared. Usually she enjoyed Chuy's earnest but cheerful demeanor. Today he made her apprehensive as he paced about her house, muttered about drive-by shooters, insisted on rearranging the furniture in her office, and added two numbers to the speed dial on her phone. He was evasive when she asked about his sudden concerns and thought he might be more talkative if she shared the casserole in her oven with him. Instead, he checked his tablet between gulps and said little.

92   J. L. Greger

His jitteriness made more sense after she overheard his phone conversation with state police and then APD officers about Jorge Lehar. As he raced from her house to get to the Lehars, he ordered her to not leave the house or answer the door until he returned. Afterwards, all she could do was to cuddle Bug as she whispered, "What's next?"

The phone's ring jangled Sara's tense nerves more. Sanders skipped any greeting. "As usual, you have sifted through a lot of data and offered options that make sense to me. Thank you. Now let's talk about an area where you are less careful — your own personal safety. Have you varied your walks? I hope you've used the disguises Xave suggested?"

"Pretty hard to do in my own neighborhood without my neighbors thinking I'm loony."

Sanders snorted. "I assume you rearranged your office so you no longer sit in front of window."

"Yes, Chuy helped me."

"Where are you staying tonight?"

"Here."

Sanders coughed, "I assume Chuy is with you. Put him on the phone."

"He left about twenty minutes ago to rescue the parents of Jorge Lehar, the man who organized the shooters."

Silence. Then she heard Sanders speak to someone. More muffled noises. "When you see him, tell him to call me immediately."

She heard the whistling sound of shots and the crash of falling glass from the front of her house. She snatched Bug, screamed for Sanders to send help, and ran to the bathroom attached to her bedroom, closing doors as she went. She called the second speed dial number Chuy gave her.

The gunshots were closer now. They were pouring through the side windows. Someone was battering her exterior door on the side of her house.

She looked around her bathroom and dove into a large walk-in closet. She shoved boxes of Christmas decorations forward to create a niche for Bug and herself at the back of the closet. Then she dragged the boxes in front of the hiding place and pulled clothes on hangers along the closet rod to further hide her location. As she shrunk down around Bug, he licked her hands

Bullets splintered the exterior door. She heard the voices of two men speaking Spanish. Gunshots now came from inside the house. In her office probably. A door crashed open. More shots. Expletives in Spanish. She guessed they'd found the mannequin.

Another door splintered under a rain of bullets. The next shots seemed to echo. She thought they were from the garage.

Heavy steps thudded through her living room and kitchen toward the bedroom suite. Gunshots whistled through the door to the suite.

Sirens. She hoped she wasn't imagining them. Maybe the shooters would flee and leave their task unfinished, but she doubted they would.

Gunshots in the bedroom. Some muffled. Maybe they were shooting through the mattress. Heavy breathing. Were they looking under the bed? Now shots in the bathroom. The glass door of the shower splintered onto the tile floor. She knew the closets were next.

"Put down your guns. You're surrounded and we will shoot."

Sara recognized the voice of the Mercado Police Chief Gil Andrews. He had rescued her before. She hoped he wasn't too late this time. More gunfire as the shooters blasted both closets and the closed door to toilet stall. She scrunched down, but knew the next round of bullets was apt to be lower and would hit her and Bug.

More shots but from different guns.

Footsteps.

"Chief, they're bleeding bad."

"Cuff them anyway." Gil's growl softened. "Sara, Sara. Are you here?" The door of her closet was thrown open.

She opened her mouth, but no words came out. She pushed the boxes, and Christmas decorations spilled out as she crawled forward. When she looked up, Gil leaned forward ready to drag her out of the rubble. She tried to smile but sobbed instead. She leaned back and picked up Bug. "I thought Bug and I were goners."

Gil pulled her over the ornaments and dragged her to her feet. " I don't see any blood. Are you and the dog okay?"

She nodded.

Gil's face reddened. "Wait until I get my hands on Chuy. Should never have left you alone. Thought I trained him better than to make a rookie mistake." He put his heavy arm over her shoulder. "Your instincts were good."

"Wouldn't have been good enough without you." She was glad he continued to stand close because she felt woozy. After she stopped swaying, he pulled her from the closet into the bathroom, as Bug stayed plastered against her chest.

There was nowhere to step without treading on shards of glass, splintered wood from doors, blood, or bodies. Sara gulped as she looked around the room. Clothes shredded by gunfire fell on top of one body in front of the other closet.

"Guess Sanders was right. I can't stay here tonight." She pointed with her foot at Jorge's body. "Did he say anything useful?"

A local policeman, who was bent over the body, looked up. "Chief did his usual. Disabled this one but didn't kill him. So far, all he's moaned is "fire." I'm not as good a shot. I aimed at the other one's heart. He's dead."

Jorge began to choke and claw at his neck. Gil said, "I may have collapsed his lung. Better lift his head a bit."

The policeman shoved his hand under Jorge's neck and lifted his head. Jorge stopped coughing, but continued to scratch at his neck and pull on a silver chain about his neck. The officer squirmed a bit. "Hey Chief, looks at this pendant, probably a religious medal. Seems to want it off." The policeman fingered the silver medal. "Looks new. Odd cross, I've never seen before."

"Touch only the edges." Gil bent down. "I've seen that wavy cross on medals for firemen. Bag it carefully." He stood. "Think they call it a St. Florian cross."

CHAPTER 18: Sergeant Chuy Bargas

Chuy received a terse phone message from Gil Andrews as he turned the next to last corner before the Lehar's house. "Sara's alive. One shooter is dead. Jorge is hanging on." A pause. "Talk to you after you're through at the Lehar's house." Gil hung up before Chuy could reply.

Chuy felt sweat wash down his back. When his old boss was terse, he was explosively angry. Chuy gulped. All he could do now was manage the next situation.

No one from APD had called him even though at least two cars should have arrived at the Lehar's house twenty minutes ago. He hoped the couple was okay.

He turned the last corner. His hopes vanished. Two police cruisers, a crime lab van, and an ambulance sat in front of the house, but no one was rushing.

When he opened the blue door to the patio, he was greeted by the odor of blood. Through the open door to the house, he saw a technician leaning over Mrs. Lehar's body. A rosary dripped from her hand. The grout on the floor near her torso was stained dark red.

An APD officer stepped forward. "Looks like they've were dead for at least an hour before we arrived." He paused. "Before you go in, I have to ask you about your whereabouts this morning."

Chuy flushed but quickly recounted his morning.

The APD officer nodded. "That's what we reconstructed, too. Think. Did you pass the killers when you left here? Were there cars on the street?"

Chuy thought for a moment. "Vehicles were parked along this street. All seemed empty." He closed his eyes. "No vans. Two or three sedans, not luxury." Pause. "They fit here. Darkish." He opened his eyes. "Nothing else. Wait. One was a Camry. Damn. Falto mentioned Jorge drove a black Camry."

"Thanks for not blowing your lid. I had to ask." The officer nodded at a technician bent over Mrs. Lehar's body. "The crime lab people arrived here ten minutes ago. The bodies are as we found them.

The killers bound his hands, gagged him, and made him kneel before they shot him in the forehead. They only gagged the woman before they shot her multiple times in the torso."

Chuy knelt by the George Lehar's body. He was always amazed how a body seemed to shrink in death. "A lot of anger from a son."

"Might not have been the son. I think the bullet wounds were made by two guns of different caliber, but the techs will have answers soon." The APD officer pointed to another technician. "I requested she dust for fingerprints. The other rooms don't show any sign of a struggle. One drawer was open in a dresser. Men's underwear and socks pushed to one side, but not sure my drawer at home would look any different."

***

Chuy swallowed hard as he left his car in front of Sara's house. Her house looked worse than he expected. A couple of shards of glass hung where the front window had been. Glass covered the front walk. At least ten neighbors stood across the street and gawked. On closer inspection, he saw the beige stucco was pockmarked with bullet holes.

The remnants of the outer door lay on gravel at the side of the house. The ambulance crew must have removed it from its hinges to expedite movement in and out of the house. The windows by the door were shattered. This stucco was pitted with bullet holes, too.

A local patrolman, logging in all visitors to the crime scene, took a quick look at Chuy. "You're brave to even show your head. Might want to look at the front office and garage before Chief Andrews sees you. He's in the back bedroom."

The door to Sara's office and the teak bookcase by the door were reduced to piles of splintered wood, shredded books, and broken mementos. Chuy wondered if the shooters had imagined Sara would be waiting with a gun when they blasted into the room. The eeriest item in the carnage was a bronze head of Lincoln with bullet holes in the side of the face. Interestingly, they hadn't shot the computer in the alcove. However, the inflatable mannequin was reduced to a puddle of shredded pink plastic.

The door to the garage was blasted off its hinges. Her gray car with its doors, including the hatch, open was peppered with bullet holes. He felt sweat run down his back. If he'd been present when the shooters attacked, he would have attempted to escape with Sara in the car.

Chuy walked back into the living room/kitchen complex, which was relatively undamaged. Sara, standing at her kitchen counter, was on the phone with her insurance agent and only acknowledged Chuy's presence quickly. She was focused on getting the agent to document the damage immediately so she could clean up the debris. Bug lay on the counter with his head only inches from Sara and whimpered occasionally.

Chuy gulped and threaded his way around blood streaks and debris as he entered the master suite. The ambulance crew had removed Jorge, but the other body remained in place while two crime technicians swarmed around it. Gil Andrews never hurried to remove dead bodies from a crime scene because he preferred to keep the scene intact as long as possible as he ruminated about it.

Gil hummed a Glen Campbell tune as he stood in the bedroom and stared at the springs and padding exploding through mutilated green and white bedding. He turned after a technician greeted Chuy. "Good thing you took your time in getting here. Gave me time to cool off and think."

Chuy thought Gil's eyes were watering when he spoke, "You couldn't have stopped them alone with your standard issue pistol. We barely did, and we had more firepower. They were crazed. I'm having them checked for drugs. Jorge babbled a couple of words repeatedly before he passed out."

"So where was Sara?"

Gil pointed to a door with only a couple of bullet holes. "She buried herself behind boxes in the back corner. Her luck almost ran out."

"Yes." Sara screamed "yes" again and again as she bounced into her bedroom. "The claims adjustor is on his way."

"Mmm." Gil nodded. "You know you can't stay here tonight."

"I know, but I'll stay until I get the house boarded up." She shrugged. "I figure it'll take several hours for Mazzone or whoever is behind this to get more shooters organized. This is as safe as I'll be here for a while." Her voice trailed off. "Maybe ever again."

A patrolman handed Sara a white legal envelope. Someone shoved this is my hand and ran."

Sara began to shake as she read the letter. Gil grabbed it from her hand. "A new threat?" He paused and chortled. "Seems the La Bendita Home Owners' Association Board held an emergency meeting." He checked his watch. "They were fast. Seems you have seventy-two hours to repair the exterior of your house or they will fine you a thousand dollars a day."

Chuy expected Sara to cry. Instead she yelled, "Those bastards are bluffing."

Gil smirked. "Of course." He scanned the letter. "This is odd. They claim the condition of your house will decrease the value of real estate in La Bendita because it 'makes our community look like a ghetto.' Must have forgotten Mazzone was their neighbor too and shot up a lot more here two years ago." His eyebrows knit together. "They suggest you shouldn't live here until your current problems are resolved because you will endanger them."

"Damn sheep. Once one gets a bad idea, they all follow. Wish I could fix them as we did lambs on the farm."

Gil looked at her quizzically. "How'd they do it in the Midwest?"

"Basically, with a rubber bands. No fuss, no mess."

Chuy choked. He had wondered what was under Sara's steely exterior. Now he knew, and he vowed not to annoy her. He was also surprised. She had expressed no animosity toward the shooters. "Hate to see what you would have done to the shooters."

Sara's face clouded. "Totally different. They were driven by fear of what Diego, Mazzone, or someone else would do to them. The Board," she paused, "or at least several of its members are driven by pettiness."

Gil convulsed in laughter. "Too bad I can't let you fix their problem. I'll talk to them. Not the first time a resident of La Bendita has brought me a complaint about your Board's decisions." He handed the letter back to Sara. "You can let your insurance agent see it, but keep it. You may need it when you sue them."

Chuy choked. Police officers generally avoided getting in the middle of neighborhood quarrels, and Gil always played it smart. He looked at Gil's face — red, lined, and hard. Gil didn't care. He was as angry as Sara.

Gil pushed Sara in front of him to the kitchen. "Chuy, why don't you give Rachel and Sanders an update." Gil dropped his arm from Sara's shoulders. "Don't worry. I'll talk to the insurance adjustor and set your Board straight, but they are right. You can't stay here. As soon as the technicians are through, pack a case or two of clothes." He left and then returned with a card. "Might as well call AAA and get them to tow your car to a shop for an estimate now. Then you won't have to bicker with the adjustor."

CHAPTER 19: Linda Almquist in the medical school on Day 8

Linda, holding a small bouquet of red carnations and yellow lilies in a red glass vase, sped into the ICU with Winston Chu at her heels. The policewoman stationed at the door and the nurses greeted her as she headed for Sally Wilson's alcove.

Linda pulled the sliding glass door open. Earlier today the alcove was filled with wilted flowers. Now it was bare except for a few mums stuck in a vase. "I noticed your flowers were drooping, so I brought you a new batch." She grabbed Sally's right hand.

Sally flashed a lopsided smile and squeezed Linda's hand twice. Linda assumed Sally was thanking her.

"Sally, I brought along a friend. Winston and I use computers to review old cases."

Winston stepped forward and licked his lips. "This new for me. Don't see this side of the hospital much." He quickly moved back toward the corner after he handed Linda several pages.

Linda held up a xerox of an old grainy photo. "Remember this man?"

Sally blinked her right eye twice.

"Good. I don't want to tire you so I'll go straight to the important question. Did you see him when you worked as a nurse in the VA?"

Two blinks.

"Mmm. Is this man the same man as in the photo Officer Elsa Grasso showed you earlier today?"

Linda sensed hesitation. The lopsided smile was now a grimace. Two blinks.

Linda slid her hand lightly across Sally's forehead. "I know you want to say more, but can't."

Two blinks.

"Did you see this man after the VA?"

Hesitation. Two blinks.

J. L. Greger

"In a hospital?"

One blink. Sally twisted her lips, almost her whole face, on the right side.

Linda looked up at the monitor and saw Sally's blood pressure was skyrocketing. "Enough for now. You've been a dear." She squeezed Sally's hand and turned before Sally saw the tears in her eyes.

Linda consulted briefly with the nurses and departed the ICU. "I need a break." She turned to Winston. "Please text Elsa and tell her we're going to the cafeteria."

He looked at her quizzically. "Boss, is that allowed? You aren't supposed to go anywhere without police. Even this trip to the ICU." He texted as they both raced down the hallway. When he finished, he grabbed her arm. "The trip away from here for a few days was good for you. You're peppier."

Linda stopped. She hadn't thought about it, but she did feel energized. She'd learned a lot at the conference in Washington. She'd also slept more soundly in Washington. Then again, Winston's verve always seemed to rub off on her.

"I always enjoy…." She stopped because she suddenly remembered Sanders and Elsa had told her repeatedly not to admit where she had gone, even if someone seemed to know, because she or Sara might have to be whisked away again.

Winston winked. "Good to keep your hiding place secret."

Elsa and a campus police officer met them at entrance to the cafeteria. "I leave you for a couple of minutes and you disappear."

Linda took a step backward and blinked. "We left a note and Winston texted you. We made a breakthrough, well sorta."

Elsa eyed the cafeteria. "This might not be the best place to discuss it."

Linda shrugged. "Might be better than my office." Linda knew despite the hubbub as the kitchen crew slammed stainless steel pans into the serving area and noisily finished preparations for dinner, the dining area would be almost empty.

Winston chuckled. "No Dean."

Linda ignored the banter between Elsa and Winston as she looked longingly at the chocolate chip cookies before she ambled to the iced tea dispenser and on to a table at the back of the dining area, without a cookie.

Elsa chose the chair next to Linda's. "Did you identify someone out of the eighty-three candidates?"

Winston took a big bite out of a chocolate chip cookie. "Threw the first list out. Started a new search. We looked for male patients who are now about Mazzone's age, who have a history of thyroid cancer, and who are veterans."

Elsa looked surprised. "Why?"

Linda played with her straw. "I made some time calculations after you told me the physician found a small surgical scar on Mazzone's neck. The timeline was right. Mazzone, as a young man, might have been assigned by the army to participate in nuclear tests in Nevada or New Mexico. Don't remember the names of the projects in the 1980s. Anyway, if he needed medical care, he might have been sent to the VA Hospital in Albuquerque when Raines and the Dean were residents there."

Elsa gasped. "I don't get the leap."

"A common symptom of overexposure to radiation is thyroid cancer, especially in children and teens. In the early 1980s, Mazzone would have been eighteen or nineteen, basically a teen. They usually treated thyroid cancer then with surgery."

"Your new list is based on lots of assumptions?"

Winston expanded his chest. "Facts not assumptions. I called a friend at the VA. Faster than official channels. She found Mazzone's name on a list of old records from 1984, but she found no evidence he ever sought medical care from a VA facility after 1984. The records prove he's a vet and was treated for thyroid cancer."

Linda flashed a smile at Winston, and then turned to Elsa. "Told you he was the best." She pushed a sheet of paper across the table to Elsa. "We assumed Mazzone sought medical care at the University Hospital sometime during the last thirty-five years. Only twenty-seven names in the University Hospital database met our criteria — a male about Mazzone's age who was a veteran and had been treated for thyroid cancer in the 1980s. Raines treated fifteen of these patients. Of course, none were named Mazzone, but he's apt to be on this list under an alias."

"Down to fifteen possibilities. Better than I expected, but why did you visit Sally?"

"While Winston talked to his friend at the VA, I kept thinking about Sally recognizing the ten-year-old photo of Mazzone you showed her yesterday. I was surprised because she never bothers her husband at work and wouldn't know his patients. Then the answer hit me. She'd been a nurse at the VA hospital when Raines and her husband were residents there. Perhaps Mazzone was her patient at the VA."

Elsa braced her head in her hands. "We're going in circles again. Are you saying Mazzone targeted Sally?"

Linda shook her head. "Oh, we forgot to tell you a couple of details. The computer technician at the VA found the name of the attending physician for the patient named Mazzone in the VA in 1984."

Elsa poised her hands above the keypad of her tablet. "Was it Raines or Dean Wilson?"

Linda frowned, "No, a name I'd never heard, but Raines and the Dean would have been residents then, not attendings. They might have treated Mazzone under his direction, but it's impossible to prove unless the Dean tells us."

"This is hopeless. Are we sure the Mazzone at the VA in 1984 is our Mazzone?"

Winston bounced in his seat. "After a lot of digging, my friend found a photo in Mazzone's old file at the VA. Scanned and sent it." He pushed across the table a grainy shot of a skinny, dark-haired young man with an army crew cut. "Look at the nose. Surprised he didn't have it fixed."

Elsa studied the photo. "Might be Mazzone. Did you show it to Sally?"

"Yes, for three reasons. One, I wanted to be sure the VA patient was our Mazzone. Two, the Dean would never admit recognizing the man in this poor-quality photo, unless Sally had already identified him." Linda looked at the ceiling.

"Your third reason?"

"Hard to explain. The nurses told me your visit yesterday upset Sally. I wanted to assess whether a photo of him as a young man also alarmed, not the right word, excited her. It did. Somehow, I don't think a nurse would remember the faces of most of her patients from thirty-five years before. There's more to this story, but I don't know how to get the answers. She admitted she saw him after he was released from the VA." Linda suddenly felt exhausted. "You'll have to take over now."

"I'm surprised you accomplished so much so quickly."

Linda teared up. "I had to. After the attack on Sara's house yesterday, I can't stop crying, unless I'm really busy."

CHAPTER 20: FBI agent Rachel Jones on Days 9 and 10

Guards brought the prisoner in. Even in an orange jumpsuit, Mazzone walked with the confidence of a man in a several thousand-dollar suit. The warden had told Rachel that the other prisoners kept their distance from Mazzone unless he signaled they might approach him by clicking his fingers and pointing at them. Unfortunately, the warden had insisted he would accompany her when she talked to Mazzone but had promised to remain silent.

Rachel wanted to catch Mazzone off guard. She began talking before he settled in his plastic chair. "We know you met Raines in the VA Hospital in Albuquerque in 1984."

Mazzone looked bored and unconcerned before his dark eyes focused on her face. She'd never faced a prisoner with so much fortitude. The eyes and smile bore no hint of fear, craziness, or spite, as she often noted in the faces of others. His visage suggested wisdom tinged with weariness. She could see why he had climbed to the top of the heap in the drug business. She fought to control her expressions to hide her thoughts.

After more than a minute of silence, he said, "You're bluffing. I don't remember the name of the old doc who treated me, but his name wasn't Raines."

"Raines was a resident on your case. You looked him up several years later at the University Hospital."

Again, a staring contest. "I don't remember."

Rachel was prepared and gave a broad smile. "One lie on your part."

He peered at her with a countenance suggesting innocence.

She added acting to the list of his skills. "You also met a nurse — a cute, young blonde called Sally at the VA." She pushed a page with an old photo of Sally in her nurse's uniform across the table. She watched Mazzone, displaying no emotion on his face, rub his thumb slowly across the photo.

J. L. Greger

"She was shot in the shootout in the Albuquerque courthouse last week."

Mazzone stopped rubbing the photo.

"She might have been all right, but she suffered a stroke. You ought to see her now. Pretty sad." She shoved the worst photo available of Sally — one with the lopsided smile.

She thought Mazzone stiffened slightly but wasn't sure.

"Funny. She couldn't talk, but she sure recognized this photo of you." She slid a copy of his 1984 army photo across the gray table toward him.

He glanced at it and returned to scanning her. "So?"

"Why did you order a hit on her?"

Mazzone folded both his big, hairy hands on the table. "I didn't. Don't try to play mind games on me. I wrote the book."

The conversation continued for another fifteen minutes. Rachel noticed Mazzone occasionally let his eyes shift from her face to the two photos of Sally. Otherwise she gained nothing new. The warden, true to his word, was silent during the interview. Surprisingly, he remained silent afterward and walked away quickly.

Rachel requested to meet with Diego before she left the facility.

***

The next day Rachel strode unannounced into Dean Wilson's office in the medical school, while Elsa argued with his secretary Audrey. Dean Wilson placed his hand over his phone and frowned. "What do you want this time?"

"Join me and Sergeant Elsa Grasso at the table." She nodded toward the large mahogany table across the room.

He appeared to ignore her. "Senator, I appreciate your help on this issue, but an emergency has arisen. I'll call you back in fifteen minutes." He typed an email and sat silently for at least thirty seconds before he ambled to the table and assumed his usual pose with his head slightly bent over his clasped hands. She had heard Linda and Elsa call it his praying posture.

As soon as Elsa bustled in, Rachel broke the silence. "We know Raines treated Mazzone for thyroid cancer. We think you knew."

Dean Wilson laid his hands flat on the table.

"Look we're trying to be nice and not do this interview in front of your wife and Associate Dean Linda Almquist."

He blinked his eyes, stood, walked to his mahogany desk, dug through the back of two drawers, and pulled out two large manila envelopes. After he returned to his seat at the table, he brought his long fingers up into the prayer position. "Raines's estate lawyer and I figured you'd eventually demand answers. What do you want to know?"

The next thirty minutes were satisfying and infuriating. He told them that during the week before Raines trial, he had visited Raines's estate lawyer once. Then he added what they didn't know. The estate lawyer gave him the keys to Raines's house and a sheet with references to pages in medical texts, which Raines wanted him to have as keepsakes. On the unaccounted night, Dean Wilson had gone to Raines's home, found the old medical texts bequeathed him, and used the sheet given him by the estate lawyer to remove items slipped between the pages of the texts.

Elsa looked uncomfortable during this confession because she'd led the search of Raines's house when Raines was arrested for two murders in the medical school. Obviously, she hadn't thumbed through the pages of his books.

He handed an envelope to Rachel. "Abel — I know you use his last name Raines — but he was my friend, so I will call him Abel. A man who was treated at our local VA hospital for thyroid cancer in the early 1980s came to see Abel in the late 1980s. He asked Abel to give him a physical focusing on the potential of any consequences of thyroid cancer and to do the consultation outside the system."

Elsa looked up. "How?"

"Don't know exactly. But Abel was supposed to give all the records to the man and retain none in the hospital system." He shrugged. "Probably possible to do before all the laws and computers. Knowing Abel, he received a sizeable cash contribution for his services."

"Nice story, but how did you learn it?"

He frowned and appeared for a moment to be at a loss for words. "I might say I found out when I looked at the file in the envelope. It appears to be a copy of the record he gave the man. It's the old style xeroxing that yellows badly with age. But...."

"You know if I catch you in a lie, you're in big trouble." Rachel smiled as she thumbed through the file and handed it to Elsa.

"About ten years ago, Abel and I went out to dinner when Sally was away for a week. He drank too much. Something he rarely did. He told me what I told you. He also claimed the man asked a lot of questions about nurses at the VA in the 1980s, especially a pretty blonde nurse called Sally." Dean Wilson waited for what he said to sink in.

Elsa gasped. Rachel frowned. "Are you telling me Mazzone not only had a long-term grudge against Raines but also against your wife?"

He shook his head in apparent disgust. "I suppose Mazzone might have wanted to get rid of Raines because he knew one of his aliases, but I doubt it. He knew Raines didn't divulge his secrets to police during the flu epidemic when Mazzone shot his way out of La Bendita."

"He might also be angry with Raines because the ineptitude of Raines's sidekick Diego Rivera got him arrested." Rachel continued, "So?"

He handed the second envelope to Rachel. All it contained was one old photo. "I don't know how Abel got it. He might have been the photographer." The picture showed a young Mazzone with his arm slung over Sally's shoulder in front of a pizzeria with a Paisano's sign. "I'd guess, judging by Sally's clothes and the look of Paisano's, the photo was taken during the first year of my residency before Sally and I were engaged."

Rachel gasped. "What does this prove?"

He brought his hands together and steepled his fingers. "Don't be dense. Sally was collateral damage. Mazzone wouldn't have hired anyone to shoot Sally. He was fond of her... at least once."

Rachel remembered how Mazzone stroked the photo of the young Sally and took peeks at both photos yesterday. She knew Dean Wilson was right. "Why are you presenting this evidence now?"

"I saw how upset Sally was last night after Linda badgered her. I've seen what my associate dean can do with the help of the computer technician Winston Chu. She can ferret out secrets better than either of you."

Rachel snorted.

He looked pleadingly at Rachel. "I don't want my wife, during the probably limited time she has left, to be haunted by questions. I don't know whether she recognized Mazzone when his picture was plastered across the *Albuquerque Journal* two years ago after he shot his way out of La Bendita during the flu epidemic." He looked at Elsa. "Possibly the truth dawned on her when you and then Linda showed her old pictures of Mazzone. I've accepted I'll probably never know the details, but I know she's been a good wife and mother."

Rachel seldom pitied a suspect, but she felt a twinge of sadness for the man. She was through with questions, but Elsa continued. "You knew Raines better than anyone. Why did Raines want you to find these pages before the trial?"

He lowered his head. "I don't know."

Elsa leaned forward. "You're hiding something. What else did you find stuck among the pages of the books?

Silence.

"We all know you're an important man in this state — the dean of the medical school and the confidant of elected officials throughout the state of New Mexico. But I'll take you down to headquarters if I don't get answers."

Rachel touched Elsa's hand. "Don't be rash?"

Elsa pushed Rachel's hand away and stared at Dean Wilson who kept his eyes focused on the table. "I talked to my bosses. We're tired of your games. They instructed me to arrest you for obstructing this investigation if I'm not totally satisfied with your answers today." She pointed a finger at him. "What else did you find among the pages of the books?"

He whispered softly. "A clipping on the Enron scandal."

"What about it?"

"Kenneth Lay wasn't officially guilty because he died before his trial ended."

Elsa sat back and seemed to think. "So?"

Silence.

"We can finish this discussion downtown. Do you have the clipping?"

"Burned it with the matches Abel left in the envelope with the clipping."

"The meaning?"

He sat upright and assumed his usual officious pose. "Obvious. He would commit suicide before the trial ended."

"How?"

"I don't know, but I assumed he wanted his death to be attributed to natural causes. Suicide would be an admission of guilt."

"What did you expect him to do?"

"Use drugs with short half lives in the body. Ones difficult to trace."

"What else did you learn or suspect after talking to the estate lawyer, being in Raines's house, and collecting the book?"

"Nothing."

Silence as Elsa drummed her finger on the table.

"Grateful after I saw the will and sad. My wife and everyone around the medical school considered Abel a snake, but he was my best friend. He deserved a few kind comments during the trial."

"It was perjury." When he didn't respond, she stood. "Do you have the keys?"

"No, I gave them back to the lawyer." For the first time in the whole discussion, Dean Wilson looked at Elsa. "If you don't believe me, ask him."

CHAPTER 21: Sanders in Washington

"I see you had to prove you were self-sufficient."

Sara ignored Sanders's comment as she parked both her rolling suitcase and Bug's case in front of the small teak table in his new office on Thursday. When she unzipped his case, Bug jumped out, shook himself, and with his tail gracefully swaying walked over to Sanders.

Sanders coughed, fumbled in his pocket, and offered a treat to Bug. "At least the dog is friendly."

Sara ignored the comment as she sorted through items in her tote and pulled out a pad of paper. "I certainly don't feel self-sufficient. I'm basically homeless. I've spent the last two days watching workman measure my windows and getting estimates." Her voice trailed higher. "You can't believe the damage. You know the car was totaled. They ruined the engine block. Then there were final straws. Gil Andrews never said he didn't trust Chuy's judgement but he stopped by my house every couple hours during the last two days. Finally, he said he'd get more work done if I left the area. And Linda told me she'd feel safer if I wasn't staying with her."

Sara sniffed as she sat in a chair at the table and motioned to Bug to come. "They're all convinced Mazzone has a hit out on me, but I don't think so. He's a mean son-of-a-bitch, but he's practical. My death doesn't help his case." Her pace was speeding up and her pitch was going higher. "Now Diego Rivera, the pretty boy Linda mentored as an assistant professor in the medical school, is a different case. He wants to build a reputation as tough guy. And I never trusted the pompous med school dean. God knows what he would do to protect his career."

He neatened his desk, checked emails, and brought his computer tablet over to the table during Sara's tirade. All the time he reminded himself not to make humorous, but appropriate, comments because they might prolong the tirade. This self-assured woman has a vulnerable side besides her dog. Finally, he said, "Have you blown off enough steam? Are you ready to settle down to work?"

J. L. Greger

He glanced over at his new prized possessions — a vintage Barcelona chair and matching ottoman covered in soft tan leather. He'd bought it in a Georgetown antique store last weekend. He cursed silently. The dog was plunked in the middle of the chair. When he moved to shoo the dog from the chair, Bug rolled his big brown eyes in Sanders's direction and seemed to dare him. Sanders knew he'd never calm Sara if he moved the dog. "Bug is ready to work. Are you?"

Sara stopped spluttering about the mess at her house and glanced at Bug on the chair. "New?" She hurried to the chair and let her hand glide over its supple leather. "I've always admired Mies van der Rohe's Barcelona chair. So sophisticated. Warmer, more inviting in tan than in black." She petted Bug. "Doesn't Bug make the chair look even more elegant?"

He cleared his throat, pleased but not surprised that she'd noticed his purchase. "Yes, to both questions." He paused. "Now to work. I've talked to my bosses. We agree. It's time for several of us to go to Cuba to lay the groundwork for a major goodwill exchange. I'd already booked a flight to Havana when…" He didn't want to set off another round of complaints by mentioning her house. "When your new problems arose. I want you to come along as an extra set of eyes and ears and to be a liaison with scientists. My trip will be low key. So, the press doesn't get wind of it."

Linda pulled a can of diet cola from her tote, popped the tab, and seemed to savor the fizz. "What do I have to do to prep?"

Sanders handed her a list. "I also made an appointment at a good kennel for Bug. My boss, the Assistant Secretary, boards her dog there when she travels. We'll leave Sunday."

As Sara studied the list, Sanders's desk phone rang. After greeting the caller, Sanders turned his back to Sara and mainly listened. Finally, he said, "I agree you need a bit of my expertise. If you plant the right data strategically, you can usually flush out hidden operatives. Give me time to talk to Sara." In a louder voice he said, "She'd never admit it, but she's adept at covert activities. Must be a skill she learned to survive in academia." He chuckled as he hung up the phone and turned to Sara.

She smiled. "Well, did I reach the right people? What do you think?"

CHAPTER 22: Sergeant Elsa Grasso on Day 11

Chuy's alarm squawked and continued its harangue until Elsa walked around his king size bed and shut it off. Chuy grabbed her wrist with one hand and raised the covers with his other arm. She allowed herself to be drawn back into the warmth. He rolled her toward him and began to nuzzle her neck behind the ears. Then he moved his lips down her neck.

"Mmm, this is nice, but you're usually eager to get to work in the morning."

Chuy progressed down from her neck to her breasts. She felt her urge to get to work on time ebb, but made one last effort. "What don't I know?"

The kissing and fondling stopped as Chuy raised himself again on one elbow. "I've been lying here for the last hour thinking while you.... you snored."

"I don't snore," she said, although she suspected he was right.

"It's a pretty snore — kinda soft and comforting." He leaned forward and gave her a quick kiss on the nose, then returned to leaning on one elbow with his hand supporting his head. "I've developed a theory about this case."

"Oh."

He sighed. "If we wait long enough, this case will solve itself. The last one left alive is the evil mastermind."

Elsa studied Chuy. He was serious. "You aren't your usual optimistic self."

"We're not making much progress on this case because we aren't recognizing leads until it's too late. Of the six shooters, only two are left alive — Falto and Jorge."

"They disprove your theory." She leaned toward him and stoked his chest. "They aren't the mastermind."

Chuy squirmed. "I'm serious. I'm afraid they'll be killed too. I've kept them under guard in the hospital, but the hospital wants to release Falto today and Jorge in probably two days. Do you think your bosses would let us send them to separate jails, not in Albuquerque, and book them under aliases?"

"I'll talk to my boss. He thinks there are leaks of info from APD, besides Lehar."

"Good." He closed his eyes. "There has to be a way to get Jorge to talk, but how? He killed his own parents to protect his secrets and those of the mastermind." He closed his eyes. "Well, for other reasons too. Jorge has a lot of pent up anger and an obsession with fire. The guard at the hospital was frightened by Jorge's yammerings and recorded them. Weird stuff. "

Elsa ran her finger in circles around his right nipple. Chuy groaned, and Elsa knew it wasn't from pleasure. "Stop groaning. We've made progress. We now think Raines hired someone to orchestrate his death. All we have to do is identify who Raines hired."

Chuy grabbed her hands and held them firmly. "We're nowhere. The most likely candidates on day one were and still are Mazzone, Diego, and Dean Wilson."

"The shootings seem too violent for Dean Wilson."

"Agreed." Chuy sat up and stared at the wall. "If we don't get a big break soon, other witnesses may be killed."

"Don't be so pessimistic."

"Both Lehars were killed on my watch. Sara would have died if not for Gil. I've never felt so lost."

Elsa twisted around in the bed and pulled her red negligee up to her hips so she could sit cross-legged facing him. She leaned forward and grabbed his shoulders to prevent him from looking away. "Granted you had a bad day." Paused, "Several bad days. We both are trying to do too much alone. I should have been with you. That's why APD prefers officers work in teams." She traced her fingers over his lips.

Chuy was obviously not in the mood to be seduced. He pulled her hand away from his lips. "I feel inadequate. Rachel and Zelda keep yelling at me. Yesterday, my boss on the New Mexico Gangs Task Force said that I'd made a rookie mistake in trying to do everything, and accordingly had failed at everything. He's re-evaluating my position on the Task Force."

Elsa ignored Chuy's last comment. "Do you realize how little Rachel has done to help us? I knew she'd fail with Mazzone, but she should have broken Diego. Now it's too late because he is holding his own with other prisoners."

"Blaming Rachel doesn't help."

Elsa brushed her lips against his cheek. "I've thought of a lead we haven't explored."

***

The Allegro Apartments at Tanoan were the home of many young professionals without children. As she and Chuy walked past the large, turquoise swimming pool, she thought it looked sad as most outdoor pools do in the late fall. The area was clean of leaves and debris but was deadly quiet. Actually, the whole complex seemed deserted. She assumed over ninety percent of the residents were at daytime jobs.

They climbed the stairs to the second floor of the taupe stucco structure and rang the doorbell. They weren't surprised when no one answered.

Elsa had requested APD officers find George Kummer last Friday after she'd seen Raines's will. She'd never seen their report. Only this morning, she realized the problem. She immediately called the manager of the apartment complex. He reported that neighbors had complained about excessive noise in Kummer's apartment over the weekend. He claimed he planned to reprimand Kummer the next time he saw him, but he hadn't seen him or his car in several days. She immediately requested a search warrant for Kummer's apartment.

Chuy used the manager's key to open the door. The apartment stunk, and dried blood stained the beige carpet. Both drew their guns as they scanned the chaos. All the drawers and doors in the kitchen were open, even the stainless steel doors of the refrigerator, oven, and dishwasher. Foam stuffing protruded from slashes in the brown leather recliner and sofa. Someone had slammed his fist or a heavy object through the living room wall. Elsa doubted scrawny George Kummer could make such a large hole.

They wasted no time examining details but followed the blood trail straight from the front door and down the hallway to first bath and bedroom on the right. Both were empty except for a few bloodstained white towels.

Next, they followed the blood trail into the second bedroom. The mattress was upended and leaned against the window, blocking the view of the pool below. The trail of blood led to a closet. Elsa stood back with gun pointed as Chuy threw open the closet door.

A smashed, empty home safe lay on the floor. A bloody hammer and screwdriver lay to the side. Only a couple of shirts hung on hangers in the closet. Either Kummer owned few clothes or he'd taken them with him. She'd seen no suitcases in the apartment.

J. L. Greger

The maple storage cabinet in the second bath was ripped from the wall. The contents of the cabinet, bottles of lotions and vials of pills, rolled on the tiled floor.

Elsa called the crime lab and put on plastic gloves before she touched objects in the trashed apartment. She figured, judging by the sour milk, the mold growth on the pizza, and general stench, no one had been in the apartment for several days. The rest of the apartment was so empty that it made a hotel room look homey.

As he left to canvas any neighbors who were home, Chuy muttered, "Another botched lead."

CHAPTER 23: Sergeant Chuy Bargas

"Didn't see this coming. Assumed George Kummer was either dead or injured." Chuy reread the email from the Albuquerque Crime Lab. The results were only preliminary, but the bloody fingerprints on the safe in George Kummer's apartment were those of Jorge and of the dead shooter from Sara's house. The blood throughout the apartment was type B positive — the same as the dead shooter. Jorge and George Kummer were type O positive. The lab crew estimated the pizza had been purchased a week ago, but weren't sure because they didn't know how many days the refrigerator door had been open. They promised more data on Monday.

Chuy decided a good way to end this miserable week was to recheck details of the Raines murder case in online police records. He found what Elsa had missed initially. APD officers, as Elsa's requested, had questioned Kummer at his apartment last Friday. Their report was brief.

> Subject not at home when officers stopped by at one p.m. Returned at seven p.m. Subject claimed he was employed full time at a private clinic during the day but can't account for his activities at night. Squirrelly, but nothing odd seen in apartment.

Officers had filed a follow-up note early Monday morning. Kummer had worked at the clinic from nine to five every day of the previous week. Elsa updated the record after she called the clinic today. She noted that Kummer had called in sick on Monday and hadn't showed up for work on Tuesday, Wednesday, or Thursday. She had also filed a missing person report for Kummer.

He drummed his desk with his fingers and planned how to avoid telling Rachel about Kummer's disappearance. She'd ream him a new aperture for not following up sooner on Kummer. He was relieved when Elsa walked in because it gave him a chance to postpone the inevitable, until he saw her face. She looked ghastly.

"Let's get out of here. Now." Elsa literally grabbed his arm and pulled him to the door. "I'll drive."

Before they entered the car, she pulled a device for detecting audio bugs from a large tote and swept the car with the device. "Seems my bosses kept you under surveillance since the shootout at Sara's house." She started the car. "So, they know all about us, but we have bigger problems."

Chuy felt sick to his stomach and could hardly look at her. He may have ruined both their careers in the last week. "I'm sorry."

"They're so worried about the apparent leaks of info on this case, they never mentioned the breech of protocol." She nodded toward the devise in her tote. "We're to sweep our office, homes, and cars before we enter."

"Did they tell my boss in the New Mexico Gangs Task Force?" Chuy pulled his hand through his thick black hair.

"No, they don't want anyone outside of the department to know their suspicions. Seems they have several officers, beside you, under surveillance. Two appear to have received large cash payments recently. They wouldn't tell me the details." She cast a quick glance at him as she drove the car from the parking lot onto the street. "No one is to know about what we're doing next. Well, with a couple of exceptions. Seems Sara and Linda concluded someone leaked info on this case, either inadvertently or intentionally, to the wrong people. They worked out a plan — a set of traps. I suspect Sanders helped them, but my boss never mentioned him. My boss only said that Sara met with him and your old boss Gil Andrews before she left for Washington yesterday."

Chuy felt his skin crawling. "Why did Sara call your boss and Gil, not us? Doesn't she trust us?"

"I don't know," she looked over at Chuy who was scratching his forehead. "I'm worried too, but now we have to set the scene for the first trap."

"Will we stop by the hospital to talk to Linda?"

Elsa looked away from the traffic on Fourth Street and gave him an impatient frown. "No, we have to acquire several props and backup at the substation on Lomas first. We've got to do everything exactly as my boss ordered. They may have set traps for us, too."

Chuy felt the vise of a headache tightening around his head. "I'm confused."

She drove with one hand and pulled a card from her purse. "Read this."

Chuy looked in disbelief at a card with Elsa's scribbles. Her handwriting was awful. He squinted at the phrases on the card "This is crazy. Why would Gil agree to hold Jorge and Falto in the Mercado jail near La Bendita?"

Elsa looked at him as if he was child, kindly but with impatience. "To save your bacon. Gil considers you his protégé, and you need help."

Chuy knew he should be thankful, but he felt nauseous. Then too, Elsa was driving faster than usual as she wove around the stop-and-go traffic on Lomas Boulevard. He looked in the glove compartment for a bag in case he regurgitated.

When she pulled the car into the parking lot by the Lomas Substation, fuzzy details in her cryptic notes became clearer. As soon as she stopped, two Hispanic men with buzz haircuts jumped into the back seat. One resembled a teenage boy with small shoulders and short stature. The other was barrel-chested and about five-ten. Chuy recognized the second man as an experienced undercover cop. Both carried stuffed duffel bags.

Elsa moved the car before the men slammed the doors shut. She instructed the undercover cops on the details of the sting as she whizzed down Lomas Boulevard toward the University Hospital followed by a marked APD car and an unmarked van. The van and the marked police car turned into the ambulance entrance while Elsa parked her car in the nearby alley.

Chuy, Elsa, and two uniformed police officers sprinted into the hospital. When they arrived at Falto's and Jorge's rooms, she ordered the surprised officers guarding Falto and Jorge to get them into orange prison coveralls immediately. Chuy had apprised the guards and the administrator in the hospital unit at noon that the transfers of prisoners would occur tomorrow. The sudden rush to complete the discharge papers for the prisoners made the staff surly. Elsa responded in kind. He'd never seen her wound so tight and wasn't sure he liked what he saw.

Within thirty minutes, they led the manacled and handcuffed prisoners out of the ward, down a back set of stairs, and into a long, windowed hallway. Most patients and visitors gave wide berth to prisoners in orange coveralls, but one man with long hair and a vacant look followed them closely. Chuy saw Elsa stiffen and grip her gun ready to pull it from the holster. He tapped the man on the shoulder and

J. L. Greger

asked him a question. Elsa sped the group forward toward the ambulance entrance.

The prisoners were loaded quickly into the back of the van. Now the passengers from Elsa's car were in the marked police car, and two different men with buzz haircuts were in Elsa's back seat. One was short and slight, and one was burly and tall.

The vehicles circled onto Lomas Boulevard and headed toward I-25 and the Mercado police station at normal speeds. Elsa held her shoulders more stiffly than usual, but her sentences were less clipped as she gave directions to her riders. Several miles before the turn off to Mercado, the driver of the van radioed, "The prisoners are ready."

The undercover cop who was now in the marked police car said, "So are we."

Chuy called Gil Andrews to warn him of their imminent arrival at the Mercado Police Station.

The transfer van pulled into a wide spot between two parked SUVs at the station. Chuy observed that Gil, as usual, had set the scene perfectly. The SUVs, one of which belonged to Gil and the other to a deputy, were not nosed against the station but parked about four feet away from it. When the van pulled up next to the building and its back doors opened, the prisoners could alight without being seen from the street. The marked police car backed up behind the van. Elsa parked her car so as decrease visibility of the marked cruiser from the street.

Chuy and a uniformed guard from the van marched two men in orange coveralls and manacles into cells in the Mercado jail. They were booked as Agustin Falto and Jorge Lehar. In reality, they were the two undercover cops who initially had been in Elsa's back seat. When Chuy returned to Elsa in the car, the second set of men in the back seat was gone.

The convoy of Elsa's car, the transfer van, and the marked APD car raced back to the APD station on Menaul Boulevard. The vehicles again parked strategically so minimize what spectators saw. Chuy and a uniformed guard from the van led two men, one small and one barrel-chested, into the station. The men dressed casually in jeans and T-shirts were booked as the burglars Pedro Hoya and Daniel Hoya. One uniformed officer stayed at the station. Chuy jumped back into Elsa's car.

The convoy's next stop was at the APD station on Roma Avenue. Chuy and the uniformed guard from the van booked Pedro Carlos, a barrel-chested, manacled man in a T-shirt and jeans, for selling major quantities of drugs and Daniel Castro, a petite man in a T-shirt and jeans, as his accomplice.

When Chuy left the station alone, the transfer van sped away. Elsa seemed more relaxed as she drove at a reasonable speed. "Now we visit Linda and Winston."

***

Winston rummaged through the clutter of his workroom to find chairs for all his visitors. He listened carefully while Elsa warned him he would be handling confidential information in a sting operation. She didn't add that no one wanted to involve him in the case but her bosses trusted no one internally in APD.

He bobbed his head at both Chuy and Elsa and in his fake pigeon English said, "No talk. I trace suspects' responses to your messages." His smile disappeared. "Remember I won't know if someone besides your suspects sees these emails?"

Elsa frowned. "I know. Phone messages would be better."

Chuy shrugged. "But I don't lie well enough to pull off the bluffs on the phone." He sent the first email to Zelda.

> Agustin Falto and Jorge Lehar were transferred today to the APD station on Menaul Boulevard under the aliases of brothers Daniel and Pedro Hoya. Do not share this information with anyone, not even Rachel Jones or anyone else from the FBI.

He turned to Elsa as he pushed the send button. "I think the warning is superfluous. Zelda doesn't share much with Rachel willingly."

Elsa gave her first laugh of the day. "It will please her."

Chuy emailed the second false message to Rachel.

> Agustin Falto and Jorge Lehar were transferred to the Mercado jail in Sandoval County today because APD wanted them outside of assistant DA Zelda Zane's jurisdiction in Bernalillo County. They think at least one person in Zelda's office is leaking secrets on the investigation.

Elsa hoped her email message to Dean Wilson would loosen his tongue.

Agustin Falto and Jorge Lehar are out of the hospital. I hope you and your wife will feel more secure. Call me if you remember any details about Dr. Raines or the days before the trial.

Then she handed cards with a new phone number and a new email address, outside the APD and the New Mexico Gangs Task Force computer systems, to Winston and to Linda. "Use these to contact us."

Chuy stood and gazed at the ceiling to conceal the tears welling in his eyes. He gulped. "I want to thank all of you for having faith in me. I... I don't know how I missed the clues so long. I guess I trusted the wrong people."

Linda patted his shoulder. "Sara, Gil, and I figured you were too polite, maybe awe-struck, around authority figures. Then Sara and I, with a little coaching from Sanders, decided we needed to become as sly as our mastermind. That meant planting a few false clues. The problem is I don't think we can maintain these subterfuges for long."

Chuy felt ashamed to ask for another favor. "I need your help in one more way. Let's go to your office."

CHAPTER 24: Sergeant Elsa Grasso on Day 12

Elsa snuggled her pillow tighter, not asleep but not awake either. In some ways this warm, relaxed coziness before the sun rose was her favorite part of the day. The sound of trumpet horns ended her reverie. She looked over at Chuy's alarm clock. Five-thirty on a Saturday morning. Too early, and it didn't blare that way. Suddenly she remembered her new phone with the distinctive ring. Only her boss, Gil Andrews, Linda, Winston Chu, Sara, and probably Sanders knew the number. "OMG".

She fumbled with the light switch and grabbed the phone from the night table, scattering pens and a book. "Hello."

Chuy, a morning person, took one look at her holding the new phone and began to get dressed.

"Sorry to wake you," said Linda, "I thought about Chuy's questions after you left yesterday. I think I know where Kummer would go."

"Where?"

"Diego Rivera's condo."

Elsa thought she must be so groggy she wasn't hearing properly. "Doesn't make sense. He sabotaged Diego's research and agreed to testify against him." To signal Chuy, she said, "Linda, why do you think George Kummer would be at Diego's apartment?"

Chuy snorted as he tied his shoes. "Crazy bastard."

"In a way, Kummer idolized Diego and wanted all Diego's possessions. Remember how he stole the keys to Diego's lab and enjoyed sitting in Diego's office. I bet he acquired the keys to Diego's condo too. You'd better hurry. Kummer might have spent the last few nights in Diego's condo, but he's not apt to stick around during daylight hours.

"Thanks."

Linda giggled. "Apologize to Chuy for the wake-up call."

***

Chuy drove while Elsa called APD's property and evidence office. They picked up the keys to Diego's condo, which they had confiscated two weeks before when they arrested Diego for plotting to kill Sara and Shantelle Eaton. They pulled up in front of a series of stucco-covered row houses a little before seven. These condos were billed as two-story homes, but they could be better described as two-bedroom apartments perched on top of a garage and an entrance.

Chuy opened the door to the condo. The entrance looked the same as the last time Elsa had been there, except the yellow crime tape was rolled in a ball at the foot of the steps. While Chuy checked the garage, Elsa climbed the stairs to the apartment.

She rubbed her eyes in surprise. She had admired Diego's neatness and enjoyed his flamboyant decorating style with black and ivory striped drapes, coffee-toned wood furniture, and turquoise upholstered pieces. Now empty pizza boxes, beer and soda cans, and crumpled paper covered the carpeted floor and all surfaces in the great room. A laptop computer sat among debris on the dining table, and a mattress was upended in front of the sliding doors to the balcony.

Someone had been here since she had searched the condo after Diego's arrest. She pulled her gun and announced her presence. Chuy, with his gun out, led the way to the first bedroom. Dozens of men's shirts and slacks were slung across a black futon. Men's underwear hung from an open suitcase perched on a desk. The closet appeared to be full of Diego's stuff or the visitor also wore mainly black. She had never seen Kummer in black. They progressed to the second bedroom. The rumpled black sheets suggested someone had slept in the bed, but no one was present now.

While Chuy checked the laptop, she called the manager of the condo. The manager was annoyed she'd roused him from bed on a Saturday morning and at first made incoherent comments. Finally, she asked the right questions. The manager wasn't concerned about the condo or Diego's belongings because the condo association had received a money order payment for the next three month's fees already. Elsa thought this was strange because she had been unable to identify any living relatives for Diego two weeks ago, except for one cousin in L.A.

In the background, Chuy stopped cursing and said with satisfaction, "I'm in." He hummed a bit. "No doubt this is Kummer's."

***

The trumpets blasted again as Elsa sat down at the dining room table across from Chuy. She tensed, dug into her jacket pocket, and answered her special phone.

"Sorry to bother you, but I'm off to Cuba tomorrow." In her usual manner, Sara cut to the chase without pleasantries. "Did our traps work?"

"Not yet. Are you sure this call can't be monitored?"

"Yeah, I'm on the safe phone in Sanders's office. I'm, actually we're both, here doing last minute prep for our trip. Tell me what you learned."

"Rachel emailed Chuy that he was a fool ten minutes after he sent her our email." Chuy looked up from the laptop that he'd found in the condo and made a face by crossing his eyes and sticking out his tongue. "Zelda emailed that she was pleased about the transfer of Jorge and Falto to the Menaul Station and asked us to inform her immediately if either Falto or Jorge Lehar even hinted of wanting to cut a deal." Elsa poked at her tablet. "One interesting item. A woman showed up at the Menaul Station and asked to see Pedro Hoya. Our police decoy refused to see her because she'd recognize our scam if she knew Jorge."

"Oh dear."

"But we have good photos of her and fingerprints. Unfortunately, she doesn't have a police or military record, and she slipped the tail in five blocks."

"So, you progressed to the second phase of our scam."

"Yes, while we wait...." Elsa stopped. There was no reason to mention that she and Chuy were waiting for lab techs to arrive at Diego's condo. It didn't seem right to have her and Chuy's strings being pulled by civilians. However, her boss had instructed her to tell Sara, she suspected really Sanders, all the details. "We've started phase two. Chuy just informed Zelda by email that another prisoner attacked Falto, and suddenly Falto remembered details and wanted to make a deal."

"And?"

"Chuy called Rachel and told her Jorge had hinted to Gil Andrews that he might have useful info. He was convincing if you didn't see his face." Chuy again made a funny face. This time wiggling his tongue as he crossed his eyes.

"What did Rachel say?"

"To ignore it. Jorge was bluffing."

"Damn. Linda and I want to return to our normal life, and we can't until this case is solved. I guess the bright spot is that someone in

J. L. Greger

Zelda's office took the bait. Can you push Rachel and Zelda a bit more with our third set of emails and calls this afternoon?"

"My boss already gave the order. Enjoy Cuba."

Elsa was checking the pockets of the clothes slung around the second bedroom when her regular phone buzzed. She listened for about a minute. "I'll send him immediately, but I can't come until someone relieves me at Diego's condo."

Chuy stepped into the room. "What's up?"

"Ever heard of life imitating fiction?"

CHAPTER 25: Ben, an undercover APD officer

Ben thought he was lucky when he was one of two police officers assigned to masquerade as Falto. His was the easiest assignment. All he had to do was observe the real Jorge, imprisoned at the Roma Station, as Chuy and Elsa waited for a response to their traps at the Mercado Police Station and the Menaul APD Station.

He changed his mind when he got into the van with Jorge Lehar on the way from the Menaul Station to the Roma Station. Jorge muttered to himself and occasionally bellowed curses. Ben deciphered enough phrases spoken in L.A. ghetto Spanglish to realize Jorge had guessed much of Elsa's ruse. However, Jorge's soliloquy was difficult to fully understand because logical comments were interspersed with chants about fire. Ben sat quietly and thought of his options as the van sped to the Roma Station. Once he entered, he would be just another prisoner. No one at the Roma Station would know his true identity.

The van stopped. Ben began to scratch his forehead, a prearranged sign of problems, as soon as Chuy appeared. Chuy missed the signal as he roughly pulled a handcuffed Jorge from the van and let the other guard lead Ben into the station.

Ben became more nervous as the processing progressed. Chuy seemed distracted. Finally, he managed to trip and fall toward Chuy. "Chuy, got to talk to you," he whispered as Chuy helped him to his feet.

Chuy seemed to come out of his fog. His eyes focused. "Prisoner needs to go to bathroom. I'll take him." The other officers growled no, but Chuy persisted.

A bit of luck. The bathroom was empty. Ben pushed past the urinal to a toilet. "Jorge is crazy — will kill anyone who gets near him. Has repeated over and over — "she'll kill me if I don't succeed.' Note he always says she not he."

"Good, get him to talk more."

Ben felt his gut convulsing. Chuy response wasn't appropriate. "Jorge has figured out the plan. Soon anyone within range of his screams will know."

Chuy looked like a caged animal as he paced about the bathroom.

"Man, you can't put him in a general holding cell."

"You have cold feet."

"Don't care what you say. I won't go in a cell with him."

Chuy's eyes lost their soft look as his pupils narrowed. "Let me think."

Ben voided the contents of his lower gut.

***

After a meal, if you could call it that, Jorge initiated a normal conversation with Ben about the slop and the plastic spoon with the noodle-like handle. Ben relaxed and approached the bars between the cells to hear well. He agreed with Jorge. Whoever had designed the plastic spoon never ate with it.

Suddenly Jorge's fingers tightened around Ben's ear and yanked hard. Ben yelped and pulled away despite excruciating pain. No guards appeared, probably because Jorge was whooping hysterically like a child playing cowboys and Indians.

***

Ben woke weary the next morning. He hadn't slept well because of the hard bed, an inflamed ear, fear, and Jorge's continual chatter, really raving in his sleep. Chuy told him at the start of the operation Jorge occasionally talked in his sleep while in the hospital. What an understatement.

Ben lay on the cot and looked at the gray ceiling as a streak of sunlight began to spill into his cell from a high narrow window. He knew the hospital guards had recorded Jorge on several nights, but few of Jorge's comments were intelligible, besides "fire, burn Mother, and she'll burn me." He might have heard a bit more last night after he asked repeatedly, "Who is she?" to Jorge. Maybe he was imagining voices in his eagerness to get out of this hellhole. He decided to ask a guard to let him see Chuy, even if it blew his cover.

***

Ben lagged behind when the guards brought him and Jorge into the yard for exercise. Time outside their cells was supposed to be a reward to prisoners. Anyone, who thought this was a reward, hadn't been around Jorge. Ben moved around the space toward a guard, careful to keep his back to the wall. He was an arm's length from a guard when Jorge let out a shriek and ran toward him. He raised his knee to kick Jorge in the groin, but somehow Jorge got his hands around his neck.

He kicked his leg forward and heard a groan, but Jorge continued to tighten his grip.

***

Ben regained consciousness with an oxygen mask over his face. He'd been injured before, but this was worse. His neck felt sore but his gut was worse. A nurse adjusted a line into his arm. "We got you in time."

"Mmm. Chuy...."

The nurse wiped his forehead with a wet cloth. "Don't talk now, until we're sure you're stabilized. The big guy put up a real fight."

Chuy shoved himself into view. "Jorge is in worse shape. The guards were a little eager to stop his attack on you."

Judging by the way he felt, Ben doubted the guards were over eager. His one eye was swollen shut and his gut ached.

"Chuy leaned close. "Did you learn anything?"

Ben nodded.

The nurse pulled Chuy back and readied a needle to insert into his line. "We'll give something to help you sleep."

"W... Wait. She controlled him by threatening to turn him in for killing his mother in a fire."

Chuy leaned close, and Ben gasped a couple of more words.

The nurse injected fluid into the line, and he drifted away from the pain.

J. L. Greger

CHAPTER 26: Sara flying to Cuba on Day 13

Sara was surprised when Sanders used a regular passport and entered the baggage check-in line for the American Airlines flight from Miami to Havana. She wondered whether he hadn't used his diplomatic passport to skip the waiting line because he knew he'd have to wait for her anyway. She doubted that explanation and began her game of trying to spot what he was up to.

Most of the crowd waiting to check bags in Miami appeared to be typical American tourists, best described as Q-tips with white at both ends — white walking shoes and white or gray hair. They were dressed comfortably in loose slacks and shirts, but unlike most tourists appeared to have moderate-sized rolling suitcases labeled with similar Chamber Explorations tags. She guessed the sponsoring group had given them strict baggage guidelines.

The other travelers in the line were more colorful. She counted thirteen carts, each with at least a thousand pounds of boxed goods precariously balanced on top. The boxes bore brand labels of computers, bathroom fixtures, air conditioners, fans, and microwave ovens. A casually dressed, Hispanic man stood by each of these carts. None appeared to have a suitcase, tote, or duffel with them.

She noted Sanders quickly lost his aloof exterior and talked to several of the men in Spanish. One man replied in English. He made the trip only twice a week. He pointed to several in the line whom he claimed made the round trip from Miami to Havana daily.

Sara assumed all the merchandise on the carts was destined for the black market in Cuba, at least not government-sanctioned stores. Although experts had been told her that the black market was alive and well in Cuba, she was surprised by this blatant movement of consumer goods from the U.S. to Cuba. Somehow, it didn't seem consistent with a trade embargo against Cuba.

Another eleven carts in the line were also piled high, although not quite as high as the first set. Suitcases were interspersed with boxes on these carts, and families were clustered around them. The men and older women in these groups were dressed casually, but the young women and girls were another story. The little girls sported brightly colored, often sparkly ribbons and bows in their curled hair and wore new or highly starched dresses with flounced skirts. Sara imagined these families planned to show off the girls to grandparents and other relatives and to deliver gifts.

Many of the young women in the family groups were dressed for Las Vegas or Times Square at night. Most wore either tiny miniskirts or skin-tight pants with high stiletto heels. Their tops left little to the imagination as they plunged dramatically either in front or back. Generally, their long nails were painted to match their ensemble. As Sara watched these young women sway on their heels, she realized the effect must be hypnotic on young men. She looked at Sanders. His lips were twitching as he stared at them. She decided the young women were hypnotic to men of any age.

Sara leaned closer to Sanders and whispered, "These women appear to be shopping for husbands, but why? Poor boys from Cuba can't buy them expensive clothes."

Sanders coughed. "They want to show their Cuban relatives that they are successful." He lowered his voice further. "I'd forgotten what I miss when I use my diplomatic passport and skip lines."

"I doubt that."

"Hmmf."

***

José Martí International Airport was a surprise. Green grass and trees were at one side of the box-like edifice, called Terminal Two, and a couple white buses and three other planes sat on the tarmac. Sara expected to see a baggage cart careen around a corner toward the plane immediately after their arrival, but none came for several minutes. When it appeared, it rolled at a leisurely pace. "I feel as if I'm stepping back in time to fly into a university town in the 1970s."

Sanders snorted. "Looks can be deceiving. This Terminal Two is mainly for chartered flights from the U.S. The other terminals are busier and older."

"I don't mind if we miss the typical old, third-world airport — hot, stinky, dirty, and with endless lines."

"This one won't meet your fantasy once you're inside. It's chaotic. You have to allow three-to four hours to clear customs and baggage check-in when you depart Cuba."

Sara nodded. She quickly realized she hadn't responded appropriately because he added, "You saw all the bathroom fixtures on the carts at the airport?"

She nodded.

"You'd think all the bathrooms in Cuba would be modern, but I'm told a half-full pail of water is kept by the toilet in many places. You have to pour the water into the toilet to flush it." He smiled. "Things often aren't what they seem in Cuba."

Sara didn't reply but thought that was true everywhere.

As they deplaned and walked up to the terminal, Sanders pointed to a group of five uniformed men with dogs. "A lot of security to greet a commercial flight."

"Mmm." Sara studied the moderate-sized dogs with flowing hair and plumed tails. The dogs were a matched set in size and body conformation, but they varied in color. Several were liver and white. Others were black and white. The guards controlled the dogs by verbal commands without holding onto leashes. Occasionally a dog would run to a grassy area for a bathroom break but would return immediately when called. She decided to ruffle Sanders' feathers. "Those are the most beautiful dogs that I've ever seen working security. Look like Springer Spaniels because they're too big to be Cockers I think."

Sanders released a slow sigh. "Not what I meant."

"I know," she whispered. "It's strange to see guards before we see baggage handlers. But I think those dogs were carefully selected. They give a gentler image than German Shepherds or typical "sniffer" dogs in the U.S., but they're smart with great tracking abilities. We're getting our first taste of sophisticated Cuban propaganda."

They walked into a noisy, hot terminal with no vacant seats and crowds milling around. Sanders whispered in her ear, "So much for sophisticated propaganda," and charged ahead.

CHAPTER 27: Sara in Havana

The smoked glass doors separated. Sara walked from the tropical sunlight into a cool, modern hotel fit for any tropical location worldwide. The floors were patterned with ivory and black marble. Palm trees, black stone columns, and black wicker chairs and sofas graced the open atrium with a bar at one end and a gift shop and business center at the other end. Black steel framed the smoke glass wall in front of her. This was Hotel Meliá in Havana.

Sara was pleased when Sanders had sent her into the hotel while he finished his business with the driver. The hotel was cooler and calmer than the car. The rather scruffy looking driver had either argued with Sanders in Spanish or told off-color jokes in English throughout the drive from the airport. Obviously, he'd been told she didn't speak Spanish. She briefly wondered what other functions he performed for the U.S. Interest Section in Cuba but decided she was letting her imagination take flight.

She checked in, pulled out a novel, and sank into a black wicker chair with thick orange pillows not far from the reception desk. She finished a chapter before she noticed Sanders was standing at the reception desk. While she hastily assembled her belongings, he strode toward the elevators and motioned for her to follow him. As they waited for the elevator, he asked her room number and said he would stop by shortly.

He exited on two; she on three. She wandered about the hallways until she deciphered the signage, which directed her from the main structure and onto a breezy, open hallway heading toward the Atlantic Ocean. When she opened her door, she was stunned by the magnificent view of the ocean.

Sanders appeared ten minutes later. "My secretary arranged for you to get a room with a view." He smiled but rushed on. "I'm going to the U.S. Interests Section. You can stay and rest."

"I'd like to see the facilities the U.S. uses because we don't have an embassy in Cuba. I can disappear in a corner with my novel. I'm ready to go." She turned and reached for her purse and a novel on the desk.

"You're booked for meetings with scientists and physicians at the Pedro Kourí National Institute of Tropical Medicine from eight to five tomorrow with your seminar at two. I expect you'll want to work on your talk now."

She hugged her purse and a novel. "I'm an old prof. Once my slides are on the memory tab, I'm good to go."

He frowned. "You're here as a scientist arranging an exchange, not as a political type using the exchange as a cover."

She frowned. "What aren't you telling me?"

"The Cubans constantly harass us at the U.S. Interest Section. In 2000, Castro put up those ugly metal arches on the plaza in front of our building with the fanciful statue of their martyred national hero José Martí holding the boy Elián, the focus of an unfortunate international custody battle in 2000. In 2006, they added more than a hundred flagpoles." He glowered but spoke more slowly. "I don't want you to be photographed going into our space." Obviously frustrated, he glared at the ceiling. "What do you do when you get to a scientific conference early?"

"Not stay in my room." She thought a bit. "Wander around the hotel and walk to some destination within twenty blocks or book a tour."

He shook his head. "Fine. Go explore but be back here," he looked at his watch, "at seven. I'll meet you for dinner in the open restaurant on the lowest level next to the waterfall."

He opened the door and started to leave but then turned toward her. "Don't walk over to the U.S. Interest Section or to Colon Cemetery."

"Studied a map. Thought I might stroll down Avenida Paseo to the Revolution Plaza and see the memorials to José Martí and Che Guevara. Figured it was a direct shot, so I wouldn't get lost." She grinned. "Even the most cynical Cuban police officer will figure I'm the typical tourist. Besides I'm want to compare Revolution Plaza to Tiananmen Square in Beijing and Red Square in Moscow."

"Seen those too?" He didn't wait for an answer. "You'll be disappointed. Less history." He walked away humming.

***

Revolution Plaza was as expected — a wide-open space of concrete surrounded by bland, box-like Soviet-style edifices with several tour buses parked to one side. The star-shaped tower, dedicated to the poet and Cuban martyr José Martí, seemed to be an imitation of the Washington Monument — only squatter, ribbed, and in gray marble. At its base, a bigger than life, marble version of Martí sat with royal palms to the side. Of more interest were the eight-story-high metal outlines of Che Guevara and another Cuban revolutionary on the sides of two structures. Sara was annoyed with herself because her knowledge of Cuban history was so skimpy that she couldn't recognize the second man. Accordingly, she traversed the wide expanse of the square, blazing in sunlight, to look for vendors of postcards and booklets on Cuba.

She was surprised by one aspect of the square. She'd never seen a tourist mecca so devoid of people and vendors. Even so, she finally found several less-than-perfect postcards, a black and white booklet on the history of Cuba, and a bottle of water but no Diet Coke. As someone who never carried a camera, she was disappointed by the cards.

She quickly retreated to the shade of palms at the edge of the plaza to enjoy her water, rest her feet, and study the booklet. She thought someone slavishly devoted to Castro wrote the hundred-page booklet, but she found the answer to her question. The second metal image was of a Camilo Cienfuegos. With a wide brim hat and full beard, he looked to be in his fifties, but according to a postcard he died before he was thirty. Che Guevara, the ultimate image of youthful revolutionary sexiness, was almost forty when he was killed in Bolivia.

As she studied the metal rendering of Che, she decided Castro had brilliantly solidified communism in Cuba through the use of the revolutionary saints depicted around the plaza without overtly aggrandizing himself. Smart.

Sara noticed the tree-lined streets were clogged with old American cars as she wandered back to the hotel. Although she recognized cars with big fins were probably made in the late 1950s, she wasn't enough into automotive history to appreciate vintage cars. However, she would have taken a photo of a small black Honda that she spied several times as she walked to and from the plaza, if she had a camera.

CHAPTER 28: Sergeant Chuy Bargas on Days 13 and 14

Chuy sneered. "The boss lady wants to see you. She's thought of a way to improve your memory. A night in a cell with Jorge." Chuy snickered as he led a quivering August Falto from his darkened cell to a mirrored interview room.

Falto bowed and whimpered as soon as he spotted Elsa seated at the table. "Ma'am, you can't put me in with Jorge. I spent part of one night with him in the hospital." He sobbed.

Elsa feigned indifference. Chuy thought she was playing her role perfectly as he pushed Falto into a chair across the table from her. She yawned and waved her hand dismissively. "You told us you knew nothing about Jorge Lehar. We don't believe you. "

"Yes, Ma'am." Falto hung his head and in a singsong manner said, "But I remember something about...." Falto swallowed repeatedly as if he couldn't say Jorge's name. Finally, he whispered, "Jorge."

"Then talk." She began to fiddle with her tablet.

Chuy poked him. "Look at the lady."

Falto lifted his head and gulped air like a swimmer when he surfaces after a dive. "Jorge talks at night. Says strange things."

"We taped his incoherent utterances. I hope you can do better."

Chuy noted Elsa duplicated Zelda's supercilious tones and Rachel's facial expressions and hand motions. The affectations must have worked. Falto stiffened with each word Elsa spoke. As they had hoped, Falto thought Elsa was the "she" Jorge screamed about. Chuy pulled Falto's head up so he gazed directly at Elsa. "Look at the lady."

"I asked him why he yelled about fire during his sleep." Falto's gulps turned into hiccups. "Said his mother died in a fire."

"Something we don't know," said Chuy.

Falto was hiccuping so violently he appeared to have trouble breathing. "Said he set the fire."

That confirmed what Ben thought he heard. "Something we don't know."

Elsa typed an email to her boss, who stood behind the mirror.

> Check for a sealed juvenile record on Jorge. Both Ben and Falto think he may have killed his birth mother in a fire.

Suddenly, she straightened and typed:

> Check whether anyone attempted to see this sealed juvenile record recently.

She stood and walked around the table to lean over Falto. "You'll have to do better. The fire occurred almost twenty years ago. If you can't, you'll get to listen again to Jorge."

When Falto grabbed for her hands, Chuy tightened his grip on Falto's arm. Falto whimpered. "He'll kill me. He'll kill me. Please..."

"Now." Chuy almost pulled Falto from the chair.

"Said a woman." Falto hiccuped loudly as he peeked a glance at Elsa. "Found him in L.A. and here. Threatened to burn him alive, all of us."

"Why?"

Falto leaned over the gray table and sobbed. "If we don't complete this job." After a minute of wailing, he looked up at Elsa. "Please don't hurt me, Ma'am. I tried to do what you ordered."

***

The next day, Chuy stared at a document on his computer screen. "Why do lab technicians have to write such boring reports? I read these two pages twice to figure out they confirmed their earlier guesses."

Elsa stopped him. "Give me the bottom line."

"Jorge and his partner broke into George Kummer's apartment the night before the shootout at Sara's house."

"Not helpful. We still don't know who assigned Jorge to act? Doubtful he was given the assignment before the ambush at the courthouse, and that means he didn't get these instructions from Raines. But that leaves Diego Rivera, assistant DA Zelda Zane, or FBI agent Rachel Jones as our puppet master. Of course, the latter two are more likely. And obviously, Falto has never seen either woman because yesterday he thought I was the woman who gave the orders to Jorge."

Chuy studied her as she returned to perusing her emails. She was beautiful with her long black hair. He especially loved the strands of

J. L. Greger

silver highlighting her temples, but he had learned the hard way that he shouldn't comment on her gray hair.

Elsa straightened in her chair. "Eureka, a break. Last week a paralegal in Zelda's office gained access to Jorge's sealed juvenile records in L.A."

Chuy was jolted out of his fantasy. "Uh, uh, so Zelda or someone in her crew might have been applying leverage on Jorge." As he returned to checking his emails, he muttered, "I always figured Zelda was too ambitious politically to do anything dumb. Wrong again."

"Wait... Please no... Damn. Damn."

Chuy swirled his chair around to face her. "What's wrong?"

"Sealed L.A. juvenile court records were hacked twice in the last two months. One of the records believed to be hacked was Jorge's."

He rose, pulled her from her chair, and twirled her around so he could wrap his arms around her and nuzzle her neck. He enjoyed the sensations, but she squirmed and pulled his hands from her arms.

"Don't, someone will see. We agreed no fun and games in the station."

Usually she enjoyed occasional hugs in the office, and he needed a little sympathy. This case kept going in circles. When the phone rang, he twirled her around and gave her a soft wet kiss on the lips before answering.

Cold sweat trickled down his back as he received more bad news. He sank onto his chair. "The psychologist we sent to talk to Jorge claims Jorge is only one step away from a complete mental collapse. No more questions for a couple of days."

He sat there exhausted. "Gives us an excuse to work only twelve hours a day, not thirteen hours, during the next two days. Probably won't matter. We're not making progress anyway."

Elsa stared at him for a moment. Instead of giving him sympathy, she rummaged through a file cabinet, opened and slammed shut drawers, and cursed. She finally pulled two folders. "I want to talk to my boss and run down a couple ideas I'm toying with."

Chuy looked at her sadly. "Don't lose confidence in me, partner. I might seem... I guess, I am a country boy, but I know how to wheedle answers out of almost anyone if given enough time."

Elsa slammed their office door shut.

CHAPTER 29: Sara at Pedro Kourí Institute of Tropical Medicine in Havana

Supper was uninspired — both the hotel food and the conversation. Sanders was silent, so Sara regaled him with the tale of her sightseeing, without mentioning the black car, while he continued to check messages on his tablet. She assumed he wasn't listening until she ordered her third can of Diet Coke. Then he remarked she must be desperate for her "caffeine fix" because she couldn't buy Diet Coke in the two small markets near the hotel.

On the way to the elevator after supper, he gave one sentence of advice about her visit to the Pedro Kourí Institute of Tropical Medicine the next day. "Don't be intent on getting answers, only at posing questions and listening."

She figured this was her last opportunity to ask questions. "Is Xave in Cuba now? Will I run into him posing as a public health official tomorrow?"

Sanders's face stiffened into the blankness of a corpse. She knew the expression signaled he would be evasive. Before he spoke, she said, "I don't want to be surprised and say the wrong thing. Should I recognize him or pretend I don't know him?"

"No, you shouldn't see him tomorrow." He lowered his voice. "You aren't apt to recognize him in his current persona," he sighed, "but if you do, try to show no recognition." He charged toward the elevator and stabbed the up button repeatedly.

***

Sara felt too nauseous to notice the scenery in Havana as the cab lurched through heavy traffic toward the Pedro Kourí Institute of Tropical Medicine. Nervousness about her seminar and dread of meeting with strangers all day were not the cause of the nausea. She was worried about the unstated purpose of her trip.

A number of the physicians and epidemiologists at the institute had published extensively on the AIDS epidemic in Cuba. They had demonstrated that homosexuals and prostitutes were major vectors of the HIV virus in Cuba. She suspected intravenous drug users were also major transmitters of the virus. Hence, she and Sanders hoped members of this institute knew the locations of pockets drug users with HIV and accordingly might be able to estimate the extent and locations of drug trafficking in Cuba.

As they planned their trip in Washington, Sanders was confident scientists would unintentionally tell her useful details about drug usage in Cuba without her actively "fishing" for it. His advice last night was consistent with his opinion, but she wasn't sure. She would be meeting with sophisticated men and women whom she feared would doubt the motives of anyone from the U.S., especially someone traveling with an experienced State Department official, such as Sanders. She gulped and exited the cab.

She walked into a room with fourteen scientists and physicians who were involved in HIV research or patient care at eight a.m. During the introductions, she realized eight members of the group had been David Rockefeller Scholars at Harvard. Accordingly, she knew those eight spoke English fluently, had spent at least several months in the U.S. at universities, and were cleared politically by the Cuban government for interactions with U.S. citizens.

The State Department, actually Sanders's office, had sent all those who agreed to meet with her a copy of her resume, copies of several of her research papers, including the one in *Science* on the Philippine flu, and a copy of the short report she'd recently prepared on the USAID committee's findings in Bolivia. Although she had studied data on the scientists and administrators she was scheduled to meet today, she was at a disadvantage. Several of those present were not on her list of invitees. She wasn't surprised. It was a typical consulting situation.

She always found she connected best with audiences when she focused on their needs not her own, but she didn't want to waste time. She started the session with a blunt question: "If you, as scientists, could have anything from the U.S., what would you pick? And don't be like American scientists and say more money. Be more specific."

The Cubans laughed but obviously had come prepared for such a question. One even noted the public health officials in Bolivia had warned them she would be frank and nosy. She felt the ambiance in the room was more like that of a job interview than of a consultation.

Sara had requested a chalkboard and chalk. The conference room was filled with state-of-the-art electronic gear and modern whiteboards with marking pens. She knew most conference rooms in Cuba were not so well equipped and figured they were showing her that they were sophisticated.

As soon as suggestions began, she grabbed a pen and wrote a summary comment on the board. At the end of one hour, she had covered all three sections of the board. During the second hour, Sara guided the group as they prioritized requests and suggestions. They also created a list of places — labs, hospitals, clinics, museums, botanical collections and gardens, aquariums, nature preserves — that she or other American scientists should visit if they wanted to understand the breadth and depth of science in Cuba.

She was both pleased and concerned when she heard whispered comments from members of the groups as they left the room: "not the typical arrogant U.S. professor" and "doubt she can deliver." What surprised her was that the comments were in English, not Spanish. The speakers wanted her to hear them.

Two of the group gave her a quick tour of the facilities as they guided her to her meeting with the members of the microbiology and parasitology sections of the institute. Researchers in these sections were interested in tuberculosis, histoplasmosis, and dengue hemorrhagic fever.

She had never studied the epidemiology of these diseases and initially assumed these investigators couldn't supply any information on illegal drug usage in Cuba. However, she had read a bit on the diseases anyway in preparation for her trip and learned her assumption might be wrong.

Thirty years ago, many physicians thought tuberculosis or TB was mainly of historic interest in the U.S. because of modern drugs. Now physicians worldwide considered TB to be a major health problem because of the emergence of drug-resistant *Mycobacterium tuberculosis* and large populations of immunosuppressed patients with HIV. The World Health Organization estimated TB was twice as prevalent in Cuba as in the U.S., but twenty-fold less prevalent than in Haiti. She suspected researchers interested in TB might also be able to speculate on the locations of heavy usage of illicit drugs in Cuba.

Histoplasmosis was a different story. Patients developed it when they breathed in the spores of a fungus found in soil and bird and bat droppings. She had assumed it was rare in the U.S. but found it was common but generally not serious among residents in the Ohio River valley. However, immunosuppressed individuals, such as HIV infected drug users, often developed serious symptoms in their lungs. Even so, she guessed the laboratory-based scientists investigating histoplasmosis at this lab were focused on the elusive goal of discovering effective fungicides and weren't interested in drug users.

A quick scan of the literature convinced her that dengue hemorrhagic fever was as nasty as its name suggested. About half of the patients infected with the virus died if the symptoms weren't treated aggressively. Although dengue certainly deserved study, she doubted the State Department would be interested in the scientists investigating it. Clinicians rarely saw dengue in the U.S., except among tourists.

Armed with this limited information, she was nervous about her ability to constructively lead the discussion in this group with such diverse interests. She started with the same questions as before. The conversation, which evolved, was fascinating and the list of needs generated was creative but focused.

***

As she prepped for the seminar on her research, she found a folded sheet of paper stuffed in the side pocket her purse.

> Meet me for drinks at six today at the El Floridita bar in
> Old Havana.

It was not signed, and she didn't remember seeing someone leave the message. It could be from a budding Casanova, someone looking for a job in the U.S., someone wanting to practice his or her English or....

CHAPTER 30: Sergeant Elsa Grasso

Elsa silently debated whether she was more annoyed with Chuy or herself. During the last two days she alternately suspected that Chuy was hiding something or that he was missing important points because he was too trusting. His trusting nature was an endearing trait in a man but not in a police officer. She, on the other hand, trusted no one completely. Sara's and Linda's plan to entice Zelda and/or Rachel into making a mistake was a reasonable one, but they underestimated how much prodding would be needed to frighten the divas.

She and her boss embellished the plan before she marched into Zelda's office without calling ahead. Zelda glowered at her until she realized Elsa was alone. "I'm glad you're alone. Do you trust your partner?"

Elsa was shaken but decided a cool response was best. "Actually, I'm here because I suspect there's a leak in your office."

Zelda stood and leaned over her desk toward Elsa. "What do you mean?"

Elsa pulled out her ever-ready tablet and a little black box from her tote and slowly took a seat. She hoped the delay would throw Zelda off-kilter and provoke candid responses. She turned on the black box and boldly set it on the desk. "A woman came to the Menaul APD Station and asked for Pedro Hoya. We think she was from your office," she paused, "or your acquaintance."

Red streaks rose up Zelda's neck as she continued to lean forward with both arms braced on her desk. "You can't be so naive to think a transfer of a prisoner from the hospital to a jail wouldn't be noticed."

"She asked for Pedro Hoya."

"So?"

Elsa enjoyed seeing the proud assistant DA lick her lips and totter a bit above her braced arms. Zelda had guessed the truth. "You were the only one given the alias."

Zelda gulped, stood erect, and walked around her desk to stand by Elsa. "Are you admitting you lied to me, a court officer? You and your partner are in big trouble."

Elsa looked at her and flashed a big smile. She hoped it infuriated Zelda. "We were under orders to find the leaks in the Raines case. Looks like we succeeded."

Zelda walked back around her desk and stared at Elsa. "Seems we both looked for leaks. I sent my maid to the Menaul APD Station to ask about Pedro Hoya. She's from the neighborhood and has relatives, actually two ex-husbands, in jail. So, she's familiar with police procedures but has never been arrested or fingerprinted."

"Convenient excuse but can you prove it?"

Zelda's nostrils flared. "Watch it, Sergeant." She reached in a desk drawer and pulled a file. "This is my maid's statement. We had it notarized immediately after she returned to my office."

Elsa studied the page. The timing was right. The maid complained the police treated her like an "aging Hispanic woman." They ignored her and sent her from line to line. When she was finally at the right desk, the officer became "solicitous" as he checked files for Pedro Hoya. He even "escorted" her to the door. She claimed she spotted a tail after she walked one block from the police station but lost him easily.

Elsa handed the sheet back to Zelda. "Did you or your maid write this statement?"

Zelda stiffened.

"Aging Hispanic woman, solicitous and escorted aren't words most maids would use."

Zelda tapped her fingers on her desk. "We have a problem of trust." Her lip quivered. "I'm curious why you brought a recorder and not your partner."

"He's busy. This is a courtesy call." Elsa was in the offensive position and planned to keep it. She glared at Zelda without flinching. "Now, let's get back to you. Why did you want your maid to speak to Pedro Hoya?"

Zelda responded so quickly that Elsa thought the answer was apt to be the truth. "I was checking the security of an important witness who is presumed to have killed his parents and orchestrated the deaths of others." She stopped tapping her fingers. "Surprisingly APD passed, but I never doubted you. Though your taste in men is questionable." She gave the toothless smile she always gave at the end of her summation in court.

Elsa decided to ignore the slur. "Who else saw Chuy's email to you?"

"No one. I erased it as soon as I read it."

"Why?"

Zelda hung her head. Her voice was uncharacteristically soft. "I thought there were leaks from my office or somewhere in the court system. Still do. It wouldn't be the first time. I heard troubling rumors about an APD investigation. Two court bailiffs resigned for no apparent reason after police talked to them. One of my aides cried for hours after you questioned her." Even more softly, "We're all nervous."

Elsa wondered whether Zelda was giving an Academy Award-winning performance or was sincere. She spoke directly at the device on the desk, "Captain, may I proceed with the next step now?"

A man's voice boomed from the device. "Good afternoon, Zelda. Yes, proceed."

The assistant DA seemed to crumple into her desk chair. "You let me think you were recording me, not doing a live feed." She straightened. "That's entrapment."

"I didn't hide the device. Now here's what I want you to do."

Elsa noted how Zelda narrowed her eyes, pinched her mouth, and clenched her fists as she listened. Those weren't signs of cooperation. Elsa pounded the number out on Zelda's desk phone and handed the receiver to Zelda.

"Hello. This is Zelda. I want to talk to Jorge Lehar. APD, as usual, isn't cooperating."

Zelda paused and listened. "Rachel, you know, the usual. Chuy is a country bumpkin, and Elsa resists suggestions until she clears them with the whole department." She glared at Elsa as she spoke. "No wonder their investigation is a leaky sieve. I want to talk to Jorge, and I know you can get me in to see him."

Zelda reached for a notepad and began to scribble notes. "Why so late?" Pause. "Oh, you have errands to do today and will have to drive from Denver tomorrow."

Her eyebrows rose higher and higher as she listened. Finally, she drew a large question mark and shoved the pad toward Elsa. She had written:

Seven p.m. Tuesday at the police station in Mercado.

Elsa watched Zelda uncharacteristically bite her lower lip. She hoped Zelda finally realized how much the APD mistrusted her and how carefully the trap was set. Of course, Zelda, knowing she'd been given false data, might guess Rachel also lacked all the facts. Elsa and her bosses had discussed their options before she set off on this fishing trip. They doubted Zelda would warn Rachel because she valued her career too much.

Zelda spoke with the cracked tremolo of an old woman, as she said, "I'll meet you there tomorrow."

Elsa felt her heart rate increase. Her bosses had bet wrong. Zelda was signaling Rachel to be cautious. She wrote on the pad. "Don't be foolish."

Zelda glanced at the note and cleared her throat. "Nothing is upsetting me." Her voice sounded normal, as she said, "My allergies act up sometimes. A lawyer who thinks he's charming sent me roses with Pampas grass as filler. I'm allergic to Pampas grass. Bye."

***

Elsa looked over her shoulder at her boss and then punched her speed dial. "Hey Rachel, we can't break Jorge. We want you to come back to Albuquerque and have a little heart-to-heart talk with him."

Rachel's voice bordered on a scream. "I'm not your babysitter. I'm busy here."

Elsa looked at her boss. He nodded. "My boss's boss talked with your supervisor in Albuquerque Ulysses Howe. He said you might as well catch up on some paperwork in your Albuquerque office and help us because you failed to break Diego or Mazzone."

"What?" Dead silence.

Elsa was thankful Rachel was quiet but knew Rachel hid extreme anger in silence. "Jorge keeps saying, actually screaming, a woman threatened him with fire." Elsa winked at her boss. "We're close to getting him to name the "she," and we thought you might want to be present."

Rachel answered immediately. "Don't question him anymore. I'll be in Albuquerque tomorrow." The phone went dead.

Her boss muttered, "And now we wait for the two rats to take our bait. We've got a lot to do before tomorrow night when they meet."

CHAPTER 31: The warden at the federal penitentiary in Florence, Colorado

The warden, usually an optimistic man, thought his prison was about to erupt. He couldn't put his finger on what made him nervous. Food fights had almost broken out twice in the cafeteria during the last week, but the cafeteria had served liver and onions one day and tuna fish casserole the next. Those were the two worst dishes on the menu. Sometimes he wished his high security prison didn't have a cafeteria and served food to inmates in their cells as they did in the supermax next door.

His personnel officer had informed him yesterday that a higher percentage than usual of the guards had called in sick during the last week, but this week was the last week of licensed deer and elk hunting in Colorado. Now, he had received a troubling call.

In one sense, he expected the call. Detainees awaiting trial in the penitentiary instead of in local jails spelled problems, probably because they received more visitors than most of the convicts on site and were new to the system. He had accepted Mazzone willingly because his extensive criminal networks made him difficult to contain anywhere but in the high security available at a penitentiary.

He had doubted Diego Rivera needed to take up space at Florence, but the FBI, specifically Rachel Jones, thought differently. Jailors in Albuquerque had carefully checked all items given to Raines while he awaited trial, and rejected almost all written materials, except crossword puzzles. Accordingly, Diego and Raines communicated through crossword puzzles. When Diego was arrested for plotting with Raines to kill several people, Rachel claimed APD was "incompetent," her word not his. He gave in to her screeches.

Rachel convinced him to assign Diego to laundry duty because she hoped threats by other prisoners would make Diego talk but it hadn't. After several days, Diego stopped sporting new bruises and cuts and began to hold his own in tussles.

The caller, an unidentified woman using a sophisticated voice changer, claimed Diego Rivera had homemade weapons. He doubted the tip but sent guards to search Diego's cell while Diego was on a work detail in the laundry. They found one homemade shiv made out of a metal spoon.

He fingered the shiv that a guard had delivered to him. He had a major security breech on his hands. Someone had manufactured the shiv from a type of spoon not used in the facility. He guessed a guard or a law officer gave Diego the spoon or the premade shiv because all others who entered the prison passed through a metal detector. He ordered guards to do body searches of Diego and the three other prisoners working in the laundry thirty minutes ago.

His phone rang. He listened to only the first few words before he sped out of his office. As he ran clutching his phone to his ear, the correctional lieutenant gave him details. After the guards completed body searches of the inmates in the laundry, they carelessly announced all were clean. Ten minutes later, the laundry manager found the three prisoners kicking Diego who was curled in a fetal position on the floor.

The warden surveyed the scene outside the laundry and decided the lieutenant had the rumpus under control. Someone had lined up the bloodied shoes and trousers of the prisoners in front of three, portable wire compartments. Two unsmiling guards with blood on their shirts completed paperwork and ignored the coughs and groans of the barelegged prisoners in the cages.

The warden stepped into the laundry. Blood was splattered over the fronts of two stainless steel washers. Blood and vomit were swirled in sudsy puddles of water on the floor. A doctor and two nurses were huddled over Diego who now lay on a gurney. A third nurse reported they were trying to stem the flow of blood from his wounds before they moved him. She added Diego had to be flown to a major trauma center for surgery because the doctor feared his spleen was ruptured.

The lieutenant and the laundry manager continued to exchange insults as the warden listened to the nurse. The lieutenant stopped yelling long enough to report all of the prisoners told the same story. "Diego fell on the slippery floor." The blood splatter on their shoes and trousers proved otherwise. The three prisoners would be isolated until Diego's fate was known.

***

Ulysses Howe called as the warden returned to his office. He sounded as authoritative as Rachel but less emotional as he instructed the warden to not allow any APD officers, FBI agents, or court officers, including assistant DA Zelda Zane, to have access to Diego or Mazzone. He groaned when the warden reported that Diego's spleen was ruptured in the melee. However, he changed his directive when the warden told him Diego would be flown to the trauma center in Albuquerque for surgery. "Update Chuy Bargas of the New Mexico Gangs Task Force. He will be my contact person."

Less than fifteen minutes later, Rachel called and announced she planned to meet with Diego and Mazzone. He told her "no." She demanded details, but he was adamant and didn't mention the incident in the laundry. Fifteen minutes later, Zelda called with a similar request. She, at least, was polite.

***

He met with the correctional lieutenant at four after he canvassed the more talkative prisoners. Everyone called Diego "a small, pretty wimp." A number of the bullies had enjoyed making Diego squeal until a couple of days ago when he turned up with a shiv. When the other prisoners in the laundry learned he was weaponless, they decided to play "kickball with Diego as the ball." No one knew how Diego got the shiv, but all the talkative prisoners thought Mazzone would know because "he knows more about the prison than anyone."

Reluctantly, the warden requested Mazzone be brought to his office. Mazzone was not physically imposing. He was about six foot and one hundred-sixty pounds with gray hair. But Mazzone walked with the easy gait of a confident man. His black eyes peered at the warden with amusement as he sat down in front of the warden's desk. "I understand you have a problem."

The warden steeled himself. Mazzone was smart. He couldn't offer much to a man who didn't need protection from other prisoners and who was charged with seven murders. Assistant DA Zelda Zane had already promised she would not ask for the death penalty if Mazzone testified against Raines and Diego at their trials. However, Zelda didn't call Mazzone to testify at the Raines's trial. If Diego died, Mazzone wouldn't have provided any useful testimony. Then too, if Zelda was involved in the recent shootout at the courthouse in Albuquerque, as the cryptic comments from Ulysses Howe hinted, her promises were worthless.

The warden smiled. "Assistant DA Zelda Zane's promises may soon be invalid."

Mazzone yawned. "Diego should survive a ruptured spleen."

The warden realized Mazzone had thought about Zelda's promises, and he was well informed about activities in the prison. "Assistant DA Zelda Zane may have her own set of problems."

Mazzone leaned forward and folded his hands together on the front of the desk. "Others have bigger problems."

"Why don't you tell me about them? It might get you what you want."

Mazzone smiled. "In due time. For now, I'll watch the game. Though, I want to talk Sara Almquist when she returns from Cuba."

The warden managed not to cough. He'd heard that Sara Almquist had been whisked away from New Mexico after the attempted ambush at her house, but he hadn't been told her location. Obviously, he needed to improve the security in his prison and isolate Mazzone more effectively.

.

CHAPTER 32: Sara at the El Floridita in Havana

The cab driver dropped her near the Museo Nacional de Bellas Artes and pointed across the maze of reconstruction projects and crowds to a sliver of salmon stucco. "El Floridita." He chugged off before she could ask a question.

She had been warned that reconstruction projects were rampant in Old Havana, but she was unprepared for the hubbub. She focused on the ground as she avoided the piles of rubble and hods of mortar spilling out of open doorways onto sidewalks and streets. When she stood in the middle of the narrow stone lane and looked up the canyon created by the ivory, gold, and gray baroque and neoclassical façades, she saw dozens of balconies and clotheslines with colorful items drying in the sun. Unfortunately, construction platforms not only blocked sidewalks but also marred the view.

When she tired of observing the architecture, she focused on the crowd. Tourists were gawking at every window and door. Locals were rushing to destinations, and workmen in hard hats were sweating and dirty as they cleaned up their work areas for the day. Not an unusual scene in any city on a hot, late afternoon.

Sara spotted two unusual characters in the tableaux. One old woman, possibly a man because white stubble erupted out of the heavy makeup on her dark chin, sat on a brightly painted chair and smoked a huge cigar. She or he wore bright red lipstick, a purple and green print bandana around her head, and a flounced red and green skirt. On closer inspection, Sara saw the cigar wasn't lit, but tourists flipped coins into the cup at the foot of the woman as they photographed her. The other character, a thin old man dressed in a 1930s style tailed tuxedo, twirled his cane as he sauntered along. At first, she thought him eccentric, but the white powder on his face and his strange whistle convinced her he was a street performer, too. However, no one tossed him coins or asked to be photographed with him. She wondered whether it would be rude to ask him whether he was a character out of Cuban folklore or a Santería persona. She decided not to risk offending him.

J. L. Greger

Sara pushed through a mob of tourists near the restaurant's door. They were debating loudly in English whether a daiquiri at La Floridita, the bar made famous by Hemingway, was worth the price.

She stopped in the open doorway and soaked up 1950s-style machismo. The heavy, dark wood bar extended along one wall, she guessed for thirty feet. Wide strips of the same dark wood framed the windows and doorways, outlined a mural above the bar, and covered the lower three feet of the walls. Both the wallpaper above the dark wood wainscoting and the mural of Havana harbor — presumably in the 1700s when sailing ships were used — above the bar were yellowed from too much exposure to smoke. However, the bar wasn't smoke-filled now. A bronze, life-size statue of a paunchy Hemingway hunched over the end of the bar. Behind him were dozens of framed photos of Hemingway and Castro. The deep olive green of the ceiling reinforced the heaviness of the room.

Sara felt sheepish as she took a seat at a small dark side table facing the main entrance. She'd bet everyone thought this décor was cool. She didn't. It tried too hard to be masculine. She was further embarrassed when the waiter in his red bibbed apron smirked as he took her order of club soda with lime.

She wondered whether she'd recognize the person who suggested they meet here? Although at least one-half of the Cubans on the street appeared to be mulattos, most of the scientists and physicians at the institute were light-skinned. She assumed the inviter was a man because he selected this bar. The problem was lots of light-skinned men who weren't obvious tourists were entering the bar.

At six-thirty, she was tired of watching giggling tourists sidle up to the Hemingway statue for a photograph and was ready to go back to the Hotel Meliá. A short, middle-aged man hurried into the bar, scanned the room, and sat down in the chair opposite of her. She recognized him immediately. She thought he'd claimed this morning to be a physician studying TB.

The man was out of breath and sweat beaded on his forehead. "I'm sorry to be late. I know you Americans value punctuality, but I had a hectic day." He wiped his bald head with a large white handkerchief. "I'm Carlos Moreno."

Sara forced a sincere smile, not a flashy one with all the teeth showing. "I recognized you. You were the quietest one all day. So, now I'm eager to hear your ideas." She resisted the urge to mention that his name hadn't been on the list of people invited to meet with her.

The waiter approached. Carlos glanced at Sara's drink. "Club soda with lime." Carlos looked around the room. "What do you think of El Floridita?"

Sara gulped. "It's famous, and I'm glad to get a chance to see it."

He nodded. "Stereotypes are usually disappointing. I bet most of the visitors here haven't read a Hemingway novel since high school." He paused. "What's your favorite Hemingway novel?"

She guessed he was testing her. She answered rapidly. *The Sun Also Rises.*"

"Ah, a romance."

"I see it more as a moral lesson. Happiness isn't getting what you want but making the most of what you have."

Carlos studied her. "You're what Americans call a straight-shooter. Odd... Odd choice for a U.S. envoy."

He was making her nervous. She interrupted, "I'm not an envoy. I'm a retired prof trying to be useful. I guess USAID liked my practical approach in Bolivia. So, the State Department sent me to talk to scientists here." She saw no need to add that she needed to get away from New Mexico for her own safety.

He snorted and took a long sip of his drink. "So, you think we're the same as Bolivia?'

She blinked. "I apologize if I gave the impression that I thought Cuba was of the same ilk as Bolivia. I know it's not."

He leaned across and tapped her arm. "No apologies needed." He watched the raucous crowd around the Hemingway statue as he sipped his drink. He leaned toward her. "I received a peculiar report from one of the clinics I supervise this morning. Funny thing, it was an HIV clinic. Many of the patients have a history of drug use."

Sara hid her eagerness. "I read that drug use wasn't a problem in Cuba."

He lifted one eyebrow. "Do you doubt our stats, too?"

She saw no polite way to contradict him politely? "Sorry, I interrupted. Go on with your story."

His brown eyes didn't blink. "Anyway, this clinic by the harbor in Santiago de Cuba sees seamen who have picked up bad habits — alcohol, drugs, smoking — during their travels. Often the men are sick physically and mentally." He leaned closer. "Someone broke into the clinic and stole medical records."

"Odd things to steal." Sara was sure she looked confused because she was. She wondered whether Sanders had acted on their theory and ordered the break in.

"Cameras at the facility showed two supposed seamen participating in the break in. They even stupidly wore the insignia of the Columbian navy, but one spoke Spanish with an accent common in the Andes, including parts of Bolivia." He stared expectantly at her.

Sara shook her head. "I'm not surprised Spanish dialects vary in South America, but I can't speak Spanish, let alone recognize dialects. I only spoke to a few public health workers in Bolivia, certainly no sailors." She thought a second. "Actually, I'm surprised anyone from landlocked Bolivia or the most of the Andes region would become a sailor. Again, what is the point of your story?"

He pulled a blurry picture from his briefcase and slid it across the table. "I thought you might recognize the men."

As he drew a photo out of his case, Sara had a premonition. She tried to freeze her facial expressions even before she looked at the photo. One glance, she knew. The shoulders and torso were right. "Pretty fuzzy." She shrugged as she wondered whether the second man in the photo was the foul-mouthed man who drove Sanders and her from the airport. She wasn't sure she could pull off this bluff. "Why the interest?"

He smiled and left the photo on the table. "Exactly, why the interest in records of patients with HIV? Who would find the data useful?" He sipped the last of his soda. "I'm guessing someone interested in the movement of drugs in Cuba. What do you think?"

Sara let her voice sound as tired as she felt. "I know it sounds simplistic, but I was hired to identify common ground for scientific exchanges between scientists in the U.S. and Cuba. I don't know anything about drug trafficking." She gulped. "Though as you may know, I discovered during the Philippine flu epidemic that one of my neighbors was a drug lord in Albuquerque. Unfortunately, I also stumbled into him in Bolivia."

"I wondered when you would admit you knew Jim Mazzone, or as we know his here as Señor Coca."

Sara bristled. "If you think I work for him, you're crazy. As far as I know, he's awaiting trial now in a prison in Colorado."

"Are you sure?"

CHAPTER 33: Sara's evening in Havana

Sara raced through the hotel. She was late for her meeting with Sanders. She flung open the door to her room and gasped.

The Atlantic Ocean, as seen through her floor-to-ceiling glass balcony doors, was navy blue at the horizon but the water gradually lightened at the shore only a couple of football fields away from the hotel. The sun was partially set and the sky was grayed shades of blue with only tinges of pink. No boats or objects ruined the view. She slammed her door shut and slid the glass balcony door open. A brisk breeze hit her as she listened to the rhythmic sound of waves lapping the shore. Not a schmaltzy sunset. A dignified, Hemingwayesque end of the day. She wished she was sharing this scene with someone special.

She left the door to the balcony open, switched on the lights, and scanned her room. A six-pack of Diet Coke sat on the bed with a large note on top.

> I'll wait at the restaurant by the falls until eight. Call if you get in later. S

She stifled a laugh. She guessed Sanders didn't want her to embarrass him again by slurping down three cans of Diet Coke at dinner.

***

The beat of a rumba throbbed as Sara stepped off the elevator. She walked toward the sound, which turned out to be the restaurant by the small waterfall. Tonight, three long tables were packed with tourists speaking English so loudly they almost drowned out the five musicians.

She scanned the crowd and barely recognized Sanders. He was slouched back comfortably in a chair with one arm draped over the chair next to him. No laptop, tie, or suit jacket was in sight. The sleeves of his white shirt were rolled to his elbows. He looked like Keanu Reeves in the Matrix movies. That was silly. Maybe, she was day dreaming because she was worn out and the sunset had been so romantic. A half glass of beer, a can of Diet Coke, and a glass of ice, but no food sat in front of him. The chair next to him offered a view of the musicians. He nodded, raised him arm slightly when she slid in, and then resumed his position. He whispered, "We'll talk when the set is over."

Water from the small waterfall misted their table slightly and she saw the sky quickly darkening above the falls. It was easy to relax, listen, and watch.

The lead singer was an ample, dark-skinned woman who continually swished her long red, tiered skirt as she sang. An athletic young man in a black T-shirt kept time with conga drums while a man with thinning, gray hair in a traditional light blue guayabera shirt strummed the guitar and sang. Two younger women sang harmony and played strange instruments. The thin, middle-aged woman stroked two hollow pieces of wood together as her body, covered in a tight black knit dress, undulated from her shoulders to her knees in time with the music. The other was only twelve or thirteen. She stood stiffly as she rubbed a rod against the roughened surface of a gourd and sang. Sara guessed the girl was daughter or niece of the lead singer because the girl lost the frozen smile on her face when the older woman stoked her hair after the song.

Before they started the next song, Sara asked Sanders whether he enjoyed Cuban music. He nodded. "I enjoy traditional Caribbean folk music and its derivatives. Unfortunately, many supposedly Cuban musical groups in the U.S. no longer use the natural claves." He seemed to realize Sara didn't recognize the word. "They're the two hollow pieces of wood played by the woman. The girl played a notched gourd, called a güiro. The plastic and metal versions used in the U.S. produce less mellow sounds."

The lead singer announced their last song would be "Guantanamera" amid cheers from the crowd. She reminded the audience that the Cuban revolutionary hero José Martí wrote the lyrics. Sara sighed internally. Cubans mentioned Martí the way the Chinese mentioned Mao in the 1980s — frequently and reverently.

The spell broke with the end of the last song, and the musical group packed their gear. Sanders straightened in his chair and brought out his laptop from his briefcase, which had been hidden under the table. A waiter rushed to their table to take their order. The noise at the tourist tables trebled.

Sara leaned closer to Sanders so he could hear her above the racket without others hearing her. "Saw a photo of Xave with our driver breaking into a clinic in Santiago de Cuba last night. Carlos Moreno seemed to think I would recognize at least one of them. Also knew I was acquainted with Mazzone. Called him Señor Coca." She forged ahead, because she wanted to impart all her new info before the waiter reappeared. "I think Moreno has guessed Xave's identity and your secret agenda. He also confirmed Mazzone has been to Cuba."

Sanders brushed his lips against her cheek. "You're good. Easy to trust you." He leaned back. "I think it's your straight-forward approach."

Sara bristled. "You mean, aging all-American blondes from the Midwest are too dumb to be devious."

His eyes became stern as he pushed her away. "Too smart to even try to be devious. Take a compliment at face value for once."

"Sorry, I appreciate the compliment. I'm... I'm in over my head again, as I was in Bolivia. Xave's days as an undercover agent are about over, though I doubt he'll accept it. And damn it, Mazzone must have another escape plan. Moreno doubted Mazzone was in prison in Colorado."

"You're right on the last two points, wrong on the first. The head of the Pedro Kourí Institute called the Chief of the Mission late this afternoon. He said you had encouraged his scientists to think about the future. He wanted you to lead one more brainstorming session."

Sara felt a giant weight lifting from her shoulders. "Maybe, I'm not just a runaway from my life in New Mexico."

He appeared to ignore her last comment. "I said you were busy at the Center of Molecular Immunology tomorrow."

Sara was surprised because Sanders generally kept her days packed when she was on assignment with him. "I'm at the center from nine to two. I could get back to the institute by three."

Sanders suddenly seemed to find something interesting on his laptop. "No, I booked you to do a bit of sightseeing tomorrow at three, and we leave the next day."

"Thanks, but I could skip the tourist sights."

He gave her a quick glance. "You'll never forgive yourself if you skip this site." He looked back at his laptop and tapped at the keys. "I'll arrange something for tomorrow night."

Sara shrugged. "No use arguing. I'm the consultant not the boss But what's so wonderful I can't miss it?"

Sanders ignored her last question as he typed and asked details about her scientific discussions during the day. She was disappointed that he didn't ask about Moreno's comments. "Is there any news from Albuquerque?"

"They set the traps for Zelda, Rachel, and Dean Wilson as you suggested. Per their usual imitation of the Keystone Kops, they're running in circles and going nowhere." He put away his tablet. "I suppose the most interesting point is that one of bad guys, Diego, is in critical condition after a prison melee."

Their meal arrived and Sanders switched gears. He began to regale her with stories of the successes and failures of cultural exchanges between the U.S. and Cuba during the last five years. The usual deep creases around his mouth disappeared when he laughed. Evidently, the sizes of the artists' egos weren't always proportional to their talents or at least their appeal to audiences in the U.S. Several artists had responded with fiery outbursts. She also soon realized that although he had worked at numerous consulates in South America during the last twenty years, he had dreamed of an assignment in Cuba.

Afterwards, he led her along the open hallway toward her room. He leaned her against her door and traced his forefinger around her eyes, nose, and chin as he talked. "Carlos Moreno is believed to be a major player in the Cuban intelligence community. I'm sure we're being watched now."

She wanted to say, "A spy would follow you, not me." Instead she said, "Then, why the romantic act?"

He whispered into her ear, "I want to whisper something to you without others hearing." Then he pulled back and studied her face. For once, he looked unsure as his lip quavered a bit. Then he again whispered in her ear. "Have a cab drop you off at the Central Chapel of the Colon Cemetery tomorrow. Join a tour group led by Andres. He's a thin, bald mulatto. Stay with the group until you get to the La Milagrosa. Then walk back to the Firefighters' Memorial. Study all sides of it. The rest will take care of itself."

"Why the melodrama? What if I'm late or get lost?"

"Not a catastrophe, be at the Firefighters' Memorial by four. Now I'm going to do something inappropriate. You're going to prove to any spectators you're not under my control by slapping me on the face and slamming your door as you go into your room."

Sara thought a joke was inappropriate but forged ahead anyway. "I hope you're not trying to tell me you're into sadomasochism. I'm not." She suppressed a giggle.

Malignancy   157

He coughed. "Hardly, but doing this right would be easier if you weren't laughing." He leaned forward, put his hands on her shoulders, and kissed her, not a peck but slowly and thoroughly.

It was hard to believe this was an act. "Nice," she whispered. Then she shoved him back as instructed. Too hard, he almost lost her balance. Embarrassed, she continued the act. "You're out of line." She scurried into her room and slammed the door.

CHAPTER 34: Sergeant Elsa Grasso on Day 15

"Not the way I want to start the day." Elsa wanted to ignore Linda's email suggesting she knew George Kummer's location. "I've wasted enough time on Kummer."

Chuy turned from his desk. "Don't be hasty. The Doughboy would make a better witness than Jorge or Falto because he speaks in coherent sentences despite his pasty white skin and unpleasant demeanor. The other two don't, and they look even shiftier. More importantly, he'll probably end up dead if we don't locate him soon."

Elsa thought for a moment. Although she doubted Kummer knew useful information, someone had sent Jorge to break into Kummer's apartment looking for him or something he possessed. If she found him, she'd dangle him in front of Rachel, Zelda, and even Dean Wilson and claim he was ready to turn important documents over to the police. Doubtful, but he might help push one of them over the edge.

Besides, a trip to the medical school would get her away from Chuy. He talked to his computer when he was bored, and it drove her crazy. Ulysses Howe, the director of the Albuquerque FBI office, had gotten a court order, and Chuy was following Zelda and Rachel through the GPS systems in their phones and cars today. Rachel appeared to be driving from Denver to Albuquerque and not using her phone. Zelda was in her office talking incessantly on the phone. Chuy was bored after only thirty minutes.

***

Linda was humming a song when Elsa strode into Linda's office. "This better be good. I'm in a hurry." She regretted her comment as she watched Linda deflate like a balloon hit by a pin.

"I know my last tip on Kummer's location was… was disappointing. This one should be better. Diego's former department head called me this morning. Janitors reported someone slept in Diego's office this weekend and even left a sleeping bag."

Elsa stood in the doorway ready to leave quickly. "What makes you think the squatter is Kummer?"

"Fits Kummer's pattern of clinging to anything of Diego's, and the department head is sure no grad students have keys to Diego's lab. They shouldn't, but grad students sometimes sleep in labs and offices when they run big experiments." She shoved a key across the desk toward Elsa.

"Have the janitors seen anyone?"

"No, but they found empty pizza boxes and soda cans in the office."

Elsa grabbed the key. "It's Kummer. If we don't find him soon, he'll die of heart disease from arteries clogged with saturated fat from pizzas."

Linda shrugged. "We can add arrested development to the list of his neuroses."

Elsa sighed. "Sorry I was grumpy. We're so short staffed now. There's no one left to monitor Diego's office."

"You forgot Winston. I bet one reason Kummer slept in Diego's office was to gain access to a computer in a private location. Chuy said you confiscated Kummer's computer from Diego's condo."

"Good idea. I don't have to get another court order because Diego's office computer is university property. No one using it has any legal reason to expect privacy."

As Elsa departed without thanking her, Linda said, "Glad I was of service."

***

"I told you Winston would get us answers." Linda seemed happier than usual, despite her office being packed like a full can of sardines. George Kummer and a campus police officer were slumped in the two chairs in front of Linda's desk. Winston sat in Linda's desk chair alternately hammering at her keyboard and pulling pages from her printer. No one but Linda bothered even to look up when Elsa entered the room.

"What brought him here?" Elsa pointed to Kummer who didn't bother to raise his head. She turned to Linda. "Please tell me that you didn't do a citizen's arrest."

Winston snorted, "Boy, what a hoot."

"He showed up in my office fifteen minutes ago. Right after Winston and I sent him an email suggesting he'd be safer in your custody than on his own. Here's a copy of the email." As Elsa scanned the note, Linda continued, "Seemed like the right thing to do after

Winston found this document." Linda handed another page to Elsa. "I called you and campus police as soon as we found it."

Elsa read only a line or two before she gasped and closed the door. She prodded Kummer. "Well?"

Kummer sunk lower in the chair. "Nowhere else to go. Police are at my apartment and Diego's condo." He groaned. "I managed all right in Diego's old office at night, but hiding out on campus during the day is rough." He gulped. "Dean Almquist's email made sense. I told him," he pointed at Winston, "how to access files not on my computer. They're in a secret account on the cloud. Lot better than the sheet you're holding."

Linda handed Elsa a pile of about twenty pages. "We underestimated him. He has considerable computer skills and has kept some riveting records."

Kummer looked up at Elsa almost in supplication. She thought, for once, he was where she wanted him. "I delivered messages," he paused, "and snooped a bit." He stared at Linda as he twisted a few strands of the red hair in his beard around his finger. "Don't forget to tell her my conditions."

Linda waited a few seconds for Elsa to peruse the top page in the pile. "Obviously, he doesn't want to be locked up with Diego or Mazzone."

"And." He twirled another strand of hair.

"He doesn't want his case prosecuted by Zelda Zane." Linda frowned. "I told him he needed a lawyer for such negotiations." She looked nervously around her packed office. "Witness protection may even be in order. I don't know."

Kummer smirked. "I figured she," he pointed to Linda, "would be better than some schmo assigned to me by Legal Protections, at least at first."

In less than five minutes, Elsa realized Kummer's cache on the cloud was enough to charge, but not necessarily convict, Zelda and Rachel for a variety of crimes. Then the whirlwind began. Elsa developed a sore throat as she made and received endless calls. By the time U.S. Marshalls arrived to escort Kummer to a safe house, her voice was raspy and her head throbbed.

Elsa appreciated how Linda handled the bedlam in her office with aplomb. She kept both Kummer and Winston focused but made them feel appreciated. When the FBI and APD computer experts swooped in, she quickly sent them to Winston's office after warning them to avoid mentioning the case in hallways where they might be overheard. Then she proceeded to make calls.

Elsa heard only snatches of Linda's conversation with the university counsel. "Dean Wilson is sometimes inconsiderate and prone to cronyism." "I believe he's too smart and cares to much about the university to have broken any laws." "The university needs to be prepared to manage potentially unpleasant comments in the press concerning previous employees of the medical school and to a lesser extent the Dean."

An hour after Elsa arrived, the small office was finally quiet. "Now all we have to do is find Rachel and Zelda. Pry something besides half-truths from Dean Wilson and elicit anything coherent from Jorge."

As Elsa moved to open the door, Linda said, "We're not through yet. I know Kummer is an obnoxious nerd, but I hope you don't prosecute him if he testifies at the upcoming trials and if he was only a gopher. He can't be all bad, he spent most of the money he's got to pay Diego's monthly condo payment."

"Lots of ifs. Can't talk now." Elsa loped off.

CHAPTER 35: Sergeant Chuy Bargas

"Please try one more time." Chuy looked around the spacious kitchen with white marble countertops, a six-burner gas range, and a mammoth double-door, stainless steel refrigerator and freezer. Assistant DA Zelda Zane lived well.

Zelda's maid drained her coffee mug. "It's like I told you. The courier delivered the box with the note on top around ten." She stretched across the kitchen island to push the empty box closer to him. "The note said I should call Miss Zelda and tell her to look for a new message on her computer and then to come home right away."

Chuy studied a new email from Elsa. The courier service claimed the package was sent from a site in Albuquerque and the delivery was paid for with cash. Elsa was already tracking the employee who accepted the package originally.

"How did Zelda act when she arrived home twenty minutes later?"

"Like I said." The maid looked defiantly at Chuy. "Miss Zelda, she was in a bad mood. She screamed at me to make her a sandwich and wrap it up as she ran into her bedroom with the package. When she came out, she was in jeans and a blue striped shirt, which she wears only on weekends. She shoved the sandwich into a big blue tote and grabbed the keys to my car. As she raced out, she ordered me to get her car washed and to pick up her dry cleaning. I was doing those errands when cops attacked me."

He scanned his emails and hoped police had found the maid's blue Honda. No such luck. "My apologies again if the officers were a bit rough with you. Call me immediately if Zelda contacts you or you remember anything else."

***

Chuy gazed back at the two-story, stone territorial-style house situated in a historic neighborhood of Albuquerque as he put the evidence bag in his trunk. He couldn't imagine why Zelda risked all of this and her political career for fifty thousand dollars.

He thought about all the new evidence on this case and felt a slight bit of satisfaction along with a lot of frustration. The APD bigwigs had been sure Zelda would cooperate yesterday. They'd been wrong, but they hatched their scheme before George Kummer's treasure trove of email messages and financial records surfaced several hours ago.

He and Elsa with help from Winston and Kummer initially had focused on emails and financial records, which mentioned Rachel's or Zelda's name. They found no record of funds being transferred to accounts in Rachel's name. As soon as they spotted fifty thousand dollars had been wire transferred from one of Raines's accounts to a new account in Zelda's name on the day he died, Chuy and APD officers began to search for Zelda. However, both he and Elsa wondered whether Zelda was being framed. The funds in the account in Zelda's name had remained untouched. Either Zelda was naive enough to believe no one would find the funds or she was unaware of the funds transfer.

Whoever had transferred funds into the account for Zelda had also transferred much larger sums from Raines's accounts to other new accounts — all with unknown names. Then they had moved the money from these new accounts into a series of accounts with different aliases. Computer experts at the FBI were searching now to find where the money finally landed and who had done the transfers.

Interestingly, Kummer's cooperative spirit had disappeared as soon as they found the account in Zelda's name. Elsa reported he was no longer answering questions.

Chuy pushed all the confusion about financial records out of his mind as he drove to the crime lab to deliver the samples — the empty box and note delivered to Zelda earlier today. He tried to focus on what motivated Zelda, the most successful assistant DA in New Mexico. He was almost to the crime lab when he received an emergency call.

New Mexico State Police had found Rachel's car parked at Dairy Delite in Springer, New Mexico. The driver, a college student, had stopped to eat. The state police learned the young man occasionally did "favors for a sexy FBI agent" when her work brought her to Denver for a few days. Last night, she had been in a rush to get to the airport when she gave him three hundred dollars and instructed him to drive her car to Albuquerque the next day. The student made several curious comments. Rachel told him to not open the trunk and to ignore any noise, including phones rings, from it. She emphasized he must drop off the car at the Mercado Police Station between fifteen and ten to seven in the evening, not later.

Chuy called Ulysses Howe for an update. He'd already determined that no woman with the last name of Jones had flown out of Denver last night or today. FBI agents in Denver were reviewing films of all passengers passing through security at the airport. So far, they had spotted no one who fit Rachel's description.

***

When the crime lab technician pulled the empty box out of the evidence bag, she gasped. "You missed a lot. Are you brain dead? I thought this was a high priority case."

Chuy felt foolish as she held up a single strand of hair with a forceps and pointed to another.

"It's gray. I'd guess it's not yours. Do you know if anyone with gray hair handled the box?"

"The maid's hair was black but looked dyed. She probably has gray hair."

The technician began to smile as she quickly examined the hair under a microscope. "What I thought. This is a Kanekalon, the modacrylic used in wigs. I'll have more of an answer in a day or two."

"May be too late, but you've given me a lead. Thanks."

"Wait, let me look at the other strand. This one Kanekalon too, but it's curly and a different shade of gray. Might be two wigs."

***

Chuy studied Elsa's most recent email. The clerk at the courier service had reported a stooped gray-haired woman had delivered the package for Zelda to the service early this morning.

He emailed Ulysses Howe.

> Zelda and Rachel are wearing gray wigs. Have your staff relook at the footage at the Denver airport for a gray-haired woman. She might be stooped. I'll check footage here of those exiting planes at the Albuquerque airport last night to see if any woman with gray hair looks like Rachel.

CHAPTER 36: Sara at Colon Cemetery in Havana

Sara hated to have to leave the Center of Molecular Immunology at two. Scientists at this biotechnology institute were doing exciting work — developing vaccines against various cancers. More specifically, they were manufacturing tumor-specific vaccines, which provoked patients' bodies to recognize specific proteins or related compounds on the surface of tumors. They hoped the patients' immune systems then would destroy the identified cells before they proliferated and the malignancies spread. In theory, the vaccines caused fewer side effects than usual cancer drugs because the patient's immune system ignored normal cells without the targeted protein. Most other cancer drugs were less specific and destroyed normal cells as well, thus weakening the patients' general health.

Scientists at the institute were proud of their patent for a vaccine against a specific type of lung cancer. Their research now focused on finding unique proteins on the surface of other, hopefully more commonly occurring, cancer cells.

Sara reviewed what she'd seen and heard as her cab moved through traffic toward Colon Cemetery. Sanders was right. Expanded scientific exchanges between the U.S. and Cuba were a wise next step in the evolving U.S. policy on Cuba. The Cuban scientists, especially in cancer immunotherapy, wanted to continue their work with scientists not only at Harvard where several of the Cuban scientists had trained, but also throughout the U.S. Equally important, the Cuban scientists were eager to have their ideas patented and to interact more with international drug companies, which in turn would encourage the development of more capitalistic opportunities in Cuba.

She had met the State Department's and her own expectations, but her stomach churned as she wondered what awaited her at Colon Cemetery. Sanders wouldn't have pushed for this so-called "tourist" rendezvous if it wasn't important.

The cab stopped at two-forty at the cemetery's main chapel, a yellow stucco structure with rococo white trim. She put on her sunglasses as soon as she stepped from the cab because the glare was blinding as sunlight was reflected from all the white limestone and marble in the memorials. She looked for shade as she wandered past one elaborately adorned mausoleum after another. There were few trees. In general, she thought this was a sunnier, hotter version of La Recoleta Cemetery in Buenos Aires, but she was no connoisseur of funerary art.

She spotted a group in front of one particularly tall memorial. The man organizing the group met Sanders's description of Andres. He quickly told them this monument was for the firemen who lost their lives in a fire in 1890. Andres spent a lot of time pointing out the images of the dead firemen in oval bas-reliefs around the base of the memorial, but Sara thought the sculpture of a nun in a headdress reminiscent of Sally Fields in the TV series *The Flying Nun* was more interesting.

As Andres led the group around the cemetery two things were obvious. First, the Cuban government was now restoring many of the tombs, which had been abandoned when wealthy Cubans fled Cuba in the 1960s. Scaffolds covered many marble tombs. Second, Andres was a top-notch guide. He explained that when he was young he thought his success was assured because he spoke fluent Russian. He humorously lamented, "While everyone else rejoiced when the Iron Curtain fell, I forgot Russian and learned English."

Despite his lively accounts of Cuban history, Sara felt she was melting in the brutal glare of the sun. However, she politely listened as Andres explained the legend of the tomb for La Milagrosa. The mother with her infant were ascribed to have healing powers. She left when the rest of the tour group joined locals in following a proscribed routine to gain the blessing of La Milagrosa.

She rushed to the firefighters' memorial and walked around it once. No one was nearby. She dreaded having to sit in the sunlight's glare for long and looked down the road to the front gate. No one was moving toward her.

"Sara. Sara."

It was an old man's raspy voice. She turned around. A man with dingy white hair slouched by the statue of the nun. She gasped as he limped toward her using a cane.

Xave's broad shoulders were hunched forward. His clothes were worn and dirty. His eyes were red-rimmed. His nose was encrusted with dried mucus, and sores festered on his face and arms. The deterioration, she saw, was more than a good makeup job.

She gulped repeatedly and rushed forward.

"Don't touch me." More softly Xave added, "Ladies don't hug bums. Here… this is for you." He handed her two drooping yellow roses with a small envelope tied about their stems with brown twine.

She blinked and decided to not ask the obvious question but instead made a positive assumption. "What a makeup job."

"Local thugs enhanced my disguise."

His eyes traced her from head to foot. She was glad she wore sunglasses so he couldn't see the pity in her eyes.

"What did Moreno have to say at El Floridita?"

Sara gasped. "How do you know?'

Xave gave her his old grin without his teeth showing. "Remember the old woman with the cigar."

Sara laughed. "I noticed she had white stubble on her chin." She frowned. "But why were you there?"

"S."

She noted he refrained from saying Sanders's name.

"S and I have channels of communication. You don't need to know details."

His head lolled on his chest as if he was too weary to hold it up.

She figured Sanders's driver was one of those channels of communications but thought Xave would be disappointed if she guessed his secrets. He didn't need more disappointment. "Moreno showed me a picture of you and another man, I think Sanders's driver, breaking into a clinic in Santiago de Cuba." She told him other details of her conversation. "The bottom line is Moreno knows who you are and surmises you are tracking the flow of drugs in Cuba. He also realizes I am acquainted with Mazzone who he calls Señor Coca."

Xave lifted his head. "That's it?"

She said more softly. "I think your days undercover here are over.

"Did S tell you to say that?"

"No, but he agreed when I said it."

Xave looked down again and muttered a few instructions before he started to shuffle away.

Sara thought this was her last chance to stop his self-destruction. "Wait. I care about you. Only a couple of weeks ago, you talked about your retirement in six months. Move up the time schedule."

He kept his back to her. "Doesn't matter to you. We don't have a future. S is more your type. I've seen how he looks at you."

She moved forward and grabbed his arm. "He's not you."

Xave turned, tore off her sunglasses, and looked into her eyes. "S can get you where you belong — doing science exchanges, planning programs — the clean stuff for the State Department." He stepped closer. It was obvious he hadn't taken a shower in several days, and his breath stank of cheap alcohol. "Take a good look at me. This is what undercover work looks like. I won't destroy you as I have others."

Tears ran down her face. "Xave, please don't throw your life away."

He yanked his arm from her grasp and shoved her glasses in his pants pocket. "Moreno probably has someone watching us now." He stumbled away. She wondered how much of the deterioration that she observed was part of his act and how much was real. She guessed she'd never know. She felt even more sadness as she realized he'd taken her glasses as a memento.

Sara stood in the blazing sun and watched him until he slipped away among the marble monuments. She looked down at the drooping yellow roses. She'd been told as a child that yellow roses meant remember me. She wondered whether Xave chose them intentionally. She felt tears well up in her eyes. He'd probably found them on one of the graves here and figured they were a way to give her the envelope. She pulled a tissue from her purse, wiped sweat off her brow and tears from her eyes as she looked around, and then laid the tissue over the stem of the roses before she pulled off the envelope. She put the envelope and tissue into her purse and trudged to the main chapel to hail a cab.

CHAPTER 37: Sara at Café del Oriente in Havana

Sanders had instructed her to be at Café del Oriente on Plaza San Francisco in Old Havana by six. She looked at her watch after she hailed a cab. She might be late.

Her curiosity grew as the cab wound through traffic. She shuffled in her purse and opened the envelope. A man's gold wedding ring fell out. She unfolded a half-page of yellow paper.

> To my gal Sara,
> Tell Moreno about Mazzone. Vouch for me. He'll believe you.
> Ask S about the ring. Have him check on L's daughter.
> Sorry, but you deserve better.
> Xave

She was disappointed. The note was so cryptic and unromantic. She assumed she wouldn't hear from Xave again and zipped the note into an inner compartment of her purse for safekeeping, but she left the ring and envelope in the main section of the purse for easy access.

The driver pointed to a corner restaurant. The stone exterior was punctuated by narrow windows, extending from the ground up two floors with a bit of a balcony between floors. The place would be at home in New York or Paris.

Inside, she was directed to climb narrow stairs to a Rococo fantasy. Crystal chandeliers hung from the pink ceiling trimmed with wedding cake white plaster. Rose-colored upholstery covered the chairs. The floor-to-ceiling draperies were pink and gold brocade. The décor might be considered too sugary for anything but a high-class women's tearoom or a bordello, except for the deep mahogany wood trim on the lower walls, around the windows, and on the chairs. The room was a splendid Latin version of Delmonico's in New York City as it must have looked in the early 1900s.

She recognized faces from her visits to the Pedro Kourí Institute and the Center of Molecular Immunology at a corner table. Sanders rose from the table and met her halfway across the room. "How's Xave?" he whispered.

"Bad. He gave me a note. Wants me to endorse him to Moreno and tell him about Mazzone."

Sanders gave a smug smile and pulled her toward the table.

She resisted. "Also said you'd explain a gold ring and check on L's daughter."

Sanders smile turned to a frown. "Coward. I'll explain later." His face and demeanor returned to his affable host persona as he led her to a seat next to Moreno. "I'm afraid this is the first decent meal Sara has gotten in Havana. I've kept her so busy she's mainly eaten in the hotel."

Moreno leaned toward Sara and winked. "That means the El Floridita Bar with me was a treat?"

Sanders quickly enthralled the other four at the table with one of his funnier stories about artists' exchanges between Cuba and the U.S. She leaned toward Moreno. "Yes, but you caught me off guard."

"Good." He winked. "I get more truthful answers then."

Sara pulled back. "I gave you truthful answers. Now, I'll give you insights on Jim Mazzone that aren't in your dossier on him." She gulped. "I'll start by saying, he's ruthless with subordinates who don't do his bidding or anyone who opposes him, but he has a weak spot for children."

Moreno glanced at Sanders. "I assume he told you to talk to me."

She rubbed her fingers over the smooth ironed surface of the white linen tablecloth. "Actually, a friend, someone I once wished was more, asked me to help you."

"I was told you talked to an old man at Colon Cemetery. They should have realized." He pulled a phone from his jacket pocket.

She put her hand over the phone. "Wait. Stop wasting your staff's time following me. I don't know Xave's plans or what he's done. I first met him when he rescued me from Mazzone in Bolivia. However, I do know Xave's goal is to stop Mazzone from moving coca through Cuba to the U.S. And I suspect one of your goals is to keep coca out of Cuba."

Sanders entertained the four others at the table throughout her conversation with Moreno, but he frequently glanced in her direction.

When Sanders raised his eyebrows in concern, she resisted the urge to summon his help and winked at him instead.

Moreno motioned to a waiter and whispered in his ear. The maître d' arrived in seconds. More whispers. Moreno stood and pulled Sara to her feet. "We're going to meet somewhere more private."

"I like it here."

Dead silence at the table.

Sanders said, "Dr. Moreno, is there a problem? Dr. Almquist should hear ideas generated by her colleagues. I'm afraid I'm no good in scientific discussions."

"She'll be back in less than fifteen minutes. Order her and me the fish of the day filleted and served with lime coulis. It's top notch here. Then you and I can talk while she and the other scientists exchange ideas." Moreno clasped her arm and led her down the steep narrow stairs and behind the large bar to a small room off the service area. Moreno pushed her onto a metal chair across a table from two men.

She decided this wasn't the time to cry or become hysterical. She took a deep breath and folded her hands on the table.

He chuckled when her hands shook. "You've heard too much American propaganda. This is going to be easy, if you cooperate. Think carefully. What did Xave Zack say in the cemetery?"

Sara internally sighed in relief. He hadn't asked to see the note. She wanted to keep the note as a memento, even though she knew it was stupid to be sentimental when she was in a pickle. She closed her eyes and pictured the note. "Tell Moreno about Mazzone. Vouch for me. Moreno will believe you."

She opened her eyes to see one man scratching notes on a pad of paper and the other typing on a tablet. Moreno stood behind them, apparently reading what they recorded. He began to ask questions in rapid order. Although he stated the questions logically, she doubted the reasoning behind them. She answered them anyway and tried to keep a calm facade.

Moreno looked at his watch. "We've been at it ten minutes. What do you want to add?"

Sara was afraid what would happen next. "I'm a scientist trying to set up a scientific exchange between our two countries. I may have stumbled into unsavory situations in the past, but I'm not into covert activities. I expect you'll now allow me to return to my dinner and not

J. L. Greger

prevent my departure from Cuba tomorrow." She decided a show of confidence was in order. "When can the scientific exchanges begin?"

"You were coached well."

Sara frowned. "No one coached me. Looks like you've seen too much propaganda, too."

The two men looked down and snickered. Moreno grabbed her arm and pulled her to her feet. "You have a problem."

Both men stopped their tittering. Sara squelched a gulp.

"You have two men interested in you. Take my advice and pick Mr. Sanders. He'll bring you back as the scientific envoy to Cuba when he becomes the Deputy Chief of Mission to Cuba. Might even marry you."

Sara gasped. She felt heat rising from her neck to her face. She was sure she blushing.

Moreno let go of her arm as he bent over convulsed in laughter. As he wiped tears from his eyes, he said, "For once, you're speechless. Now I know your weak spot."

The diners studied Sara when she returned to the table alone, but no one asked questions. She knew her apparent dispute with Moreno was ruining the evening, so she answered their unvoiced questions. "Senor Moreno is optimistic about the scientific exchanges. He was over eager about learning details that I don't think have been decided yet." She paused, "At least I don't know them, and he's not used to the honest answer of I don't know."

Sara was surprised by the response. Three of the scientists looked uncomfortably at their plates until the leader of the Center of Molecular Immunology chortled, "You're right, he doesn't believe me either when I say I don't know." They all returned to normal conversation.

When she had first returned to the table Sanders looked as if he was ready to spring into action. As she spoke, the wrinkles around his eyes and mouth disappeared. She was struck by how handsome he was when he was relaxed.

Shortly after the waiter served the entrees, Moreno strutted to the table. Before he sat down, he said, "The Cuban government is eager for the scientific exchanges to begin." He looked at the four Cuban scientists. "It's up to you to work out details with your U.S. counterparts."

CHAPTER 38: Sergeant Chuy Bargas in flight

Chuy stared at the image on his computer screen as he spoke to Ulysses Howe on the phone. "I agree. The stooped, gray-haired woman on the ten p.m. United flight to Albuquerque from Denver was Rachel. But sir, I'd rather you look at the image I sent you of the woman with black hair. Note she's humped and appears to have some sort of brace under her jacket. She boarded the United flight from Albuquerque to L.A. and should get in at three-thirty Pacific Time." He looked at his watch." The flight was due to land only a few minutes ago. The driver's license used for identification was for a Delores Gaza."

"Clothes are different. Can't see the face, but the timing is possible and L.A. is the perfect place to disappear or leave the country. Yes, I'll give the order."

***

Thirty minutes later, Chuy breathlessly answered Ulysses Howe's call. "Did you catch her?"

"The plane landed early. Damn, never happens for my flights."

Chuy couldn't think of a response. Ulysses continued as if he didn't expect one. "The so-called Delores disappeared by the time I got the alert out. We found the real Delores was injured in an auto accident a month ago and is hospitalized in a Denver long-term care facility. More importantly, the ID for the old woman who boarded the plane in Denver was for another old woman in the same facility as the real Delores. Rachel likes to go to Denver and takes every assignment that allows her to go to there. I know she followed up on leads with patients in Denver hospitals a month ago. It would have been easy for her to collect driver's licenses of patients then."

"Oh, so...."

"My staff is checking out the hospital for other ties to Rachel. They've sent me a list of other women in critical or serious condition there. I've broadcast the names to the airlines to hold anyone with one of those names from departing on a plane, but it won't be enough. I want you at LAX. You're good at seeing through Rachel's disguises."

"Er, er, how? I don't think there's a flight from Albuquerque to LAX for several hours."

"I know. I pulled strings. You can catch a military cargo flight leaving Kirtland in twenty minutes."

Chuy knew Kirtland Air Force Base was adjacent to the Albuquerque Sunport, but he had no idea where to catch the flight. "How? Where do I go?"

Ulysses guffawed. "Rachel always called you a hayseed. Nothing wrong with being a beginner." He gave instructions.

***

Chuy bounded onto the military cargo plane only five minutes before it was due to depart. Both the pilot and co-pilot were fiddling with knobs and switches and talking to the air controllers. A big-shouldered, Afro-American man with salt and pepper gray hair was seated behind the pilot. He looked up momentarily from his laptop and pointed to a fold down seat behind the co-pilot.

Chuy buckled up and waited for his fellow passenger to stop pounding the keys of his laptop and introduce himself. He looked familiar. "Can I use my laptop during the flight?"

The man ignored him. The pilot looked over his shoulder toward Chuy. "Not until we're in the air." He stretched further toward the other passenger. "Turn it off now."

The man ignored the pilot.

"I'm pulling rank. Now."

"Okay." The man turned off his computer and began to sort through pages in his briefcase.

Chuy almost choked when he heard the man's resonating bass voice. He'd seen photos of Ulysses Howe and exchanged emails and phone calls during the last week, but he'd never met him. "Mr. Howe, I'm sorry. I should have recognized you." He didn't mention that Rachel described her boss as a slow, old man. Ulysses Howe was probably in his early fifties. His face looked less wrinkled and more youthful than his gray hair might suggest.

Howe's lips quivered in amusement as he studied Chuy. "Not what you expected? Rachel told you I was a decrepit old man, didn't she?"

"Oh, no, sir." Chuy felt his Adam's apple bob in his throat. It always did when he was embarrassed.

"If we're going to work together, you have to be honest with me even when it hurts. I dislike yes-men. I appreciate smart people with ideas. Why else would I put up with Rachel's tantrums as my associate director of the Albuquerque field office?"

"Yes, sir."

Ulysses rummaged through the stack of papers on his lap as the plane lumbered down the runway and then jerked repeatedly as it made a rapid ascent. Chuy didn't remember the runway was so rough or the takeoff was so steep when he flew commercial airlines. He wished he'd had time to purchase Dramamine before the flight.

Ulysses shoved several pages at Chuy. "I don't do much field work anymore, but then I don't usually have an associate director on the lam. Here's the plan. I'm going to focus my efforts on LAX with Tom O'Hara of the L.A. branch of the FBI. You're going to comb through details from the Denver and Albuquerque offices. Your contact persons' emails are at the top of the first page." He drummed his fingers on the back of the pilot's seat.

"I know you want to get back on your computer. Wait two more minutes." The pilot under his breath hissed, "I hate VIPs."

***

Chuy found it difficult to concentrate on his assigned task. He barely kept his stomach contents in place during takeoff. Before he settled down to work on his laptop, he read Elsa's email several times.

> Chuy,
> I'm getting ready for the stake-out at the Mercado Police Department. Gil Andrews and his crew are in position. Gil and you are right. Good luck.
> Love,
> Elsa

A tear coursed down his cheek. She never signed an email with "love" before. After the squabbles of the last two days, he thought their relationship was over.

"Police found a black wig in the garbage in the woman's bathroom nearest the gate for the flight from Albuquerque to LAX," Ulysses announced. "They sent it to a lab to check for Rachel's DNA from sloughed hair, sweat, or skin."

It took Chuy several minutes to figured out that when Ulysses spoke, he wasn't addressing anyone in particular and didn't expect responses to his announcements. Chuy clicked the keys of his computer. Two minutes later, he said, "The college kid working for Rachel said that she stowed only a small rolling case by her hotel door in Denver. She can only have so many disguises in the small case. If she pitched the black hair, I think she'll wear the gray wig again."

"Agreed."

"If she plans to leave the country on her next flight as you expect, she'll need the passport of an old woman, a document harder to find than driver's licenses in a hospital." Chuy glanced at Ulysses who had not looked up from his computer. "So, I have the Denver office checking whether she has elderly relatives… aunts, grandmothers, or a mother with passports."

"Good. Agents in LA checked the rosters for all flights out of LAX in the next eight hours. No one with a name from the targeted Denver hospital is flying."

Chuy was surprised when he saw Rachel's history in a file Ulysses had forwarded to him. No wonder she was always a bit sullen. Her birth certificate indicated her father was unknown. She had spent several months in two foster homes during her teen years.

Ulysses cleared his throat. "There are over nine hundred nonstop flights out of LAX to foreign countries weekly. I figure she'll try to leave LAX in the next eight hours because she knows she can't hide from security sweeps of the airport between two and four in the morning, when the crowds dwindle to a few stragglers."

Chuy continued to work until the cabin was silent for several minutes. He looked over at Ulysses, who appeared to be in suspended animation with his mouth agape and eyes shut.

Suddenly, Ulysses came out of the trance and spoke rapidly. "I think she'll choose the flight carefully. She'll pick a country, which hasn't signed a U.S. extradition treaty, like China, Russia, India, Viet Nam, an Arab nation, or much of South America. However, with enough money, she could disappear in France, Switzerland, or the Balkans. They're checking all flights to those countries between now and three in the morning. Chuy, any ideas for reducing this list to a manageable size?"

"No, but her Spanish is good. Afraid I'm coming up empty. Her only living relative appears to be her mother. No passport has ever been issued to her. But Lydia Jones has been institutionalized several times over the last twenty years for mental instability."

"Did you check for a passport with her mother's maiden name?"

"Jones is her maiden name and the name she appears to use, but she was married twice. I'm looking for her ex-husbands' names."

Ulysses's groans turned into a "Eureka" as he scanned his screen. "We're making progress. They've identified twenty-five commercials flights meeting my criteria: nonstop to another country where extradition would be difficult and leaving in the next eight hours." He read off the names: "Seoul, Taipei City, Manila, Mexico City, Guadalajara, Puerto Vallarta, Cancún, San José in Costa Rica, Guatemala City, Panama City, and Lima."

Chuy stifled a groan. "Awful lot of flights to delay and you still might not catch her. What if she hired a private jet?"

Ulysses's eyes narrowed. "You just delivered a double punch. We're running computer searches for passengers on private jets, but without knowledge of her alias, it's hopeless. LAX administration has already balked about delays. The flights leave from three of LAX's terminals. Only about one-half of them depart from Tom Bradley International Terminal, which is the easiest one to isolate. Would be easier if we were searching for arrivals not departures because all international arrivals come to the international terminal."

As the plane bounced and skidded to a stop, Chuy realized he was trading motion sickness for the nausea that he experienced when he was panicky. He also thought this might be the last time he could say something important. "Mr. Howe, thanks. I know I've made mistakes or at least acted too slowly in the last few days, and many have doubted me. Thanks for trusting me anyway."

Ulysses chuckled. "I figured you and your partner were my best bet after I saw that both Zelda and Rachel showed such an aversion to you."

J. L. Greger

CHAPTER 39: Sergeant Elsa Grasso

Elsa parked her unmarked car in front of a laundromat about a block away from the Mercado Police Station on Baca Calle. She glanced at the laundry basket, which sat where Chuy usually sat, and missed his constant commentary.

At least, the debate was over. Gil Andrews thought he and three officers from the Mercado Police Department along with the two undercover cops, who had posed as Jorge and Falto for the last four days in his jail, were sufficient if APD kept two squad cars in the vicinity.

The APD had allocated four cars to protect the Mercado Police Station. She checked her watch. Fifteen minutes to seven. She saw a pickup truck with two officers parked in front of the clinic directly across Baca Calle from the police station. She couldn't see a third car parked on the main street of Mercado fifty feet before the intersection with Baca Calle, but she heard occasional comments on her radio as they reported vehicles turning onto Baca Calle. A fourth unmarked car was pulled to the side of the road not far from the I-25 exit to Mercado. Gil called it "overkill."

Everyone agreed on one point. They wished Rachel had chosen to meet Zelda at six, not seven, because the sun set around six-thirty. Mercado hadn't invested much in streetlights. However, the parking lot by the police station was well lit.

A state police officer dressed in the plaid shirt and baseball cap parked Rachel's car in front of the station and entered the edifice at twelve to seven. Elsa smiled as she remembered how easy it was to get the college kid's shirt and cap.

The kid had been defiant with the New Mexico State Police. He stopped using his line, "Rachel has more authority than you do," after technicians from the New Mexico State Crime Lab found a bomb hidden in the trunk of Rachel's car. He practically ripped his shirt and cap off for police to use after they told him the bomb was set to go off at exactly seven.

The bomb and its timing were puzzling. If technicians hadn't found it, the bomb would have demolished the car, but it wasn't big enough to inflict severe damage on adjacent buildings. If the college kid followed Rachel's instructions, he would have been safely in the police station at the time of the explosion. Her bosses at APD figured Rachel planned to detonate the bomb to distract police, so she had time to sneak in by a back route and kill Jorge during the confusion. Gil, after a conversation with Chuy, opined Rachel had seen though the police trap. She had concocted ways to waste police efforts while she flew out of the country.

Ulysses Howe had agreed with Gil Andrews and focused FBI efforts on tracking Rachel through airports. However, he agreed APD needed to follow Zelda and monitor the developments at the Mercado Police Department, just in case he was wrong

Gil convinced Ulysses Howe at the last minute to fly Chuy to L.A. Gil had also called Elsa twenty minutes before Chuy's flight. "Before we mop up a minor scene here, you better email Chuy and wish him good luck in L.A. You've been pretty rough on his pride." She bit her tongue. Instead of arguing with Gil, she did what he suggested.

Elsa looked at her watch. Ten to seven. Her mind wasn't on the job because she was worried about Chuy and regretted several remarks she made to him during the last couple of days. He would never have complained to Gil, but he must have seemed so depressed that Gil noticed. Not surprising. Gil thought of Chuy as a son, not as a past employee or a colleague. At least she had sent an email to Chuy before his flight took off.

At three minutes to seven, the third APD car reported a blue Honda was turning the corner onto Baca Calle. The driver quickly turned off the lights after parking the car next to Rachel's vehicle but remained in the car for two minutes.

Elsa wondered whether Zelda was waiting for a signal. Then she had a brainstorm. Although Rachel's bomb wasn't powerful enough to destroy the building, it probably would have destroyed a car parked next to it. What if Rachel had told Zelda to stay in the car until seven? The bomb could have been Rachel's attempt to eliminate Zelda as well as to create a diversion. Elsa shivered as she thought about the hatred that must have driven Rachel.

A short individual slowly climbed out of the Honda. Elsa was too far away to identify her as Zelda. The woman officer in the truck said the individual had gray hair but otherwise fit Zelda's description.

At one minute after seven, the silence in Elsa's car was broken by Gil's voice. "Zelda Zane in her usual cock-sure way demanded to see Jorge." Gil chuckled. "I frisked her and gave her a two-sentence explanation of the situation. She's now moping in a jell cell."

Elsa's throat tightened. Zelda could sue him for false arrest. "What did you charge her with?"

"Nothing. I told her the safest place in the house was in a cell if Rachel came in with guns blazing. You should have seen her scurry." He seemed to have covered the mike as he talked to someone else because muffled sounds emanated from her radio for the next minute. "Told Zelda about the bomb." He chuckled. "She was upset and rushed to the bathroom. She's sobbing now and keeps waving a note at us. Claims it was in the package she received at home before noon today. My quick assessment is she doesn't know Rachel's location. As I said before, Rachel isn't going to show."

"Stay in position and stay sharp for another ten minutes." Elsa emailed an update to her bosses and Ulysses Howe. Then she sent another email to Chuy.

> Chuy,
> The ball is your court. We have Zelda, but doubt she knows anything useful. Ben, the undercover agent at Roma Station, heard right. The mastermind is the blonde.
> Love,
> Elsa.

***

Elsa closed the door of the interview room and told the two APD officers, whom she had not sent home an hour ago with the rest of the APD crew, to monitor Zelda. She wandered down the hallway of the almost deserted station to Gil's office. He was leaning back in an old leather recliner in his office reading *Adventures of Huckleberry Finn*. "I think I'll scream if I hear Zelda say one more time, 'Rachel duped me,' or, 'Lots of people will celebrate my fall.' She's a modern version of the old Chatty Cathy dolls who blurted out one of about ten lines every time you pulled their string."

Gil snorted. "Finally cut the string on my daughter's doll." He closed his book and leaned forward. "I reread this book occasionally.

Helps me to put things in perspective. Something Zelda isn't doing. She gains little by worrying now about what others think of her."

Elsa sank into a nearby chair, which looked as if Gil had gotten if from Goodwill. "As far as I can see, she broke no major laws. Granted she was foolish not to talk to the police as soon as she saw the email on the accounts transfer. The problem is: I don't know if I believe her."

"Why?"

"First off, it's hard to believe a woman as smart as Zelda would make the stupid mistake of not calling the police as soon as she got the email about the account. Second, she seems pathetic sitting in the interview room. That's not the Zelda I know. Before she came here today, she sat at the Sonic drive-in on Alameda in the gray, curly wig and sucked peanut butter-chocolate milkshakes and made a list of people she mistrusted."

"Must be a long list."

Elsa handed him the list. "It includes most of the investigators, lawyers, and court officials connected to the Raines's trial, except Rachel. Doesn't make sense. You should see them fight. What do you think?"

He pulled his reading glasses into place and studied the list. "When Sara first suggested the sting with the prisoners, I thought it might work because no one talks to Zelda or Rachel if they can avoid it. I suspect Rachel earned Zelda's trust by telling her a secret." He pushed his reading glasses back onto the top of his head.

Elsa wiggled in the chair to find a spot where a spring wasn't poking her. "During the last hour of questioning, Zelda claimed that Rachel told her that Ulysses Howe sometimes pried into bank records of court officers without getting warrants first. Doubt that's true. Otherwise, I don't think they shared confidences."

"Mmm," he leaned back and hummed a Glen Campbell song. Suddenly he pushed forward. "Think. Zelda fell into the traps we laid because she believed what you told her. Your name wasn't on her list either, but most men connected with the case are named. Why wouldn't she believe Rachel, another woman?"

"She's a clever lawyer, not a hysterical feminist."

"Aha, you overrate legal training. It doesn't erase basic beliefs. What else?"

"You saw the note Rachel gave Zelda with the wig. It was so contrived." She gave him another copy of the note.

Zelda,

We'll get all our questions answered tonight at seven when we talk to Jorge. I'm afraid others will try to stop us.

Follow these precautions: Turn off your cell phone. Don't email anyone. Drive a car without a GPS system. Avoid being recognized. The wig should help. Don't arrive at the Mercado Police Station before one or two minutes before seven. Wait in your car for me to arrive until five minutes after seven.

We'll solve who killed Raines tonight, despite the APD's efforts to hide the facts.

R

"A bit cloak and dagger." Gil stood and reshelved his book. "I'm surprised Zelda fell for it, but she's smart enough to know you don't have a case against her. You might as well cut her loose."

"That's what I thought too." Elsa dragged herself toward the door. She was tired of failing in this case.

"Don't feel bad. When the story of this incident gets out, Zelda will be the laughingstock of the New Mexico court system. Both you with the sting and Rachel with her note outsmarted her. No jury has ever handed her a worse verdict. Of course, the story won't ever see the light of day if Chuy and the FBI don't find Rachel."

CHAPTER 40: Sergeant Chuy Bargas at Los Angeles International Airport (LAX)

Tom O'Hara was a lanky, nervous man with thinning red hair. He forced Chuy and Ulysses Howe to sprint with him to the nearest stop for the LAX Shuttle. He gasped as he ran, "Mr. Howe, be reasonable. You want us to sort through twenty-five flights with about five thousand people to find a Caucasian woman with an unknown hair color, indeterminate age and height, and no name."

"At least, we've potentially narrowed our search to one in about a thousand," panted Howe. "Best odds of today."

In the distance, a shuttle bus moved away from the stop. All three men stopped running.

Tom sighed. "Next one should be here in ten minutes. Might as well slow down. Although it doesn't look it, the shuttle is usually faster than a cab during busy times."

As they waited, Tom listed details about the logistics of what he called the "find Rachel" operation. FBI agents, airport security staff, and Los Angeles police were monitoring electronically all people entering and, to a lesser extent, leaving secure areas in the airport. Alerts with pictures of Rachel as she looked normally and in the disguise that she used on the flight from Denver to Albuquerque had been sent to airports and police in the U.S. and worldwide. FBI staff had also sent messages to all private carriers out of LAX and other southern California airports. Local police had sent out alerts to cab companies and limousine services. "The problem is the descriptions of her are so vague that they're useless."

Ulysses snorted. "Not useless, but close to useless, because Rachel is a master of disguises."

Tom continued with his recitation. "Three FBI agents with three airport security officers have already monitored the boarding of flights departing for Dubai, Mexico City, Paris, and Istanbul. "The next two hours are relatively easy to man. We have flights to Lima, Guatemala City, Manila, Mexico City, Cancún, and Bogota. Then all hell breaks loose. Twelve direct flights to foreign destinations leave between nine and midnight. Most of the flights are packed." Pause. "And the late-night crowds are grouchier than most passengers."

As the shuttle arrived, Tom said, "We're going to Terminal 3. We have a room near their departure areas because we're monitoring several flights out of Terminal 3, and it's an easy walk to the Tom Bradley International Terminal."

***

Chuy stood next to the American Airlines agent as she accepted the boarding passes of each passenger in coach. If it was a man or a non-Caucasian woman, he remained silent. He asked each Caucasian woman a question, usually, "Will you be staying in Lima?" and attempted to see her eyes as she answered. Chuy knew he was delaying the boarding process, so he winked at the women. Most were annoyed. After the first fifty, he stopped trying to be charming. He noticed the FBI agent checking passengers to first- and business-class seemed more successful. No one yelled at him.

Chuy studied the stragglers while agents identified the "no shows." The FBI agent emailed the names of the "no shows" to the "find Rachel" headquarters. Immediately after the doors to the American Airlines plane were slammed shut, Chuy and his entourage of an FBI agent and two airport security guards bolted off to the gate where the Philippine Air flight to Manila was parked.

The crowd at the gate for the flight to Manila was restless, and the airline agents grumpy because boarding should have started five minutes earlier. As the FBI agent spoke to the airline staff at the gate, Chuy literally looked over the crowd. He breathed a sigh of relief. The women were petite. Rachel couldn't contort her body to look as short and not be severely stooped. He twittered Ulysses. "Anyone can monitor this flight. Rachel will stand out."

Five minutes later an FBI agent replaced Chuy at the gate, and Chuy trotted to the "find Rachel" headquarters.

***

Chuy looked around the small room with almost floor to ceiling windows on one side. Three agents were pecking at their computer keyboards. Ulysses was pacing around the room, occasionally looking over their shoulders, as he barked orders into his phone. Tom and a woman agent served as receptionists as they responded to incoming calls and directed most of them to others. A coffee urn, an ice bucket with cans of diet sodas, and sandwiches sat on a cart by the door, but no one at the tables was eating or drinking. Chuy grabbed a ham and cheese sandwich. He'd not eaten since noon, and the opportunity might not occur again for hours.

Tom covered the phone receiver with his hand. "How was it?"

"Impossible. She'll bolt if she sees me. And I couldn't check them fast enough on the flight." Chuy paused, "Better use FBI agents or police she doesn't know to check out the passengers."

Ulysses nodded.

Tom announced. "We checked the background of the 'no shows' on all the departed flights. So far, we've noted one is also booked on the flight to Cancún. Not logical to book a flight to Manila and an alternate to Cancún."

Ulysses strode over to Tom and motioned Chuy to follow. "What's the name?"

"Loretta Healy."

Tom pulled up the passport photo of a gray-haired woman, who lived in Phoenix. "We don't have any evidence of her clearing the passport control yet for her flight at ten-fifteen, but it's only nine." His computer beeped. "Here are the passport photos of the other no-shows who are adult Caucasian women."

Chuy sighed. "No clear family resemblances to Rachel."

Ulysses coughed. "Agreed, but Rachel is pretty talented at disguises." He tapped his finger on the table. "Alert security to watch for these six women too."

***

Chuy was lounging in a chair in the Terminal 3 near the gate for the next flight to Guatemala City. A casual observer might think he was reading a newspaper. A more astute observer would notice his earbud and the way his eyes constantly scanned the crowd as he occasionally talked to himself. He hoped Rachel was too tired to be an astute observer anymore.

Chuy was pleased Ulysses had listened to his advice and ordered two women officers to circulate through bathrooms near the gates. He saw one of the women officers come out of a bathroom two hundred feet away.

He gasped. A woman standing at the Starbucks counter about one hundred feet away looked similar to Rachel from the rear with shapely, high buns. He alerted the woman officer to turn around and come back toward Starbucks and look closely at the women with long brown hair in black slacks. The woman sitting next to him stood. As she assembled her luggage, she spilled her coffee on Chuy. He jumped to his feet.

In his ear, "What woman with long brown hair?"

Chuy looked back at the Starbuck's counter, he scanned the other counters. The brown-haired woman was gone.

He thought he saw a woman with brown hair running toward the exit from the terminal. He ran after her and instructed the woman officer to do the same. He alerted airport security at the far end of the terminal to stop any tall, brown-haired women leaving Terminal 3 as he jostled his way through the crowd.

Again, he thought he saw the brown hair. The distance between them was widening. Rachel was better at shoving women and children aside than he was. His musing must have distracted him, and he found himself tripping over a duffle bag dragged by a teenage boy as he jumped to avoid colliding with an old woman with a wheelie bag. When he regained his balance, the brown-haired woman was gone.

He saw two gates with no flights posted. He didn't see the woman among the twenty men and women milling in the area. He ran past these gates toward the terminal exit.

At the exit to the secured area, security officers guarded six brown-haired women in an area generally reserved for those being frisked as they entered a secure area. None were Rachel.

Chuy guessed his mistake and ran back to the gates not in use and began to question the people there. Three had seen a woman with long brown hair. They had assumed she worked for the airlines because she had disappeared behind the counter. They thought she looked for supplies because eventually she reappeared, put on a captain's hat, and walked away.

He radioed the security at the gate to keep detaining tall women with brown hair, including staff and flight crews. He radioed for the woman agent to check the bathrooms and look in the garbage for pilots' hats and wigs.

Chuy was relieved when he heard Howe's announcement on his earbud. More staff members were arriving at the security checkpoint at the end of the terminal. Two more women agents would circulate through the bathrooms. Airline staff members were warned to look for unfamiliar faces among their ranks. Four airport security officers were assigned to talk to all vendors and check storage rooms.

Chuy was panting hard as he slowed down. Rachel, if she was the brown-haired woman, was trapped somewhere in the terminal. He radioed Howe. "Rachel knows our tactics. She'll change her appearance by tying the long brown hair up to look short or by replacing her wig. I'm going to get on the Guatemala City flight and give everyone a once over."

***

Chuy was exhausted when he exited the flight ready to leave for Guatemala City. His shins and thighs were bruised from running into objects projecting suddenly in front of him in the terminal and then the aisles of the plane. The only positive thing he could say on the radio was, "I'm glad I'm not an airline steward on packed international flights."

The earbud stopped crackling. A woman's voice said, "I found a long dark brown wig stuffed in a receptacle in a bathroom near Gate 39." More crackling.

Chuy wasn't used to wearing an earbud for long periods of time. He found the background noise raised his tension, and he felt the vise of a headache circling his head and slowly tightening.

Tom Ohara's voice reverberated in his ear as he instructed a guard, "Check out the boarding of a flight to Cancún at Gate 32."

Chuy composed himself as he attempted to resume his veneer as an un-hurried traveler. As he purchased a newspaper to replace the one he lost, Howe's voice resounded in his ear. "Appears Sanders and Sara in Cuba have come up with the clue we need — the name on the passport Rachel will use."

CHAPTER 41: Sara at the Malecón

A knock on her door. There was no window or peephole. "Who's there?"

"Sanders."

Sara opened the door. The creases around his mouth changed from a frown to a smile as he looked her up and down. After the dinner at Café del Oriente, she had taken a shower and changed to a pair of shorts and tee shirt without a bra. "Put on shoes and join me for a walk to the Malecón." When she started to reply, he raised a finger in front of his mouth to silence her. Then he started to tell her the history of the Malecón or sea wall along the Atlantic in Havana.

He continued his story as they walked down several flights of back stairs. As they walked through a maze of manicured paths on the grounds of Hotel Meliá toward the Atlantic Ocean, the roar of the ocean grew louder. Sanders didn't try to yell above the sound of crashing waves. Finally, they stood at the Malecón surveying the dark Atlantic. "I wanted privacy for this conversation. I thought your room might be bugged. We'd better sit down." He sighed and gulped repeatedly as he looked alternately at his hands and the ocean.

She couldn't figure out what was wrong with him. He didn't usually act nervous. "I thought dinner ended well. Will there be problems tomorrow?"

"No, this is about Xave "He should have you told this. Remember, I warned you he was unlucky."

"He told me about a girl in Viet Nam."

"He was kid then." He began to speak rapidly. "He recruited several women in Iraq and Kuwait during the first Gulf War to obtain data about troop deployments. One of them, a wife of a colonel in the Iraqi army, and Xave's sergeant were executed by stoning." A tic on the side of Sanders's mouth began to pulsate. "Seems the sergeant was mistaken for Xave."

Sara couldn't decide whether the tic showed Sanders was nervous or was an involuntary reflex caused by his desire to laugh. She couldn't sort her emotions either. Mainly relief because she had survived in Bolivia, considering Xave's track record. Annoyance because Xave made her feel inadequate in Washington and again today by not admitting the truth. Amusement at the ridiculous situation. Mainly, she felt sad but not enough to cry, at least not now.

Her silence seemed to unnerve Sanders, and he stood and began to pace. "Xave comforted the sergeant's wife afterwards. I shouldn't be the one telling you this, but I assume he wants you to know because he gave you his ring." He sat on the wall again. "Anyway, he married her without much thought. I don't know whether they were ever happy, but they were arrested for disturbing the peace several times during their drinking binges and flamboyant fights. His solution to their marital problems was to take one assignment after another overseas."

Sara expelled a long gasp.

"What can I say? He's an irresponsible but charming, rogue. He can always gain a woman's cooperation, unless he's married to her." More softly, "Though you're his best catch."

Sara began to giggle. She grabbed his hands and pulled him to sit on the wall beside her. "You don't need to apologize. I'm not an innocent schoolgirl. He's not the first man who forgot to tell me important pieces of his history. Tell him he doesn't have to bury himself in Cuba to avoid me."

The lines around Sanders's eyes and mouth lessened. He squeezed her hands.

"More importantly I appreciate how solicitous you've been with me." She loosened his grip and turned his palms upward and traced her pointer finger across his palm. "You got me out of Albuquerque and have acted like a mother hen to me during our visit to Cuba."

He snorted and pulled his hands away. "Is that how you see me? As a mother hen?"

"Poor choice of words." She wished she could see his face better in the moonlight because his voice had lost its usual confident ring. "You've worked hard all your life and are about to get what you deserve. Moreno thinks you'll become the Deputy Chief of Mission to Cuba."

"Idle speculation." Sanders's voice sounded hoarse as if his allergies had kicked in or he was ready to cry.

She traced her hand along the corner of his eyes. There were no tears. "I don't want to jeopardize your chances. Somehow, I have become a liability here. Probably because of my association with Xave and Mazzone. I'm sorry."

"You're no liability."

"You don't have to be gallant." Her finger moved across his lips. They were wet.

He pushed her away. "Now I've got to clean up the rest of the chaos Xave created. I've done a lot of checking during the last two hours. I knew Xave's wife Lydia had a child. Long before Xave met her, but I never knew any details. Xave's note made me think."

Sara sucked in a deep breath of sea air. Sanders didn't make a big deal out of unimportant details.

"He, really all of us, should have caught this sooner, but Lydia's daughter uses her middle name. She's Laura Rachel Jones, the FBI agent in Albuquerque."

Sara felt as if someone hit her in the gut, and she was unable to speak for several seconds. "Makes sense, I guess. Rachel was pleasant when I first met her during the flu epidemic two years ago, but seemed hostile toward me after I returned from Bolivia. I take it she and Xave dislike each other."

"Hate would be a better word. She testified in court how his reckless behavior destroyed her mother, claiming he owed her mother support when they divorced ten years ago. The court agreed."

She stood because the stone wall suddenly seemed hard and scratchy. "Any more bad news?"

"No. Quite the contrary. The FBI think Rachel will use documents with some derivative of her mother's name Lydia Loretta Jones Healy Zack to board planes out of L.A."

Sara felt confused. "Wait. What am I missing?"

"A lot." He updated her on the continuing search for Rachel in the L.A. airport. He concluded by adding, "We'll fly to Washington tomorrow so you can pick up Bug before you fly to Albuquerque. Then Elsa Grasso will drive you to the federal prison in Florence. "Seems Mazzone knows the details about the shootout at the courthouse, but insists he'll only tell you. Are you willing? "

"Of course, I want to get my life back to the way it was."

He put his arm over her shoulder. "Hopefully with a few changes?"

CHAPTER 42: Sergeant Chuy Bargas at LAX

Only the first-class passengers were boarding the flight to Cancún, but at least two hundred passengers and their bags were already in a line snaking past the row of seats where Chuy was seated. He wondered how airline representatives faced these mobs day after day. Here in the midst of the crowd, he smelled the sweat of the hot, tired people waiting to board the jet. He wanted to slink away and hide. Instead he stood and stretched while craning his neck to see down the line.

A voice from his earbud reminded him Loretta Healy had booked a seat on this flight but hadn't checked any baggage. Not surprising. If Rachel was traveling as Loretta Healy, she would have on a gray wig now. A number of women with gray hair were in the line. He advanced down the line, bumping into women of the right height to make them look his way. Several women asked if he was drunk. He saw no one of interest.

Then he saw a woman kitty-corner across the terminal from the gate for the flight to Cancún. A stooped woman, dressed all in black, wore a black scarf around her head and stood by the counter for a domestic flight, which had left ten minutes before for Houston. The head shape was right. He calculated her height if she stood straight. About right. He averted his eyes so he could watch the woman in black but not arouse her suspicions. "Look at the stooped woman with the black head scarf at the Delta flight to Houston. Don't spook her." He heard Tom give orders through his earbud.

He casually stepped away from the line to the Cancún flight. It was cooler away from the crowd. He advanced toward the mystery woman always keeping himself between her and the distant exit to the terminal. He saw a man in a red hoodie swinging a duffle bag as he hustled toward the woman. Chuy recognized him as an FBI agent. The man used the duffle to clear people from his path. Chuy thought he would use this technique if he ever had to get through crowds an airport again. The woman in black ducked behind the wall in back of the counter.

J. L. Greger

A siren went off and the red light above the gate for the Houston flight began to flash.

The agent in the red hoodie raced around the wall behind the counter. In his ear, Chuy heard, "Emergency exit is open. I need back up."

A woman's voice announced, "Open emergency door might be a ruse, I'll check the jetway." Chuy saw a teenage girl in a Goth costume slide behind the barrier at the same gate. She was one of the agents checking the bathrooms.

Chatter from his earbud suggested Rachel would be caught quickly by airport security if she exited through the emergency door and went down the metal steps to the tarmac. He saw lights popping up on the tarmac. Passengers in the throng were pointing toward the lights. He threaded his way through the crowd, always keeping himself between the terminal exit at the security checkpoint and where he last spotted the woman in black.

The red light over another external exit began to blink as a siren wailed. This exit was farther from the security checkpoint at the other end of the terminal. He said, "She's moving counterclockwise around this end of the terminal."

Ulysses took over from Tom on the radio and instructed crews to move more lights to the tarmac at the end of the terminal and ordered airport security to man all emergency exits in the terminal.

Chuy saw two more emergency exits between the second blinking light and the gate for the flight to Cancún. The FBI agent checking passengers to Cancún must have observed movements at one of the doors because he started to run to one of the exits.

Chuy muttered, "Go back to Gate 32. Keep checking passengers as they load on the Cancún flight. Rachel might be trying to create confusion so she can board unnoticed."

A man said through his earpiece, "A black scarf was found on the ground by the second gate. She exited through the second doorway."

A few seconds later, a woman said, "Don't be too sure. The scarf's too small to wrap her head."

Chuy's eyes kept scanning the terminal, focusing primarily on the two remaining exits while three LA police officers roped off the area behind him with yellow streamers. The voices emitting from his earbud became less distinct as the throng became noisier. Many in the crowd were booing because they were unable to move.

Chuy and three other officers moved toward the two unopened exits. The agitated passengers were unwilling to step aside and jostled the four men trying to walk through the crowd. He feared they might stampede like cattle.

"Wish we could use dogs to flush her out." He heard a few snickers from his earbud.

One of the open doors slammed shut. The mob suddenly surged forward in panic. Chuy, keeping his eyes on the two closed exit doors, stumbled twice as he tripped on a bag once and over a screaming child the second time. He realized that even if he saw Rachel, he couldn't reach her if the crowd stampeded. He plodded forward.

Suddenly, he saw something black slither along the floor. Rachel was crawling toward the exit gate twenty feet from him. He ruthlessly shoved a mother and screaming child aside as he sped to the gate. The door opened. A siren shrieked. He slid forward like a batter running to first base and clenched a leg.

He heard a horrific screech as he felt himself hurtling forward out the door. Something was wrong. Instead of being dragged down rough metal stairs by the escapee, they were falling. Falling.

CHAPTER 43: Sara in Florence, Colorado on Day 16

Sara sat on the FBI's Gulfstream V with Bug licking the dust and sweat of Cuba off her arms and hands. She was exhausted. Sanders had arranged for his aide to be waiting with Bug at Washington Dulles International Airport when he and Sara arrived from Miami. The aide had shoved boarding passes at her and propelled her and Bug to their flight. In the rush, Sanders promised to call Sara tomorrow around noon.

A diminutive FBI agent had met her at the Albuquerque airport and announced Elsa was indisposed. He proudly announced that he would escort her to the federal penitentiary in Florence, Colorado and whisked her to this private jet without any more explanation. Now, he bent over his laptop pecked out emails, talked into his headset, and generally ignored her. It was just as well, she was too tired to talk. She also wanted to think: Why did Mazzone want to see her?

She heard some racket outside the plane and two APD officers walked on the plane followed by man a foot taller. He reached out to shake Sara's hand. "I'm Ulysses Howe. Call me Ulysses. I don't usually travel in this luxury, but the FBI director felt sorry for me because I've lost all the key people on this investigation. He let me use this plane, provided it was back in Washington by two tomorrow afternoon."

The plane door slammed shut. The pilot recited a shortened version of the standard memorized lines used by commercial airline stewards.

"Your sister and I met with both Sally and Dean Wilson today. The man doesn't deserve either of those women."

"Will he be charged with abetting murder?"

He guffawed. "You're blunter than your sister. Unfortunately, the university counsel negotiated with the DA's office. Dean Wilson won't be charged, if he cooperates fully." Ulysses drummed his fingers on the armrest, shook his head, and asked the short FBI employee for an update.

The young man cleared his throat. "The warden has bent rules so we, I mean you sir, Sara, and the police officers, can meet with Mazzone even though it's after visiting hours." The agent briefed them on the procedures to be followed when entering the high security prison at Florence.

Ulysses pulled a file out of his briefcase. "Here's what we must do. We don't want Mazzone to know that no one, except George Kummer, is left to testify against him. The warden is convinced Mazzone has ears everywhere. Accordingly, we've kept the following information from the press. Diego Rivera is lying in a morgue in Albuquerque with a false name on his toe tag. Similarly, Rachel is in a morgue in L.A., and Chuy is in critical condition in an L.A. hospital."

Sara winced. "How was Chuy injured?"

"The tarmac crew at LAX wanted to guarantee Rachel's capture so they removed the metal stairs from the emergency exits. Usually a two- or three-story fall isn't fatal, but she fell head first with Chuy holding onto her leg. The only good thing about the last twelve hours is Rachel broke Chuy's fall. He should recover at least partially." He looked at his watch. "Elsa is with him now. Accordingly, you get me and a jet, instead of Elsa and a car, to transport you to Florence."

"What about Jorge, the lead gunman at my house? Did he identify Rachel as the person who hired him? Did he mention Mazzone or Diego?"

"Psychiatrists are working with him, but he has few lucid moments. However, it's clear a blonde woman, probably Rachel, controlled him by threatening him with fire."

"Mmm, has Falto, the only other surviving shooter, been helpful?"

"Yes, but the only person he can identify is Jorge." He sighed. "Assistant DA Zelda Zane tendered her resignation."

Sara leaned forward. "Was she in on this mess?"

"We don't think so, but she was embarrassed that she fell for the ruse you, your sister, and Elsa set up and that she followed Rachel's advice." He paused, "Too bad. Nasty little woman but a savvy prosecutor."

Sara sighed. "Nasty is the wrong word. Zelda is what she has to be to succeed as an assistant DA."

Ulysses flinched. "I agree. That's why I asked the DA to not accept her resignation and sent a sympathetic note to her. Maybe this experience will make Zelda a wiser, more compassionate prosecutor."

He cleared his throat and studied his file. "Time to practice our lines. We want to maximize what we learn from Mazzone without letting him guess our secrets."

"It would help if I understood why he wanted to see me."

Ulysses looked askance. "I hoped you knew."

***

The red brick prison at Florence could pass as a badly designed school until you noticed the guard tower. However, it appeared sinister to Sara on this cloudy afternoon. She couldn't keep her imagination under control. She had left the hotel in Havana more than twenty-four hour before and slept little on flights. All she could think of was George Raft in an old prison movie as she was led into the high security prison.

Now, she sat on one side of a room split by a clear, obviously thick, room divider. Ulysses sat to her left, the warden on her right. The two APD officers were seated in green plastic chairs behind them. Prison guards stood near the exit. Sara had requested two plastic glasses and two cans of Diet Coke be placed on the shelf by the lone window on the divider.

When Mazzone, clad in an orange jumpsuit, strolled into the small room on the other side of the wall, Sara immediately spoke. "Hello, Jim. You haven't shaved your head recently. You look better."

He walked up to the divider and peered at her. "You look tired and wrinkled. Must have flown from Cuba today."

"Be kind. I remembered you drank Diet Coke." She popped the can, filled the two glasses, shoved one through the window, and closed it.

Mazzone walked along the divider and studied everyone. "Where are your usual sidekicks — Elsa and Chuy?"

She knew she wasn't much of an actress, but she managed to look nonchalant as she smiled. "Busy and out-ranked. Have you met Ulysses Howe, the director of the Albuquerque office of the FBI?"

Mazzone eyed Ulysses and sat down on a green plastic chair as if it was an easy chair.

As preplanned, Sara went on the offensive immediately. "Rachel claims you planned the "wild west" shows in Albuquerque and at my home. I don't believe her, but Ulysses does. Why don't you set him straight?" Sara sipped her beverage.

"Why should I bother?"

"You weren't asked to testify in the Raines trial. May not get to testify at all, so assistant DA Zelda Zane's promises could be moot."

Mazzone shrugged. "Zelda'll need my testimony eventually. Let's get back to Rachel. Exactly what did she say?"

Sara winked at him. "Time for you to talk.'

"Don't want to?"

She slid her chair back as if she was ready to leave. Again, a preplanned move. "You asked for the meeting."

Mazzone leaned back. "Poor Raines was dying of pancreatic cancer. Shame, he was a damn good doc. Saved me." He pulled his hands through his thick gray hair. "Asked for advice on a hypothetical situation through his gopher Diego Rivera."

"What did you tell him?"

Mazzone leaned back and yawned. "I told him about an FBI agent desperate for cash to cover her mother's medical bills and the son of an officer in APD. The son owed me big time. That's all."

"Are you sure?"

The corners of Mazzone's lips slowly edged upward. "I told him an easy way to motivate the officer's son." Sara must have looked confused, because he quickly added, "The son was afraid of fire. I mean crazy afraid."

"How did Raines pay for these hints?"

Mazzone leaned forward. "I owed him for saving my life."

"Rachel tells a different story." Sara sipped her soda, so did Mazzone. "I think if I was stuck in here, I'd want to get a soda daily."

Mazzone laughed. "I'm not a cheap date. You're used to slumming with Xave."

Sara willed the muscles in her face not to move. "Did you ever meet with Rachel before you were arrested in Bolivia?"

He shook his head. "She's too unpredictable."

Ulysses started to write a note but stopped when Sara asked, "Then how did you communicate with her and Raines?"

"Diego coded info into crosswords puzzles, which were delivered to Raines in jail, by a series of dumb bimbos." He uncharacteristically looked down. "Diego talked to me and Rachel when necessary." He jerked his head up. "Bet you wonder whether Raines planned the attacks on you." He leered and nodded toward Ulysses. "Now it's time for your friend to make a few promises to me."

Ulysses promised neither state nor federal officials would request the death sentence for Mazzone, if his clues and testimony led to the conviction of Rachel Jones, Diego Rivera, George Kummer, Jorge Lehar, Augustin Falto, and Dean Ethan Wilson. Sara almost giggled during Ulysses's spiel because the only two to be brought to trial were Falto and George Kummer. Jorge would be declared mentally incompetent and the rest, except for Dean Wilson, were dead.

As soon as they finished their exchange, Sara zoned in on a new bit of information that FBI agents had uncovered. "How did George Kummer play into the scheme?"

Mazzone stared at her. "He didn't"

"Are you sure?" She stared back, but he didn't flinch. "We know he's your cousin."

Mazzone sighed, "I told Raines, when he asked for hypothetical advice to let George Kummer, not Rachel, handle the money he'd stashed away in overseas bank accounts. Kummer's more honest. Rachel embellished the plan." He leaned back again and yawned. "Guess you getting her ex-step daddy's attention set her off. Though she hated all what she called 'tight ass bitches' — Zelda, Elsa, and you." He emptied the glass. "Bet she went after them too. She bragged to Diego that she'd ruin them or their lovers before she killed them."

Sara took a sip of her beverage and hoped he didn't notice her hands were trembling slightly.

Mazzone finished his soda. "Why didn't you ask about Diego? Rachel planted clues so you'd conclude he was the mastermind behind the shootings. You must have figured that out." He scratched his chin. "Bet he's dead."

Sara kept her voice steady as she lied, "Not that I know."

Mazzone leaned forward and peered at her. "You don't lie well. Too bad about Diego. Although death might be better than the life he would have here, especially since Rachel wouldn't be able to slip him another shiv."

Ulysses slid a note to Sara. She nodded. "How was Dean Wilson involved?"

Mazzone shrugged. "He wasn't. Well, except for a bribe in the will to encourage a little perjury."

"Weren't you worried about your nephew George Kummer?"

Mazzone looked surprised. "Not really." He gulped the last of his soda. "I knew your sister, dripping with motherly sympathy, would protect him." He leaned back and stretched. "I'm bored. You about through?"

Sara thought of the list of rehearsed questions and bundled the rest together. "Why did you agree to see Rachel after you were imprisoned here?"

"No choice. She holds grudges longer than most of my business associates." Mazzone shrugged. "Besides, I enjoyed her kitten with a whip routine."

"Why did you ask to see me? I'm not exactly your favorite person, and I'm not exciting like Rachel."

He snorted. "Wanted to set the record straight before Rachel lied her way into being found innocent. Knew as a do-gooder, you'd be obliged to protect me." He stood. "Remember I only advised on hypothetical questions, no matter what she claims."

Sara suddenly felt safe for the first time in the last two weeks. The warden and Ulysses Howe had succeeded in isolating Mazzone. He didn't know Rachel was dead.

CHAPTER 44: Sara at home on Day 17

Sara cradled Bug in her arms as she looked out her front window. The neighborhood looked the same, except the bright yellow of the cottonwood trees had dulled since the last time she stood here. Then, workmen had been sweeping shards of glass splintered by a rain of Jorge's bullets and putting a sheets of plywood into the voids left by the broken windows.

When two APD police officers delivered Bug and her home after their flight from Florence at ten last night, she and Bug had crawled into bed without studying the repairs. Now, as she stumbled about her house, she found less evidence remained of the shooting rampage. She knew she should be happy, but she felt much of her world remained topsy-turvy.

She kept musing. If scientists can develop a vaccine to stop or at least slow the spread of cancer in the body, why can't society develop ways to block the uncontrolled spread or of illicit drugs? During the last few weeks she'd seen this malignancy, known as the drug trade, destroy a number of lives, including Xave's.

Linda called at eleven with bad news about her meeting with the president of the university this morning. Linda thought he resembled a hyena admiring a dead carcass as he eagerly talked about uses of funds from the "Raines endowment." He hemmed and hawed at her suggestions to name the endowed professorship in medicine after Sally Wilson rather than Dean Wilson and to convert the endowed professorship in Raines's name into funds to foster the research development of assistant professors. Linda was sure he wouldn't select her to be the interim dean to replace Dean Wilson. When Sara suggested she take the afternoon off, Linda reeled off a long "to do" list but agreed to meet Sara for supper.

As Bug nuzzled her hands, Sara thought the best way to feel better was to focus on the good aspects of her life. She punched buttons on her phone. "Gil, thanks for overseeing the repairs on my house. The house looks much better. You certainly went past your duties as the local police chief."

"That's what friends do. Have you read the *Albuquerque Journal* this morning yet? Ulysses Howe must have been busy on the flight back from Florence."

"Wasn't much to do from what I heard of his phone conversations on the plane. He, some boss at APD, and the DA debated the charges against George Kummer and finally agreed he was an accomplice in the murder of Raines and the attempted murders of Linda, Sally, and me. They wanted a long list because they guessed Kummer was the heir apparent to Mazzone's business."

"Good. Elsa called with even better news. The doctors say Chuy will make a full recovery. He's also decided to return to the Mercado Police Department because they're getting married. They don't think working together every day would be wise."

His continued ramblings comforted Sara. She was happy that at least some of the pieces of her life in New Mexico were falling back into place.

Her phone rang at noon. "Where do you want to go for lunch?"

Sara knew she was sleep deprived, but the question was illogical. "Sanders, what are you talking about?"

"Open your door and you'll see."

She felt dizzy when she opened her new front door. "What brought you here?"

As Sanders stepped inside, Bug twirled on his back feet to get attention. "At least, Bug gave me a proper greeting." He planted a kiss on Sara's cheek. "Last night, actually early this morning, Ulysses Howe informed me that your meeting with Mazzone went well."

Sara tried to smile but she couldn't. "It was an anticlimax. All our efforts probably didn't even slow the malignancy of the drug trade. Mazzone's business will go on largely untouched, although I don't see what all his money can buy him in prison."

Sanders put an arm on her shoulder and pulled her to sit with him on the sofa. "Take a deep breath." The furrows on his forehead deepened. "Xave and Shantelle Eaton are going deep undercover to work on a cooperative venture with the Cuban government to stop Mazzone and other drug lords from moving cocaine from South America through Cuba to the U.S. He asked me to thank you for helping him to gain the trust of the Cubans and to forgive him for not realizing sooner that Rachel would be threatened by you." Sanders

J. L. Greger

looked down. "Damn Xave. He delights in making my life difficult. And to consider him always as a friend."

Sara didn't want Sanders to see her cry so she stood and went to the refrigerator to extract two sodas. After a minute, Sanders followed. He turned Sara around and put his arms around her waist. "I'm sorry."

"No apologies are necessary. Xave's right. I'm not the type of woman to be attached to a man living on the edge as he does." She pulled away and turned to face him. "I'm in a funk today."

He pulled her toward him and kissed her forehead. "So am I. Thought we might go for lunch and shop for a car for you. Maybe I could meet your sister too."

She blinked in surprise.

"You need a car because Jorge destroyed your last one. Right? I like cars."

She couldn't hide her disbelief. "I doubt you're into Subaru Foresters or other practical small SUVs."

"Okay, I came to convince you that you should accept a part time job with the State Department to continue what you've started in Bolivia and Cuba. You'd save my secretary the work of filing all your temporary assignments."

She enjoyed seeing him without his usual self-assured veneer, but knew she'd better not dangle him long. "I don't want to move from New Mexico."

"I know, but I hoped to give you a reason for wanting to be in Washington more."

She draped her arms around his neck. "I already have a reason."

SCIENTIFIC QUESTIONS

Why the title *Malignancy*?

After a shiver, most of us would define malignancy as the uncontrolled growth of tumor cells with metastasis (spread) of the abnormal cancer cells to other parts of the body. However, any deteriorating hurtful situation could be called a malignancy.

I titled this novel *Malignancy* for two reasons. One, I featured exciting new avenues of fighting cancer in this book. Two, my heroine Sara Almquist continues to duel with drug lord Jim Mazzone. I think the illegal drug trade qualifies as a malignancy of society. PBS reporters estimated that the illegal drug industry was an expanding global business, already worth four hundred billion dollars in 2014 (1).

Why mention cancer research in thriller set partially in Cuba?

My tour guide in Cuba in 2013 bragged that the Cubans had patented a drug for cancer. I didn't believe her and checked. She was right. The drug — a cancer vaccine, the health statistics, and the Cuban research institutes mentioned in this novel are real. Maybe, you'd like a few more facts.

• Most cancer chemo- and radiation therapies focus on destroying cells in patients' tumors. Unfortunately, these treatments often kill normal cells too and cause severe side effects, like nausea and weight loss. The new so-called therapeutic cancer vaccines rev up patients' own immune systems to produce white blood cells (mainly T cells), which recognize substances found on the surface of tumor cells but not on the surface of normal cells. These white blood cells then slay the cancer cells, but not the normal cells (2, 3).

• Currently scientist worldwide, not just in Cuba, are developing and evaluating cancer immunotherapy drugs. So far, all are specific to limited types of tumors. Even so, the editors of *Science* named cancer immunotherapy the scientific 'breakthrough of the year" in 2013 (2). As of March 2018, the FDA has approved immunotherapies as treatments for nearly twenty cancers.

 • Researchers at the Center of Molecular Immunology in Havana and scientists in Argentina developed the therapeutic cancer vaccine Racotumomab to treat one type of lung cancer (non-small cell lung cancer). The vaccine targets complex lipid complexes found on the surface of certain cancer cells. A multicenter clinical trial is now evaluating the drug's effectiveness (4, 5).

Are scientists, like Sara Almquist, ever involved in diplomatic efforts?

The U.S. State Department has an Office of Science and Technology Advisor. In June 2014, the leaders in the American Association for the Advancement of Science (AAAS) called for increased "science diplomacy with Cuba" (6).

For more details, check these out.

1. http://www.pbs.org/wgbh/pages/frontline/shows/drugs/business.
2. Couzin-Frankel J. Cancer Immunotherapy. *Science* 342 (6165): 1432-3 in 2013.
3. Green J & Ariyan C. 2014. Deploying the body's army. *Scientist* 28 (4): 35-39 in 2014.
4. Hernández AM et al. Anti-neuGcGM3 antibodies, actively elicited by idiotypic vaccination in non-small cell lung cancer patients, induce tumor cell death by an oncosis4-like mechanism. *Journal of Immunology* 186: 3735-3744 in 2011.
5. https://www.en.wikipedia.org/wiki/Racotumomab.
6. Fink GR, et al. Science diplomacy with Cuba. *Science* 344 (6188): 1065 in 2014.

THE END

ABOUT THE AUTHOR

J.L. Greger is a biology professor and research administrator from the University of Wisconsin-Madison turned novelist. She has consulted on scientific issues worldwide and loves to travel. Thus, she likes to include both science and her travel experiences in her thriller/mystery novels: *The Flu Is Coming*, *Murder: A Way to Lose* (1st prize in 2016 Public Safety Writers' [PSWA] book contest and finalist for a 2016 NM/Arizona book award), *Ignore the Pain*, *Riddled with Clues* (finalist for a 2017 NM/Arizona book award), *She Didn't Know Her Place*, and others.

Her short story collections: *Other People's Mothers* (finalist for a 2017 NM/Arizona book award) and *The Good Old Days* focus on families.

Her website is **http://www.jlgreger.com.**